Deemed 'the father of the sci[...] **Austin Freeman** had a long an[...] a writer of detective fiction. He [...] tailor who went on to train as a pharmacist. After graduating as a surgeon at the Middlesex Hospital Medical College, Freeman taught for a while and joined the colonial service, offering his skills as an assistant surgeon along the Gold Coast of Africa. He became embroiled in a diplomatic mission when a British expeditionary party was sent to investigate the activities of the French. Through his tact and formidable intelligence, a massacre was narrowly avoided. His future was assured in the colonial service. However, after becoming ill with blackwater fever, Freeman was sent back to England to recover and, finding his finances precarious, embarked on a career as acting physician in Holloway Prison. In desperation, he turned to writing and went on to dominate the world of British detective fiction, taking pride in testing different criminal techniques. So keen were his powers as a writer that part of one of his best novels was written in a bomb shelter.

BY THE SAME AUTHOR
ALL PUBLISHED BY HOUSE OF STRATUS

Felo De Se

R Austin Freeman

HOUSE OF
STRATUS

This edition published in 2001 by House of Stratus, an imprint of
House of Stratus Ltd, Thirsk Industrial Park, York Road, Thirsk,
North Yorkshire, YO7 3BX, UK.

www.houseofstratus.com

Typeset, printed and bound by House of Stratus.

A catalogue record for this book is available from the British Library
and the Library of Congress.

ISBN 0-7551-0357-2

To
My Brother Robert

PART ONE
THE GAMBLER

Narrated by Robert Mortimer

'

CHAPTER ONE

The Man in the Porch

There is something almost uncanny in the transformation which falls upon the City of London when all the offices are closed and their denizens have departed to their suburban homes. Throughout the working hours of the working days, the streets resound with the roar of traffic and the pavements are packed with a seething, hurrying multitude. But when the evening closes in, a strange quiet descends upon the streets, and the silent, deserted by-ways take on the semblance of thoroughfares in some city of the dead.

The mention of by-ways reminds me of another characteristic of this part of London. Modern, commonplace, and dull as is the aspect of the main streets, in the areas behind and between them are hidden innumerable quaint and curious survivals from the past; antique taverns lurking in queer, crooked alleys and little scraps of ancient churchyards, green with the grass that sprang up afresh amidst the ashes of the Great Fire.

With one of these curious "hinterlands" – an area bounded by Cornhill, Gracechurch Street, Lombard Street, and Birchin Lane, and intersected by a maze of courts and alleys – I became intimately acquainted, since I usually crossed it at least twice a day going to and from the branch of Perkins' Bank at which I was employed as a cashier. For the sake of change and interest, I varied my route from day to day – all the alleys communicated and one served as well as another – but the one that I favoured most was

3

the very unfrequented passage which took me through the tiny churchyard of St Michael's. I think the place appealed to me specially because somewhere under the turf reposes old Thomas Stow, grandfather of the famous John, laid here in the year 1527 according to his wish "to be buried in the litell Grene Churchyard of the Parysshe Church of Seynt Myghel in Cornehyll, betwene the Crosse and the Church Wall, nigh the wall as may be." Many a time, as I passed along the paved walk, had I tried to locate his grave; but the Great Fire must have made an end of both Cross and wall.

I have referred thus particularly to this "haunt of ancient peace" because it was there, on an autumn evening in the year 1929, that there befell the adventure that has set me to the writing of this narrative; an adventure which, for me, changed the scene in a moment from a haunt of peace to a place of gruesome and tragic memories.

It was close upon eight o'clock when I emerged from the bank and started rather wearily on my way homeward. It had been a long day, for there had been various arrears to dispose of which had kept us hard at work hours after the bank had closed its doors; and it had been a dull, depressing day, for the sky had been so densely overcast that no single gleam of sunlight had been able to break through, and we had perforce kept the lamps alight all day. Even now, as I came out and shut the door behind me, twilight seemed to have descended on the City, though the sun had barely set and it was not yet time for the street lamps to be lit.

I stood for a moment looking up the gloomy, twilit street, hesitating as to which way to go. Our branch was in Gracechurch Street close to the corner of Lombard Street, and both thoroughfares were equally convenient. Eventually, I chose Gracechurch Street, and, crossing to the west side, walked up it until I came to the little opening of Bell Yard. Turning into the dark entry, I trudged up the narrow passage, cogitating rather vaguely and wishing that I had provided something better than the scanty cold supper that I knew awaited me at my lodgings. But I was tired and chilly and empty; I had not had enough food during the day, owing to the pressure of work; so that the needs of the body tended to assert themselves to the exclusion of more elevated thoughts.

At the top of the yard I turned into the little tunnel-like covered passage that led through into Castle Court and brought me out by the railings of the churchyard. Skirting them, I went on to the entrance to the paved walk and passed in up a couple of steps and through the open gateway, noting that even "the litell Grene Churchyard" looked dull and drab under the lowering sky and that lights were twinkling in the office windows beyond the grass plot and in those of the tavern at the side.

At the end of the paved walk is a long flower-bed against the wall of St Michael's Church, and, just short of this, the arched entrance to another tunnel-like covered passage into which, near its middle, the deep south porch of the church opens. I was about to step down into the passage – which is below the level of the churchyard – when I noticed a hat lying on the flower-bed close up in the corner. It lay crown downwards with its silk lining exposed, and, as it appeared to be in perfectly good condition, I picked it up to examine it. It was quite a good hat; a grey soft felt, nearly new, and the initials AW, legibly written on the white lining, suggested that the owner had set some value on it. But where was the owner? And how on earth came this hat to be lying abandoned by the wayside? A man may drop a glove or a handkerchief or a tobacco pouch and be unaware of his loss; but surely the most absent-minded of men could hardly lose his hat without noticing the fact. And then the further question arose: what does one do with a derelict hat? Of course, I could have dropped it where I had found it; but from this my natural thriftiness and responsibility revolted. It was too good a hat to have been casually flung away by its owner, and, since Fate had appointed me its custodian, the duty seemed to devolve on me to restore it.

I stood for a few moments holding the hat and looking through the dark passage at the shape of light at the farther end, but no one was in sight; and I now recalled that I had not met a soul since I entered Bell Yard from Gracechurch Street. Still wondering how I should set about discovering the owner of the hat, I stepped down into the passage and began to walk along it; but when I reached the middle and came opposite the church porch, my problem seemed to solve itself in a rather startling fashion; for, glancing into the porch, I saw, dimly but quite distinctly in its shadowy depths, a man sitting on the lowest of the three steps that lead up to the church door. He was leaning back against the jamb limply and helplessly as if he were asleep or, more probably, drunk, the latter probability being rather confirmed by a stout walking-stick with a large ivory knob, which had fallen beside him, and what looked like a rimless eyeglass which lay on the stone floor between his feet. But what was more to my present purpose was the fact that not only was he bare-headed, but that no hat was visible. This, then, was doubtless the owner of the derelict.

Holding the latter conspicuously, I stepped into the cavern-like porch, and, addressing the man in a rather loud tone, enquired whether he had lost a hat. As he made no reply or any sign of having heard me, I was disposed to lay the hat down by his side and retire, when it occurred to me that he might possibly have had some kind of fit or seizure. On this I approached closer, and, stooping over him, listened for the sound of his breathing. But I could hear nothing nor could I make out any movement of its chest.

As he was sitting, or sprawling, with his legs spread out, his shoulders supported by the jamb of the door and his head drooping forward on his chest, his face was almost hidden from me. But I now knelt down beside him, and, taking my petrol lighter from my pocket, held it close to his face. And then, as the gleam of the flame fell on him, I sprang up with a gasp of horror. The man's eyes were wide open, staring before him with an intensity that was in hideous contrast to his limp and passive posture. And the face was unmistakably the face of a dead man.

Dropping the hat by his side, I ran through the passage into St Michael's Alley and down this to Cornhill. At the entrance to the alley I stood for a moment looking up and down the street. In the distance, near the Royal Exchange, I could see a white-sleeved policeman directing the traffic, and I was about to start off towards him when, glancing eastward, I saw a constable approaching along the pavement. At once I hurried away in his direction and we met nearly opposite St Peter's Church. A few words conveyed my information and secured his very complete attention.

"A dead man, you say. Whereabouts did you see him?"

"He is lying in the south porch of St Michael's Church, just up the alley."

"Well," said he, "you had better come along and show me"; and without further parley he started forward with long, swinging strides that gave me some trouble to keep up with him. Back along Cornhill we went and up the alley until we came to the arched entrance to the passage, and here the constable produced his lantern and switched on the light. As we came opposite the porch and my companion threw a beam of light into it, the cave-like interior was rendered clearly visible with the dead man sitting, or reclining, just as I had left, him.

"Yes," said the constable, "there don't seem to be much doubt about his being dead." Nevertheless, he put his ear close to the man's face, raising the head gently, and felt for the pulse at the wrist. Then he stood up and looked at me.

"I'd better get on the phone," said he, "and report to the station. They'll have to send an ambulance to take him to the mortuary. Will you stay here until I come back? I shan't be more than a minute or two."

Without waiting for an answer, he strode out of the passage and disappeared down the alley, leaving me to pace up and down in the gathering gloom or to stand and gaze out on the darkening churchyard. It was a dismal business, and very disturbing to the nerves I found it; for I am rather sensitive to horrors of any kind, and, being now tired and physically exhausted, I was more than

ordinarily susceptible. I had suffered a severe shock, and its effect
was still with me as I kept my vigil, now glancing with horrid
fascination at the shadowy figure in the dark porch, and now
stealing away to the entrance to be out of sight of it. Once, a man
came in from the offices across the churchyard, but he hurried
through into the alley, brushing past me and all unaware of that
dim and ghostly presence.

After the lapse of two or three incredibly long minutes the
constable reappeared, and, almost at the moment of his arrival, the
lights were switched on and a lamp in the vault of the passage
exactly opposite the porch threw a bright light on the dead man.

"Ah!" the officer commented cheerfully, "that's better. Now
we can see what we are about." He stepped up to the body,
and, stooping over it, cast the light from his lantern on the step
behind it.

"There's something there on the stone step," he remarked;
"some broken glass and some metal things. I can't quite see what
they are, but we'd better not meddle with them until the people
from the station arrive. But while we are waiting for the
ambulance I'll just jot down a few particulars." He produced a
large note-book, and, taking an attentive look at me, added: "We'll
begin with your name, address and occupation."

I gave him these, and he then enquired how I came to discover
the body. I had not much to tell, but, such as my story was, he
wrote it down verbatim in his note-book and made me show him
the exact spot where I had found the hat; of which spot he entered
a description in his book. When he had completed his notes, he
read out to me what he had written; and on my confirming
its correctness, he handed me his pencil and asked me to add
my signature.

He had just returned the note-book to his pocket when an
inspector appeared at the alley entrance of the passage, closely
followed by two constables carrying a stretcher and one or two
idlers who had probably been attracted by the ambulance. The

inspector walked briskly up to the porch, and, having cast a quick glance at the dead man, turned to the constable.

"I suppose," said he, "you have got all the particulars. Which is the man who discovered the body?"

"This is the gentleman, sir," the constable replied, introducing me; "Mr Robert Mortimer; and this is his statement."

He produced his note-book and presented it, open, to his superior; who stood under the lamp and ran his eye over the statement.

"Yes," he said when he had finished reading and returned the book to its owner, "that's all right. Not much in it except the hat. Just show me where you found it."

I conducted him up into the churchyard and pointed out the corner of the flower-bed where the hat had been lying. He looked at it attentively and then glanced down the passage, remarking that the dead man had apparently come down from Castle Court. "By the way," he added, "I suppose you don't recognise him?"

"No," I replied, "he is a total stranger to me."

"Ah, well," said he, "I expect we shall be able to find out who he is in time for the inquest."

His reference to the inquest prompted me to ask if I should be wanted to give evidence.

"Certainly," he replied. "You haven't much to tell, but the little that you have may be important."

We were now back at the porch, on the floor of which the stretcher had been placed. At a word from the inspector the two bearers lifted the corpse on to it, and, having laid the hat on the body and covered it with a waterproof sheet, grasped the handles of the stretcher, stood up, and marched away with their burden, followed by the spectators.

The raising of the body had brought into view the objects which the constable had observed and which now appeared to be the fragments of a broken hypodermic syringe. These the inspector collected with scrupulous care, spreading his handkerchief on the upper step to receive them and picking up even the minute splinters of glass that had scattered when the syringe was dropped. When he had gathered up every particle that was visible, and taken up some drops of moisture with a piece of blotting-paper, he made his collection into a neat parcel and put it in his pocket. Then he cast a rapid but searching glance over the floor and walls of the porch, and, apparently observing nothing worth noting, began to walk towards the alley.

"I wonder," he said as we turned into it and came in sight of the waiting ambulance, "how long that poor fellow had been lying there when you first saw him. Not very long, I should say. Couldn't have been. Somebody must have noticed him. However, I expect the doctor will be able to tell us how long he has been dead. And you had better note down all that you can remember of the circumstances so that you can be clear about it at the inquest."

Here we came out into Cornhill, where the ambulance had been drawn up opposite the church, and the inspector, having wished me "good night", pushed his way through the considerable crowd that had collected and took his place in the ambulance beside the driver. Just as the vehicle was moving away and I was about to do the same, a voice from behind me enquired:

"What's the excitement? Motor accident?"

I seemed to recognise the voice, which had a slight Scottish intonation, and when I turned to answer I recognised the speaker. He was a Mr Gillum, one of the bank's customers with whom I had often done business.

"No," I replied, "I don't know what it was, but the dead man looked perfectly horrible. I can't get his face out of my mind."

"Oh, but that won't do," said Gillum. "It has given you a bad shake up, but you've got to try to forget it."

"I know," said I, "but just now I'm rather upset. This affair caught me at the wrong time, after a long, tiring day."

"Yes," he agreed, "you do look a bit pale and shaky. Better come along with me and have a drink. That will steady your nerves."

"I am rather afraid of drinks at the moment," said I. "You see, I have had a long day and not very much in the way of food."

"Ah!" said he, "there you are. Horrors on an empty stomach. That's all wrong, you know. Now I'm going to prescribe for you. You will just come and have a bit of dinner and a bottle of wine with me. That will set you up and will give me the great pleasure of your society."

Now I must admit that a bit of dinner and a bottle of wine sounded gratefully in my ears, but I was reluctant to accept hospitality which my means did not admit conveniently of my returning. A somewhat extravagant taste in books absorbed the surplus of my modest income and left me rather short of pocket-money. However, Gillum would take no denial. Probably he grasped the position completely. At any rate, he brushed aside my half-hearted refusal without ceremony and, even while I was protesting, he hailed a prowling taxi, opened the door and bundled me in. I heard him give the address of a restaurant in Old Compton Street. Then he got in beside me and slammed the door.

"Now," said he, as the taxi trundled off, "for 'the gay and festive scenes and halls of dazzling light'; and oblivion to the demmed unpleasant body."

CHAPTER TWO

John Gillum

As the taxi pursued its unimpeded way westward through the half-populated streets, I reflected on the curious circumstances that had made me the guest of a man who was virtually a stranger to me, and I was disposed to consider what I knew of him. I use the word "disposed" advisedly, for, in fact, my mind was principally occupied by my late experiences, and the considerations which I here set down for the reader's information are those that might have occurred to me rather than those that actually did.

I had now been acquainted with John Gillum for some six months; ever since, in fact, I had been transferred to the Gracechurch Street branch of the bank. But our acquaintance was of the slightest. He was one of the bank's customers and I was a cashier. His visits to the bank were rather more frequent than those of most of our customers and on slack days he would linger to exchange a few words or even to chat for a while. Nevertheless, our relations hardly tended to grow in intimacy; for though he was a bright, gay, and rather humorous man, quite amusing to talk to, his conversation persistently concerned itself with racing matters and the odds on, or against, particular horses, a subject in which I was profoundly uninterested. In truth, despite our rather frequent meetings, his personality made so little impression on me that, if I had been asked to describe him, I could have said no more than that he was a tallish, rather good-looking man with black hair and beard which contrasted rather noticeably with his blue eyes, that he spoke with a slight Scotch accent and that two of his upper front teeth had been rather extensively filled with gold. This latter characteristic did, indeed, attract my notice rather unduly; for, though gold is a beautiful material (and one that a banker might be expected to regard with respectful appreciation), these golden teeth rather jarred on me and I found it difficult to avoid looking at them as we talked.

Yet even in those days I felt a certain interest in our customer; but it was a purely professional interest. As cashier, I naturally knew all about his account and his ways of dealing with his money, and on both, and especially his financial habits, I occasionally speculated with mild curiosity. For his habits were not quite normal, or at least were not like those of most other private customers. The latter usually make most of their payments by cheque. But Gillum seemed to make most of his in cash. It is true that he appeared to pay most of his tradespeople by cheque, but from time to time, and at pretty frequent intervals, he would present a "self" cheque for a really considerable sum – one, or even two or three hundred pounds, and occasionally a bigger sum still – and take the whole of it away in pound notes.

It was rather remarkable, in fact very much so when I came to look over the ledger and note the fluctuations of his account. For at fairly regular intervals he paid in really large cheques – up to a thousand pounds – mostly drawn upon an Australian bank, which for a time swelled his account to very substantial proportions. But, by degrees, and not very small degrees, his balance dwindled until he seemed on the verge of an overdraft, and then another big cheque would be paid in and give him a fresh start.

Now there is nothing remarkable in the fluctuation of an account when the customer receives payment periodically in large sums and pays out steadily in the small amounts which represent the ordinary expenses of living. But when I came to cast up Gillum's account, it was evident that the great bulk of his expenditure was in the form of cash. And it seemed additional to the ordinary domestic payments, as I have said; and I found myself wondering what on earth he could be doing with his money. He could not be making investments, or even "operating" on the Stock Exchange, for those transactions would have been settled by cheque. Apparently he was making some sort of payments which had to be made in cash.

Of course it was no business of mine. Still, it was a curious and interesting problem. What sort of payments were these that he was making? Now when a man pays away at pretty regular intervals considerable sums in cash, the inference is that he is having some sort of dealings with someone who either will not accept a cheque or is not a safe person to be trusted with one. But a person who will not accept payment by an undoubtedly sound cheque is a person who is anxious to avoid evidence that a payment has been made. Such anxiety suggests a secret and probably unlawful transaction; and in practice, such a transaction is usually connected with the offence known as "demanding money with menaces." So, as I cast up the very large amounts that Gillum had drawn out in cash, I asked myself, "Is he a gambler, or has he fallen into the clutches of a blackmailer?" The probability of the latter explanation was suggested by certain large withdrawals at approximately quarterly periods, and also by the fact that Gillum not only took payment almost exclusively in pound notes, but also showed a marked preference for notes that had been in circulation as compared with new notes, of the serial numbers of which the bank would have a record. Still, the two possibilities were not mutually exclusive. A gambler is by no means an unlikely person to be the subject of blackmail.

Such, then, were the reflections that might have occupied my mind had it not been fully engaged with my recent adventure. As it was, the short journey was beguiled by brief spells of scrappy and disjointed conversation which lasted until the taxi drew up opposite the brilliantly lighted entrance of the restaurant and a majestic person in the uniform of a Liberian admiral hurried forward to open the door. We both stepped out, and when Gillum had paid the taxi-driver – extravagantly, as I gathered from the man's demeanour – we followed the admiral into a wide hall where we were transferred to the custody of other and less gorgeous myrmidons.

Giamborini's Restaurant was an establishment of a kind that was beyond my experience, as it was certainly beyond my means. It oozed luxury and splendour at every pore. The basin of precious marble in which I purged myself of the by-products of the London atmosphere was of a magnificence that almost called for an apology for washing in it; the floor of delicate Florentine mosaic seemed too precious to stand upon in common boots; while as to the dining-saloon, I can recall it only as a bewildering vision of marble and gilding, of vast mirrors, fretted ceilings and stately columns – apparently composed of gold and polished Gorgonzola – and multitudinous chandeliers of a brilliancy that justified Dick Swiveller's description, lately quoted by Gillum. I found it a little oppressive and was disposed to compare it (not entirely to its advantage) with the homely Soho restaurants that I remembered in the far-off pre-war days.

A good many of the tables were unoccupied, though the company was larger than I should have expected, for the hour was rather late for dinner but not late enough for theatre suppers. Of the guests present, the men were mostly in evening dress, and so, I suppose, were the women, judging by the considerable areas of their persons that were uncovered by clothing. As to their social status I could form no definite opinion, but the general impression conveyed by their appearance was that they hardly represented the cream of the British aristocracy. But perhaps I was prejudiced by the prevailing magnificence.

"What are you going to have, Mortimer?" my host asked as we took our seats at the table to which we had been conducted. "Gin and It, cocktail, or sherry? You prefer sherry. Good. So do I. It is wine that maketh glad the heart of man, not these chemical concoctions."

He selected from the wine list the particular brand of sherry that commended itself to him and then gave a few general directions which were duly noted. As the waiter was turning away, he added: "I suppose you haven't got such a thing as an evening paper about you?"

The waiter had not. But there was no difficulty. He would get one immediately. Was there any particular paper that would be preferred?

"No," replied Gillum, "any evening paper will do."

Thereupon the waiter bustled away with the peculiar quick mincing gait characteristic of his craft; a gait specially and admirably adapted to the rapid conveyance of loaded trays. In a minute or two he came skating back with a newspaper under his arm and a tray of hors-d'œuvres and two brimming glasses of sherry miraculously balanced on his free hand. Gillum at once opened the paper, while I fixed a ravenous eye on the various and lurid contents of the tray. As I had expected, he turned immediately to the racing news. But he did not read the column. After a single brief glance, he folded up the paper and laid it aside with the remark, uttered quite impassively: "No luck."

"I hope you haven't dropped any money," said I, searching for the least inedible contents of the tray.

"Nothing to write home about," he replied. "Fifty."

"Fifty!" I repeated. "You don't mean fifty pounds?"

"Yes," he replied calmly. "Why not? You can't expect to bring it off every time."

"But fifty pounds!" I exclaimed, appalled by this horrid waste of money. "Why, it would furnish a small library."

He laughed indulgently. "That's the bookworm's view of the case but it isn't mine. I've had my little flutter and I'm not complaining; and let me tell you, Mortimer, that I have just barely missed winning a thousand pounds."

I was on the point of remarking that a miss is as good as a mile, but, as that truth has been propounded on some previous occasions, I refrained and asked: "When you say that you have just barely missed winning a thousand pounds, what exactly do you mean? How do you know that you nearly won that amount?"

"It is perfectly simple, my dear fellow," said he. "I laid fifty pounds on the double event at twenty to one against. That is to say, I backed two particular horses to win two particular races. Now, one of my horses won his race all right. The other ought to have done the same. But he didn't. He came in second. So I lost. But you see how near a thing it was."

"Then," said I, "if you had backed the two horses separately, I suppose you would have won on the whole transaction?"

"I suppose I should," he admitted, "but there would have been nothing in it. The horse that won was the favourite. But the double event was a real sporting chance. Twenty to one against. And you see how near I was to bringing it off."

"Nevertheless," I objected, "you lost. And you went into the business with the knowledge, not only that you might lose, but that the chances that you would lose were estimated at twenty to one. I should have supposed that no sane man would have taken such a chance as that."

He looked at me with a broad smile that displayed his golden teeth to great disadvantage.

"Thus saith the banker," he commented. "But you are taking a perverted view of the transaction. You are considering it as an investor might; as a means of realising the greatest profit with the smallest risk. That is the purely commercial standpoint. But I am not engaged in commerce; I am engaged in sport – in gambling, if you prefer the expression. Now the essence of the sport of gambling is the possibility that you may lose. If you were certain to win every time, it might be highly profitable but it would be uncommonly poor fun. Believe me, Mortimer, the heart and soul of the game is the chance of losing."

He spoke quite gravely and earnestly and the statement put me, for the moment, rather at a loss for a reply. For, in its mad way, it was true, and yet, from a practical point of view, it was nonsense. Meanwhile, the waiter brought and placed before us a strangely sophisticated dish, based, I believe, on fish, and then proceeded to fill our glasses with champagne. It was, I think, quite good champagne, though I am no authority, my extreme dissipation, in the ordinary way, not going beyond the traditional "chop and a pint of claret." At any rate, it was highly stimulating, and when Gillum had raised his glass and, with a toast "to the next double event," emptied it and insisted on my doing likewise, the last traces of my depression vanished.

"I admit, Gillum," said I, resuming the discussion, that there is a certain amount of truth in what you say. But we must try to keep some sense of proportion. Fifty pounds is a devil of a price for the fun of a little flutter. Surely you could have got your sport at a cheaper rate than that."

"But that is just what you can't do," said he. "What you don't seem to realise is that the intensity of the thrill is strictly proportionate to the amount of the possible loss, and, of course, of the possible gain. I could have laid five shillings on the double event and been secure from appreciable loss. But then I should have stood to gain a mere fiver. No, my young friend, you can't get a respectable thrill for five bob. And there is another thing that you are over-looking. You speak as if I lost every time. But I don't. Sometimes I win. If I never won, it would be a dull game and I expect I shouldn't go on."

"I think you would," said I. "You would always be hoping that at last you would get your money back."

"Perhaps you are right," he conceded. "It is certainly the fact that a genuine gambler is not put out by a succession of losses. The oftener he loses the more dogged he becomes."

"So I have always understood," said I. "But to come to your own case, you say that sometimes you win. How often do you win? Taking your betting transactions as a whole, how does the balance stand? Are you in pocket or out?"

"Out, of course," he replied promptly. "Everybody is, excepting the bookies. And they don't do it for sport, but just as a cold-blooded matter of business. They don't lose, in ordinary circumstances, and they don't win to a considerable extent. They just balance their books and make a comfortable living. But, of course, the fact that the bookies are in pocket by the transaction is clear proof that the backers, as a whole, must be out."

There seemed to me something very odd and rather abnormal in the reasonable and lucid way in which he discussed this absurdity. I had the sort of feeling that one might have had in discussing insane delusions with a lunatic. But I returned to the charge, futile as I knew the discussion to be.

"Very well," said I, "you agree that the balance of profit and loss is against you. How much, you know better than I do, but I suspect that your losses, from month to month, are pretty heavy." (Of course, I did not "suspect." I knew. The bank's books told the story.) "You must be paying very considerable sums for your little flutters and I put it to you, isn't it a most monstrous waste of money?"

He laughed cheerfully and refilled our glasses.

"I see," he replied, "that you are an incorrigible financier. You are taking a completely perverted view of the matter. You speak of waste of money. But what, after all, is money?"

"If you are asking me that as a banker," I replied, "I can only say that I don't know. I know what money was before the war, but now that the politicians and financial theorists have taken it over, it has become something quite different and I don't profess to understand it."

"That isn't quite what I meant," said he. "I was referring to money in general terms. What is it? It is simply a means of obtaining certain satisfactions or pleasures. No one wants money for itself excepting a miser."

"You can rule out misers," said I. "They are an extinct race. A miser doesn't hoard paper vouchers which have only a conventional and temporary value."

"No, I suppose not," he agreed. "At any rate, I am not a miser" (which was most unquestionably true), "and I have no use for money excepting as a means of obtaining satisfactions. And that is

19

the rational use of money. I put it to you, Mortimer, if a man has money and there are certain things that he desires and that money will buy, is it not obviously reasonable that he should exchange the thing that he doesn't want for the things that he does? You speak of waste of money. But is it wasted when it is being used for the very purpose for which it exists? Take, for instance, this bottle of champagne – which, by the way, is getting low and needs replacing. Now, I think we like champagne."

"I do, certainly," I admitted.

"I am glad you do. So do I. And we can get it in exchange for your despised paper vouchers. Accordingly, like sensible men, we make the exchange; and I submit that it is a reasonable and profitable transaction. For if, as you suggest, the money is a mere fleeting convention, the champagne for which we have exchanged it isn't. It is real champagne."

Seeing that we had already emptied one bottle, the cogency of this argument did not impress me. Probably I should have proceeded to rebut it, but at this point an interruption occurred and the discussion broke off.

When we had entered the room, I had noticed a party of three persons, two men and a woman, at a table in a corner. They had caught my attention because we had evidently caught theirs. But I don't think that Gillum observed them; and when we had seated ourselves, as his back was towards them, they were outside his range of vision whereas I was nearly facing them; and throughout our meal I found myself from time to time looking in their direction, attracted as before by the occasional glances that they cast in ours. It seemed to me that they must be acquainted with Gillum, for there was otherwise nothing noticeable in our appearance. At any rate, they were obviously interested in us and I received the impression that we were being discussed.

They did not prepossess me favourably. I cannot say exactly why, but there was an indefinable something about them that jarred on me. The men did not look like gentlemen, and the woman, dressed in the extreme of an unbecoming fashion, was so heavily and coarsely made up as to extinguish any good looks that she might have had. Everything about her seemed to be artificial. Her hair was of an unnatural colour, her cheeks were visibly painted, and her lips were plastered with crude vermilion like the lips of a circus clown.

That these people were acquaintances of Gillum's became evident when they rose to depart, for they steered a course across the room which brought them opposite our table. And here they halted; and, for the first time, Gillum became aware of their presence. His expression did not convey to me that he was overjoyed, but as the lady bestowed on him the kind of leer that is known as "giving the glad eye," he made shift to produce a responsive smile.

"Now, don't let us interrupt your dinner," said she, as he rose to shake hands. "But, as you cut us dead when you came in, we have just come across to say 'howdy' and let you know that we saw you. We are now off to the club. Shall you be coming along presently?"

Gillum was inclined to be evasive. "I don't quite know what the programme is," he replied. "It depends on what my guest would like to do."

"Bring him along with you," said she, "and let him see the ball roll. I'm sure he'd enjoy it, wouldn't you?" As she asked the question, she turned to me with the peculiar cat-like grin that one sees in newspaper portraits of young women, with a distinct tendency to the "glad eye"; and I noticed that it seemed a rather tired eye and slightly puffy about the lower lids.

"I am not really an enthusiast in regard to billiards," I replied, "and I am no player. But it is interesting enough to look on at a good game."

Apparently I had said something funny, for the lady greeted my answer with a gay – and rather strident – laugh, and the two men, who had been looking on in silence, broke into sour grins. But Gillum, also smiling, evidently wished to get rid of his acquaintances for he interposed with the air of closing the conversation.

"Well, we shall see what we feel like when we have dined. I won't make any engagement now."

The lady took the hint graciously enough. "Very well, Jack," said she. "We will leave you in peace and hope to see you later;" and with this and another smile which embraced us both, she moved off with her two companions, neither of whom seemed to take any notice of Gillum.

"What was the joke?" I asked when they had gone. "And what club was she referring to?"

"It isn't really a club," replied Gillum. "It is what, I suppose, you would call a gambling hell; a place where you can stake your money at trente et quarante, rouge et noir, chemin de fer, or any of the regular gambling games. The joke was that the ball she meant was not a billiard ball but the little ball that rolls round the roulette wheel. It wasn't a particularly amusing joke."

"No," I agreed. "And are these people connected with the club?"

"Very much so," he replied. "That tall chappie – the one with the squint – runs the place, and I should think he does fairly well out of it. He is a Frenchman of the name of Foucault."

"He doesn't look a particularly amiable person," I remarked, recalling the rather sulky way in which he had looked on at the interview.

Gillum laughed. "He is a silly ass," said he, "as jealous as the devil; and as Madame's manners are, as you saw, of the distinctly coquettish, slap and tickle order, there is pretty constant trouble. But he needn't worry. There is no harm in the fair Marie. Her engaging wiles are all in the way of business."

"Do you spend much time at the club?" I asked.

"I drop in there pretty frequently," he replied.

"And I suppose you drop a fair amount of money."

"I suppose I do. But not so much as you would think. You orthodox financiers seem to imagine that a gambler always loses, but that is quite a mistake. The luck isn't always on the one side.

Sometimes I pick up a little windfall that pays my expenses for quite a long time."

"Still," said I, "the balance must be against you in the long run."

"I have already admitted," he replied, "that I lose on my gambling transactions as a whole, and probably I lose, in the long run, at the club, though it isn't so easy to keep accounts of what I do there. But supposing that the balance is against me. What about it? Foucault runs the club to make a profit. But he can only make a profit if the players make a loss. What they lose to the bank is, in effect, their payment to him for the entertainment that he supplies. Hang it all, Mortimer, you can't expect to get your fun for nothing."

"Some people do," said I, "the people, I mean, who have infallible systems. I gather that you don't use a system."

"Well," he replied cautiously, "I haven't managed yet to devise a system that really works, but I have given some thought to the matter. There ought to be some way of ascertaining how the laws of chance operate, and if one could discover that, one would have the means of circumventing them."

"You haven't tried the plan of doubling the stakes when you lose?"

"Yes, I have; and I must admit that, for sheer excitement, there is nothing like it. Your real, rabid gambler loves it — and usually cleans himself out. But for a sane and sober gambler it is not practicable. There are too many snags. To begin with, at the best you only get your money back plus the amount of the first stake. Consequently, the first stake must be a fairly large one or there is nothing in it. But if you start with a substantial stake and the luck is against you, you are up in enormous figures before you know where you are. For instance, supposing you are playing roulette and you lay a hundred pounds on manque or impair or any of the even chances. If you lose four times in succession, which would not be extraordinary, you have dropped fifteen hundred pounds; and the danger is that you may empty your pocket before the winning coup comes round. Then you have lost the lot. But there is another snag. The bank won't let you go on doubling as long as you like. There is a limit set to each kind of bet, and when you reach that limit you are not allowed to double any more. If you go on playing you have got to go back to a flat stake, in which case it is impossible for you to win back what you have lost. So, regarded as a serious method of play, the doubling racket is no go."

"It seems astonishing," said I, "that anyone should practise it. But perhaps they don't."

"Oh, don't they?" said Gillum. "You must understand, Mortimer, that to the real, perfect gambler, the charm of the game is the risk of losing. The bigger the risk, the greater the thrill. Plenty of people at the club, particularly the roulette players, double the stakes when they lose; and there is a temptation, you know, when you have lost, to take another chance in the hope of getting your money back. But it is a bad plan, because you stand to lose so much more than you stand to gain."

"Don't some people double on their winnings?" I asked.

"Ah," said he, "but that is quite a different kind of affair. There is some sense in that because it is quite the opposite of the other method. If you win you win, you don't merely get your money back; and if you eventually lose, you have only lost your original stake – plus your winnings, of course. Supposing you take an even chance at roulette, say you put a hundred pounds on red and you win; and suppose that you leave the stake and the winnings – two hundred pounds – on the table as a fresh stake. If the red turns up again you take up four hundred, of which one hundred is your original stake. You have won three hundred. But if you lose, you have only lost a hundred, plus the three that you had won. From a gambler's point of view it is quite a sound method."

"Yes," I agreed, "I see that, at least, you start with the knowledge of the amount that you stand to lose. But the whole thing is beyond my comprehension. I can't begin to understand the state of mind of a man who is prepared to risk his money in a transaction over which he has no control and in respect to which no judgment, calculation or prevision is possible."

He laughed gaily and refilled our glasses.

"You are a banker to the finger-tips, Mortimer," said he; "and, as you happen to be my banker, I am not disposed to quarrel with your eminently correct outlook. I suppose you have never seen a gambling den."

"Never," I replied; "and I am an absolute ignoramus on the subject of gambling. I hardly know how to play the common card games."

"I think you ought to know what these shows are like," said he. "I can assure you that, as a mere spectacle, a regular gaming house is worth seeing. What do you say to strolling round to the club with me when we have had our coffee? It's too late to do anything else."

It was really too late to do anything but go home and go to bed. But I could hardly, in the circumstances, suggest that course. Nor, in fact, was I particularly disposed to; for the excellent dinner and the equally excellent wine had produced a state of exhilaration that made me not disinclined for adventure. In my normal state, nothing would have induced me to set foot in a gambling den. Now I fell in readily enough with Gillum's suggestion.

"But shan't I be expected to play?" I enquired. "Because I am not going to."

"That will be all right," he replied. "I shall explain to Madame, and she will see that you are left in peace. But you understand that this is an unregistered club and that you will keep your own counsel about your visit there. I shall have to guarantee your secrecy."

I gave the necessary undertaking and Gillum then held the wine bottle up to the light.

"There's half a bottle left," said he, making as if to refill my glass. "Won't you really? Not another half-glass? Well, I don't think I will, either. We will just have our coffee and a cognac and then toddle round to the club and see the ball roll."

CHAPTER THREE

The Gaming House

From Giamborini's we strolled forth into Wardour Street, and, proceeding in a southerly direction, presently turned into Gerrard Street. I knew the place slightly and on my occasional passage through it had found a certain bookish interest in contrasting its present faded and shabby aspect with that which it must have presented in the days when Dryden was a resident, and, later, when the Literary Club with Johnson, Reynolds, Goldsmith and Gibbon, held its meetings here.

"Queer old street," Gillum commented, looking about him disparagingly. "Quite fashionable, I believe, at one time, but it is down on its luck nowadays. Very mixed population, too. All sorts of odd clubs, British and foreign, and tradesmen who seem to have survived from the Stone Age. There is a fellow somewhere along here who makes spurs. Think of it. Spurs! In the twentieth century. This is our show."

He halted at a doorway which, shabby and grimy as it was, yet preserved some vestiges of its former dignity, and having run his eye over an assortment of bell-handles, put his finger on an electric button which surmounted them and pressed several times at irregular intervals.

"Are you ringing out a code message?" I asked.

"Well, yes, in a way," he replied. There is a particular kind of ring that the regular members give just to let the people upstairs know that it isn't a stranger. There is always the possibility of a raid and our friends like to have time to make the necessary arrangements."

The idea of a police raid was not a pleasant one and the suggestion tended rather to damp my enthusiasm. I expressed the hope that this would not happen to be the occasion of one.

"No, indeed," said Gillum. "It would be unfortunate for you. Wouldn't increase your prestige at the bank. But you needn't worry. There has never been any trouble since I have known the place. I have sometimes suspected that Foucault has some sort of discreet understanding with the authorities, but in any case, I know there is a bolt hole through into the next house where an Italian club has its premises."

This did not sound very reassuring. I felt the exhilarating effects of the champagne evaporating rapidly; and when at length the door was opened, the aspect of the janitor did not produce a favourable impression. He was a big, powerful man, with a heavy jaw and beetling brows and a strong suggestion of the professional pugilist. He carried an electric lamp, the light of which he cast on us while he inspected us critically. Then the truculent expression faded suddenly from his face and a cheerful Irish voice exclaimed:

"Whoy, it's Mr Gillum. Good evening, sorr. And the other gentleman, would he be a friend of yours?"

"Yes," replied Gillum, "it's all right, Cassidy. All's well and the lights are burning brightly, sir."

Mr Cassidy chuckled as he let us in and shut the door.

"Many's the time," said he, "as I've spoken them same wurrds in the days when I used the sea. What did ye say the gentleman's name was?"

"His name is Mortimer," replied Gillum.

"To be sure it is," said Cassidy, adding, as he threw his light downwards: "Kape your oyes on the stairs, sorr. There's a tread loose at the turn."

The stairs were, in fact, in somewhat indifferent repair, but I noticed as the light flickered over them that this had once been quite a handsome staircase though a trifle narrow; and even now the fine moulded handrail and the graceful twisted balusters redeemed its extreme shabbiness. At the top of the second flight we came to a bare landing with a door facing us. This Cassidy opened, and, having admitted us, passed in himself, crossed the room and disappeared through another doorway, presumably to report our arrival and identity.

I looked round the room which we had entered and was conscious of a faint sense of anti-climax. It was so very ordinary and so very innocent; much like the interior of the cheaper kind of old-fashioned Soho restaurant. At the farther end of the room was a large sideboard, presided over by a man in a white coat and cap and piled with a variety of food, including a ham, a number of different types of sausage, a great stack of sandwiches and long French loaves. On a shelf behind was a long row of bottles of mineral waters but on the sideboard I noted several champagne bottles, a few of whisky, and some of absinthe and other liqueurs.

The room was moderately full of people; full enough to have given Mr Cassidy considerable occupation if they had been admitted separately. Some of them were lounging about, talking; others were seated at little tables, taking food rather hurriedly, and some were actually drinking ginger ale, though most of them were provided with wine, whisky or Dutch gin. One or two of the tables were furnished with chess-boards and sets of dominoes, but none of them appeared to be in use. Apparently their function was purely psychological. They were part of the "make-up" of the establishment.

I had not much time to examine the company, but a rapid inspection conveyed to me the impression that they were all rather abnormal and slightly disreputable. There was an air of eagerness, anxiety and excitement about them, mingled, in some cases, with a sort of wild hilarity. Those at the tables gobbled their food as if they were hastily stoking up and were anxious to get the business over. Particularly I noticed a group of four men standing by the sideboard devouring sandwiches wolfishly and gulping champagne from tumblers. But, as I said, I had little time to observe them, for, after a brief pause and a curious glance round the room, Gillum conducted me to a door near the farther end from which Cassidy emerged as we approached.

There was certainly nothing innocent about the room that we now entered. A single glance convicted it. The roulette table alone furnished evidence to which there could be no answer, and the groups of haggard, intent men and women gathered round the card tables that filled most of the room, if less conclusive to a possible raider, were unmistakable, seen as I saw them.

From one of these tables the lady of the restaurant rose, and laying down her cards, came to meet us.

"So you have persuaded Mr Mortimer to come," she said, bestowing a gracious smile on me and offering an extensive sample of teeth for my inspection (apparently she had got my name from Mr Cassidy).

"Yes," replied Gillum, "but he has only come as a spectator. I have just brought him round to show him the ropes in case he may feel disposed for an evening's sport later on."

"That is very good of you, Jack," said she. "Of course, he can please himself as to whether he plays or not. Perhaps, when he has looked on for a while, he may feel inclined to try his luck. People who come to look on very often do."

"I have no doubt they do," said Gillum with a sly smile. "The complaint is catching and fools who come to scoff remain to play."

"I hope Mr Mortimer hasn't come to scoff," said she; and when I had protested with more emphasis than sincerity she asked: "Where is your pupil going to take his first lesson?"

"Well," he replied, "as he knows practically nothing about card games, I think roulette will suit him best. Besides, it is the beginner's game and it is the most typical game of chance."

"That's true," Madame agreed, "though it seems to me a dull game, if you can call it a game at all. Let us find a couple of chairs so that you and your pupil can sit together; and then, when Mr Mortimer is comfortably settled, I want to have a few words with you."

We secured two chairs and placed them in a vacant space at the end of the table by the compartment distinguished by a red lozenge on the green cloth. Then Madame introduced me to the croupier, whom she addressed as Hyman – his surname I found later to be Goldfarb – and when Gillum had placed his hat on his chair, she linked her arm with his and led him away among the multitude of card tables.

Left to myself, I first disposed of my hat and stick under my chair, as I noticed that several other men had done, though there was a large hat rack in the adjoining room. Then I proceeded to make my observations.

There was plenty to observe, and it was all strange and novel to me. There were, for instance, the various players, most of them seated at the table, though some preferred to stand and hover about behind the chairs, and there was the croupier, a pleasant-faced Jew, calm, impassive and courteous, though obviously very much "on the spot"; and there were the parties of players at the card tables, most of whom I could see from my position without appearing to spy on them.

I considered them one by one. My next neighbour was an elderly woman whom I judged to be French, who sat like a graven image, silently and immovably intent on her game. She seemed to have the disease in a chronic form, for she played mechanically without a sign of satisfaction when she won or annoyance when she lost. At each spin of the wheel she laid a ten-shilling note on the space before which she sat – that marked with the red lozenge. If she won, she put the note that she had gained into a little handbag and held the other in readiness for the next turn of the wheel; if she lost, she fished a note out of the bag for the next coup. So she went on as long as I observed her; always the same stake on the same spot. It looked deadly dull, and it was not gambling at all in any proper sense; for, by the ordinary laws of chance, it was almost impossible for her either to win or lose to an appreciable extent. So fatuous her proceedings seemed that I almost felt more respect for her next-door neighbour, a small

German who might, from his appearance, have been a waiter. He certainly took risks, for his formula was two numbers "à cheval," and he kept to the same two numbers. As the odds against him were seventeen to one, he naturally lost with great regularity; and when he lost cursed under his breath – but not very far under – shook his head and grimaced angrily. I think he must have been pretty near the end of his resources, for I saw him take out a wallet and look into it anxiously. But at this moment his magic number was announced, whereat he gave a yell of ecstasy, grabbed up his winnings, stuffed them into his wallet excepting one pound note, which he laid on the same spot as before and lost within a minute.

From the roulette table my attention wandered to the other occupants of the room and occasionally to Gillum and Madame, who walked slowly to and fro at the end of the room conversing earnestly. Nor was I the only observer. Several of the card-players cast a glance from time to time at the pair, and the three occupants of the table from which Madame had risen made no secret of their interest. Two of these I could not see very well but M. Foucault sat facing me; and never have I seen a more evil expression than that which his countenance bore as he watched them. He was not a pleasant-looking man at the best, and a slight squint did not improve matters; but now his aspect was positively villainous.

Not that his manifest anger was without provocation, for Madame's oglings and her caressing manner towards Gillum, regardless of the company, would have been offensive to the most tolerant of husbands. She might have been Gillum's lover – and not a very reticent lover at that. It is true that Gillum took it all very coolly with no sign of responsive demonstrations; but I felt that he was being more than indiscreet. Obviously, in his association with this woman, who seemed of set purpose to exasperate her husband, he was taking the risk of serious trouble.

Presently, to my relief, they strolled over to Foucault's table and while Madame resumed her seat, Gillum drew up a spare chair and sat down facing her husband. Apparently the lady was giving some sort of explanation for she spoke volubly, leaning across the table to avoid raising her voice, while the others leaned forward to listen, and Foucault appeared to be gazing simultaneously at his wife and Gillum – an optical illusion, of course, due to his "swivel eye."

The discussion did not last long, and it was evidently quite an amicable affair, for when Gillum stood up, he shook hands with them all, including the grim-faced Foucault, before turning away to rejoin me; and I noted the leave-taking with considerable satisfaction, for it was getting alarmingly late and I began to feel that I had had enough of this not very thrilling form of entertainment.

"Yes," Gillum agreed, when I ventured on a hint to that effect, "time's getting on and you've to be at the bank as fresh as a lark tomorrow morning. But we must have one little flutter before we go. What shall it be? Shall we try an experiment with the doubling plan that we were discussing at dinner?"

Without waiting for an answer he laid a pound note on the red beside the ten-shilling note that the elderly lady had just put down. I watched with unexpected interest as the revolving wheel was checked and the little white ball clattered round the dial, and was sensibly disappointed when it settled at last in compartment 21. For 21 happened unfortunately to be black. But Gillum was as indifferent as the old lady, and while Mr Goldfarb raked in the bank's winnings and paid out to the players who had won, he calmly selected two fresh notes from his bulging wallet.

Once more the wheel was spun, the ball was thrown out on to the revolving surface, then the croupier chanted "Rien ne va plus" and checked the wheel, Gillum laid down his two notes, and a dozen pairs of eyes anxiously followed the travels of the dancing ball. At length it dropped into compartment 32 – black again; and Gillum sorted out four pound notes from his wallet.

So it went on for a while. Regardless of the law of probability, the ball persisted in dropping into black compartments, and at each failure Gillum doubled his stake. I watched the proceedings with ridiculous anxiety. At the fourth losing coup when the croupier raked in eight of Gillum's pound notes, I noted mentally that my friend was already fifteen pounds out of pocket. If he lost the next coup, that fifteen would become thirty-one. It was positively harrowing to a thrifty man like myself, accustomed to keep a rigid account of every shilling that I spent.

However, he did not lose this time. My anxious eye following the ball, saw it eventually settle in compartment four which was red; and the croupier's rake, instead of sweeping away Gillum's sixteen pounds, added to them another sixteen.

"There, you see," said Gillum; "I am one pound to the good; and that is all I should have gained if I had gone on till doomsday. But I am a gainer to the extent that I have got back what I had lost."

He began to pick up the notes, counting them as he did so. Among them there had been four ten-shilling notes, but now there were only three; the explanation of which was that the old lady, when she had gathered up her two notes, had quietly added to them one of Gillum's. I saw her do it, and so did he; and he now ventured, with the utmost delicacy, to point out the little inadvertency. The lady gazed at him stonily, and I think was about to contest the matter, but at this moment a shout from the farther end of the room, followed by a crash and the sound of shattering glass, effectually diverted our attention.

I looked round quickly and saw two men, each grasping the other by the hair and both yelling like Bedlamites, one accusing the other – in Italian – of being a cheat and the other retorting – in French – that his accuser was a liar. A table and two chairs had been capsized, and very soon, as the combatants gyrated wildly and clawed at each other, more tables were capsized. Then the occupants of those tables joined in the fray with suitable vocal accompaniments and in a moment pandemonium reigned in the previously quiet room. As Foucault and his two friends sprang up and charged into the midst of the mêlée, the door burst open and Cassidy rushed in like an angry bull.

"We'd better clear out of this," said Gillum. "If they keep up this hullabaloo they'll bring the police up."

As I agreed heartily, he grabbed up his winnings (but I observed that there were now only two ten-shilling notes) and we retrieved our hats from under the chairs and stole out as well as we could through the little crowd of spectators from the restaurant-room who had gathered round the door to look on at the battle. With the aid of my pocket lamp we made the perilous passage of the stairs – not forgetting the loose tread – and at last emerged safely into the street.

"My word!" exclaimed Gillum, as we crossed the road the more completely to sever our connection with the club, "how those dagoes do yell when they have a bit of a scrap. Just listen to them."

There was not much need to listen for the uproar was such that windows were opening and various nightbirds were appearing from the doors of adjacent houses. Evidently, it was desirable for us to get out of the neighbourhood as quickly as possible; which we did, walking briskly but with no outward sign of undue hurry until we were safely out in Wardour Street, where we turned to the left and headed for Leicester Square. Here we had the good fortune to encounter a prowling, nocturnal taxi, the driver of which Gillum hailed by voice and gesture. As the vehicle drew up at the kerb he turned to me and asked: "Whereabouts do you hang out, Mortimer?"

"I live at Highbury," I replied.

"Yes, but that's a trifle vague. What's the exact address?" I gave him my full postal address which he communicated to the driver. "And," he added, "you can drop me at Clifford's Inn Passage, opposite the Inner Temple Gate. Will that do for the whole journey?"

"That" appeared to be a ten-shilling note and the driver replied that "it would do very well, thank you, sir"; whereupon we got in and the cab trundled away towards the Strand. I made some ineffectual efforts to refund my share of the payment, but Gillum declared that the calculation was beyond his arithmetic and suggested that we should work it out on some more suitable occasion. We were still arguing the point when the cab stopped in the shadow of St Dunstan's Church and Gillum got out.

"Well, good night, Mortimer," said he, "or good morning, to be more exact. I hope you have had a pleasant and instructive evening. You have certainly had a full one what with corpses, illegal gambling, and the battle of the dagoes."

He shut the door and waved his hand, and the taxi resumed its journey, turning up Fetter Lane and later heading for Gray's Inn Road. Now that I was alone, I felt a strong disposition to go to sleep; but by an effort I managed to keep awake and watch the familiar landmarks as they slipped by until, in a surprisingly short time, the taxi drew up at the gate of the "eligible suburban residence" which enshrined the two rooms that served me as a home. The driver actually got out to open the door for me – possibly suspecting some temporary disability, or perhaps as a demonstration of his satisfaction with the fare. At any rate, he gave me a cheerful "good night" and I inserted my latch-key with ease and precision as the clock of a neighbouring church was striking two.

CHAPTER FOUR
Abel Webb, Deceased

The events of the evening which I had spent with Gillum gave me a good deal to think about. There was no longer any mystery as to what he did with the large sums that he drew from the bank. He just gambled them away. As to how much it was possible for an inveterate gambler like Gillum to drop in any one transaction, I could form no guess. Apparently there was no limit excepting the total amount that the gambler possessed. I had heard and read of players who had lost thousands in a single game, but it had always seemed to me incredible. Now, however, judging by what I had seen, and still more by what Gillum had said, I felt that nothing could overstate the monstrous truth.

The reflection was a sad and depressing one. It made me quite unhappy. For Gillum was no longer a mere customer. He had become an acquaintance, almost a friend, and I had found him a pleasant, likeable man, and apparently a man of good intelligence apart from his insane hobby. It really distressed me to think of a man with his brilliant opportunities frittering away the means of achievement in this puerile sport. And then, what of the future? If his source of supply was a permanent one he might go on indefinitely, simply flinging away his income as fast as he received it. But suppose it were not a stable, continuing income. Suppose it should dwindle or cease? What then? It was pretty certain that this relatively wealthy man would very soon be reduced to actual poverty.

But the mystery of Gillum's expenditure was not completely solved. Apart from the big drafts in cash at irregular intervals there were those regular, periodic drafts which I had regarded with such suspicion. Had our evening's experiences thrown any light on them? I could not say positively that they had. And yet there was at least a suggestion. The whole atmosphere of that sordid gaming house with its deeply shady frequenters: the sinister-looking proprietor – manifestly hostile to Gillum – the painted Jezebel, his wife, the ruffian Cassidy, obviously a paid bully, and finally, Gillum's long and mysterious conference with Madame; if these did not actually offer a suggestion of blackmail, they did at least suggest the very conditions in which blackmail is apt to occur.

From Gillum and his affairs my thoughts turned at intervals to the dead man who had been the means of our introduction. I had read a brief notice of the discovery in the morning paper and had expected to receive on the same day a summons to attend the inquest. Actually, I did not receive it until the evening of the second day, when I found it awaiting me at my lodgings, requiring my attendance on the following day at two o'clock in the afternoon. Accordingly, on my arrival at the office in the morning, I showed it to our manager, and, having received his authority to absent myself from the bank, duly presented myself at the time and place appointed.

The body had been identified as that of a man named Abel Webb, and that was all that was said about him in the first place. Further particulars were left to transpire in the evidence.

There is no need for me to describe the proceedings in detail apart from the essentials. The coroner opened with a concise statement of the matter which formed the subject of the inquiry, the jury were then conducted to the mortuary to view the body, and when they had returned and taken their places the coroner proceeded to deal with the evidence.

"I think," said he, "that we had better begin by calling Mr Mortimer. His evidence is of no great importance but it comes first in the order of time."

My name was accordingly called, and when I had given the necessary particulars concerning myself, the coroner said:

"Now, Mr Mortimer, just tell us how you came to be connected with the subject of this inquiry. We can ask any necessary questions later."

Thus directed, I gave a plain and rather bald account of my discovery of the body and the circumstances leading thereto, to which the jury listened with eager interest; naturally enough, since the coroner's statement had given but the barest indication of the nature of the case.

"We understand," said the coroner, "that you did not recognise deceased as a person whom you had ever seen before?"

"That is so," I replied. "The man was a stranger to me."

"Would it have been possible for anyone passing along the alley as you did to fail to notice the body?"

"Yes," I replied, "and not only possible but rather probable. It was dark in the alley and still darker in the church porch. I am not sure that I should have seen the body myself but for the fact that I had found the hat and was on the look-out for the owner. Moreover, I was walking very slowly at the moment when I saw the body."

"You think, then, that a person walking at an ordinary pace and not closely observing his surroundings, might have passed the porch without seeing the body?"

"I think it extremely likely," I answered. "In fact, while I was waiting for the constable, a man did actually pass through without noticing the body. He was certainly in a great hurry, but I think if he had not been, he still might not have noticed anything."

"That," said the coroner, addressing the jury, "is, of course, only an opinion, but it agrees with the facts to which the witness has deposed; and the point may be of some importance. Does anything further occur to you, Mr Mortimer, or do you think that you have told us all that you have to tell?"

"I think I have told you all I know about the matter," I replied; whereupon the coroner, having invited the jury to ask any questions that they wished to ask and receiving no response, the depositions were read and signed and the next witness called.

Constable Walter Allen of the City Police, having completed the preliminaries, deposed as follows:

"I was on duty in Cornhill on the evening of Monday the ninth of September. At eight-two p.m. on that evening I was accosted by the last witness, Mr Robert Mortimer, who informed me that he had seen the dead body of a man lying in the passage leading from St Michael's Alley to the churchyard. I went with him at once to the place mentioned and there saw the body of deceased in the church porch. The body was partly sitting and partly lying. It was seated on the lowest of the three steps and was leaning back in the corner against the church door. I examined the body sufficiently to assure myself that the man was really dead and then I went away and telephoned to the station in Old Jewry, reporting the discovery and returned to the passage to wait until I was relieved."

"You have heard what the last witness said about the darkness of the passage," said the coroner. "Do you agree that it would have been possible for anyone to pass through the passage without noticing the body?"

"Yes," the constable replied, "I do. It was growing dark out in the street, and in the passage, which is a sort of tunnel, the light was very dim; and in the porch, which is about eight feet deep, it was practically dark. A person might easily have passed through the covered passage without seeing the body in the porch."

This completed the constable's evidence, and as he retired, the name of Inspector Pryor was called; whereupon that officer came forward, and having been sworn, proceeded to give his testimony with professional conciseness and precision. Taking up the thread of the constable's story, he confirmed the description of the body and its position in the porch and agreed that it might have been lying there unnoticed for some time – perhaps as long as half an hour – before it was discovered.

"Were you able," the coroner asked, "to form any opinion as to how deceased met with his death?"

"Yes. When the body had been put on the stretcher, I examined the place where it had been lying and there I found the pieces of a broken hypodermic syringe and some drops of liquid on the stone step. The fragments of the syringe gave off a smell rather like bitter almonds and so did the liquid, which I took up with a piece of clean blotting-paper. The fragments of the syringe are in this box but the blotting-paper was handed to the medical officer."

He handed a small cardboard box to the coroner who opened it, peered in, sniffed at it, and passed it on to the jury. Then he asked:

"Were there any finger-prints on the fragments of the syringe?"

"Only a few smears that were quite undecipherable. I examined the button of the plunger very carefully, but even there I could find nothing but a smear."

"You were able to ascertain the identity of deceased?"

"Yes, there were a number of letters in his pocket addressed to Abel Webb, Esq. which enabled us to make the necessary enquiries."

"Besides the syringe, did you find anything on the spot that could throw light on this mysterious affair. Any signs of a struggle, for instance?"

"Nothing whatever," was the reply. "But as to a struggle, seeing that the floor of the passage is paved and that of the porch tiled, there would hardly be any traces even if a struggle had occurred."

"No," said the coroner, "I suppose there would not." He reflected for a few moments, and then, as there was apparently nothing more to be got out of the Inspector, he intimated that the examination was concluded; and when the depositions had been read and signed, the officer retired.

"I think," said the coroner, "that, as I see that Dr Ripley is present, we had better take the medical evidence next so as not to detain the doctor unnecessarily."

The new witness, a small, very alert-looking gentleman, having been sworn and having stated his name and professional qualifications, looked enquiringly at the coroner; who, after a brief glance at his notes, opened the examination.

"Perhaps, Doctor," said he, "it would save time if you were to give us your evidence in the form of a statement. You saw the body, I think, shortly after the discovery."

"Yes," replied the witness. "On Monday evening, the ninth of September, at eight-fifty-six, I received a summons by telephone from the police to go to the mortuary to examine a body which had just been brought in. I went at once and arrived there at five minutes past nine. There I found the body of the deceased which had been undressed and laid on the mortuary table. At the first glance I formed the provisional opinion that deceased had died as a result of poisoning by hydrocyanic acid or some cyanide compound. The face, and especially the lips, were of a distinct violet colour. The eyes were wide open, set in a fixed stare. The jaws were firmly closed and there was slight stiffening of the muscles at the back of the neck. The hands were tightly clenched and the fingernails were blue. These are the usual appearances in cases of cyanide poisoning, but the froth on the lips, which nearly always occurs in such cases, was absent.

I examined the body for bruises or other signs of violence, but there were none, excepting that on the left thigh, a couple of inches from the groin, was a very distinct puncture which looked as if it had been made with a hypodermic needle of unusually large size. I was shown a broken syringe which had been found close to the body. It was not an ordinary hypodermic syringe but a larger kind; what is known as a serum syringe; and the needle was not a regular serum needle, but a longer and stouter form with a larger bore, such as is used by veterinary surgeons. I produce for your inspection an exactly similar syringe, but fitted with an ordinary

41

serum needle, which you can compare with the broken syringe that was handed to you by the inspector."

He laid the syringe on the table and paused while the coroner and the jury compared it with the fragments in the box. When they had made the comparison and put the two syringes aside, he resumed:

"The broken syringe and the needle both contained minute quantities of a clear liquid, which I collected in a pipette for subsequent analysis. But, at the time, I could tell by the characteristic smell of bitter almonds that it was one of the cyanide compounds."

"So that, in effect," said the coroner, "you had then established the cause of death."

"Yes," was the reply, "there was practically no room for doubt. The body showed the distinctive appearances of cyanide poisoning. There was no froth on the lips, which suggested that the poison had not been swallowed. There was the mark of a hypodermic needle, and there was a syringe containing traces of a cyanide compound. It was all perfectly consistent."

"You subsequently made a post–mortem examination?"

"Yes; and, as it is very important in cases of poisoning by hydrocyanic acid or cyanide, I made the post-mortem the same night. But first I analysed the liquid in the pipette; which I found to be a concentrated solution of potassium cyanide."

"Did the post-mortem throw any fresh light on the case?"

"Not very much, but it converted the inference into an ascertained fact. I can say with certainty that deceased died from the effects of a very large dose of potassium cyanide injected into the upper part of the thigh – the region which is known as Scarpa's Triangle. But one, possibly important, fact came to light, which was that the needle of the syringe entered the great vein of the thigh – the femoral vein."

"In what respect is that fact of importance?" the coroner asked.

"In its bearing on the rapidity with which the poison will have taken effect. Five grains of potassium cyanide will, if swallowed, produce death in about a quarter of an hour. The same quantity injected hypodermically would cause death in a minute or two at the most; while if it were injected into one of the great veins, death would probably follow in a matter of seconds. Now, in the present case, a much larger quantity was discharged directly into this great vein; from which I infer that death must have occurred practically instantaneously."

"Is it possible to say how much was injected?"

"Not in exact terms. I made only a qualitative analysis. Anything like an exact estimate of quantity would have involved a long and complicated procedure and it would have served no useful purpose. But I can say confidently, that the amount of cyanide injected was at least ten grains."

"When you first saw the body, did you form any opinion as to how long deceased had been dead?"

"Yes. Judging principally by the temperature of the body, I should say that he had been dead about an hour."

"You mentioned some stiffening of the muscles – apparently rigor mortis. Would that occur so soon after death?"

"The clenching of the jaws and hands was not due to rigor mortis. It was really cadaveric spasm and will have occurred at the moment of death. But the stiffening of the neck muscles did indicate the beginning of rigor mortis and was, of course, much earlier than in the average of cases. But there is nothing remarkable in this early onset. It very commonly occurs in cases of violent death and especially of suicide. I don't think deceased had been dead more than about an hour."

The coroner wrote down this statement and appeared to scan the preceding evidence before putting the next question. At length he looked up and turned to the witness.

"You say that death was due to poison injected by means of a syringe. Could that injection have been administered by deceased himself?"

"Yes. The site chosen was not a very convenient one for self-administration but it was well within reach, and self-administration would not have been difficult."

"So far as you could judge from your examination, was there anything that suggested either that deceased had or had not administered the poison to himself?"

"In a medical sense and in terms of mere physical possibility, there was no evidence one way or the other."

The coroner looked at the witness critically, and then remarked:

"I seem to detect a note of doubt and reservation in your answer. Is that not so?"

"Perhaps it is," the doctor replied. "But I am here as a medical witness and my evidence is properly restricted to what I know, or can reasonably infer from my examination of the body."

"That is a highly correct attitude, Doctor," said the coroner with a faint smile, "but I don't think we need be quite so particular. Have you any opinion, medical or other, as to whether deceased did or did not administer the poison to himself?"

"I have," the witness replied promptly. "My opinion is that he did not administer the poison to himself."

"That is perfectly definite," said the coroner, "and I am sure the jury would like to hear your reasons for that opinion, as I should myself."

"My opinion," said Dr Ripley, "is based upon the circumstances of the deceased's death. Either he killed himself or was killed by some other person. There is no question of accident or misadventure. It is either suicide or homicide. If we consider the theory of suicide, we are confronted by two anomalies. The first is the syringe. Why should deceased have used a hypodermic syringe? There is no reason at all. In the case of morphia there would be a reason; for the poison acts comparatively slowly, and large doses, if swallowed, tend to cause vomiting and so defeat the suicide's ends. But cyanide poisons act very rapidly and tend to produce death before the stomach becomes disturbed. Suicide by means of potassium cyanide is not uncommon, but the usual method is to swallow one or more tablets; and this is quite efficient for the purpose. I have never before heard of a syringe being used for this poison.

"The conditions in the case of homicide are exactly the reverse. You can't compel a man to swallow a tablet or even a liquid poison. But you can stick a hypodermic needle into him even if he has time to resist. And then the peculiarities of this particular syringe are adapted to homicide but not at all to suicide. The big veterinary needle would cause considerable pain in insertion. Its only advantage, its large bore, enabling the syringe to be discharged rapidly, would be of no benefit to the suicide; but it would be of vital importance to a murderer, who would want to get the business over as quickly as possible and make off.

"The other anomaly is the place where the death occurred. Why should a suicide, having provided himself with the poison and the syringe, go forth to use them in a public thoroughfare when he could have done the business without disturbance in his own premises? And why, if he chose a public place, should he have selected a dark corner in an unfrequented passage? To a suicide, the solitude and obscurity of the place would offer no advantage. But to a murderer, those conditions would be essential; for he would want to get clear of the neighbourhood before the body was discovered. In short, the mode of death, the means used, and the place selected, were all unadapted to suicide, but perfectly adapted to homicide."

As the doctor concluded his exposition, a murmur of approval arose from the jury, and the coroner, who also appeared to be deeply impressed, commented:

"Dr Ripley has given us, in a very ingenious and cogent argument, his reasons for taking a particular view of this case, and I am sure that when we come to consider the evidence as a whole, we shall give them due weight. And now, as he is a busy man, I think we ought not to detain him any longer, unless any of you wish for further information."

He looked enquiringly at the jury, and the foreman, in response to the implied invitation, signified that he would like to put a question.

"The doctor," said he, "has referred to the solitude and obscurity of the place where the body was found. I should like to ask him if he has any personal acquaintance with that place."

"Yes," replied the witness, "I know it very well indeed. My practice is in the City of London and I am perfectly familiar with all the courts and alleys that form the short cuts from one main thoroughfare to others. As to St Michael's Alley, I think that hardly a week passes in which I do not pass through it at least once."

"And if you pass through it," said the foreman, "I suppose other people do."

"Undoubtedly," the witness agreed; "and in the daytime a fair number of people pass up and down the alley, although after business hours, when the City has emptied, it is very little frequented. But the point is that when I go up the alley I go straight up to Castle Court; I don't turn off through the covered passage. And other people do the same, and for the same reason, which is that the covered passage also leads to Castle Court but by a less direct route. The only people who habitually use the covered passage are those who are employed in the office building that faces the churchyard. When they have gone, there are probably periods of half an hour or more during which not a soul passes through that passage."

The foreman expressed himself as quite satisfied with the explanation and thanked the witness, who was then released to go about his business. When he had departed, the name of Alfred Stowell was called and a middle-aged, gentlemanly man came forward and took his place at the table. Mr Stowell, having been sworn, gave his particulars, describing himself as the manager of

The Cope Refrigerating Company, of Gracechurch Street, London.

"You have viewed the body of deceased," said the coroner. "Did you recognise it as that of anyone whom you knew?"

"Yes. It is the body of Mr Abel Webb, lately my assistant manager."

"How long had he been with you?

"Less than two months. He took up his duties with us on the twenty-second of last July."

"Do you know how he was employed before he came to you?"

"He was in the service of the Commonwealth and Dominion Steamship Company and had been for about ten years. He had served as purser on several of their ships and it was on account of his experience in that capacity that my firm engaged him."

"I don't quite follow that. In what way is a purser's experience of value to you?"

"The ships of the Commonwealth Line are engaged in the frozen meat trade, and Mr Webb had a rather special knowledge of refrigerating plant, as well as of the trade in general."

"What sort of person was deceased — as to temperament, I mean? Did he strike you as a man who might possibly take his own life?"

"Most certainly not," the witness replied. "He was of a singularly cheerful and happy disposition and very pleased with his new occupation after the long years at sea."

"Have you any reason to suppose that he was in financial difficulties or in any way troubled about money?"

"No reason at all. Quite the contrary, in fact. I gathered from certain remarks that he let fall that he was in very comfortable circumstances. He was a bachelor without any dependants or responsibilities and had been steadily saving money all the time that he was at sea. That is what I understood from him. Of course, I have no first-hand knowledge of his affairs."

"So far as you know, had deceased any enemies?"

"I am not aware that he had, and I have no reason to suppose that he had. In the excellent testimonial from his late employers he was described as an amiable and kindly man who was universally liked. I know no more than that."

"Do you know of anything that could throw light on the manner and circumstances of his death?"

"Nothing whatever," was the reply; and as this seemed to conclude the evidence, the coroner asked the jury the usual question, and when the depositions had been signed the witness was released.

For some time after he had retired, the coroner sat scanning his notes with a manifestly dissatisfied air. At length he confided his difficulties to the jury.

"There is no denying," said he, "that the evidence which we have heard has left this mysterious affair to a great extent unelucidated; and the question arises as to whether it is advisable to adjourn the inquiry and endeavour to obtain further evidence. On the whole, as the police have not succeeded in discovering any of deceased's relatives, I am disposed to think that nothing would be gained by an adjournment. The further elucidation, if it is possible, seems to lie outside our province and within that of the police. Accordingly, I think it will be best for us to try to find a verdict on the evidence which is before us. It is unnecessary for me to recapitulate that evidence. It was all very clearly given and you have followed it closely and attentively. The question that you have to decide is: Who injected the poison? If deceased injected it himself, it is obviously a case of suicide. If you decide that it was injected by some other person you will have to find a verdict of wilful murder, since the injection could not have been given for any lawful purpose.

"The difficulty of deciding between suicide and murder is that there is no positive evidence of either. The medical evidence is to the effect that suicide was physically possible and that murder was physically possible. That is all that we have in the way of positive evidence. And in considering the medical evidence we must be careful to keep the facts separate from the opinions. The facts sworn to by the medical witness we can accept confidently; but the witness' opinions, weighty though they are, can be accepted only so far as your judgment confirms them. It is you who have to find the verdict, and that verdict must be based on the evidence which you have heard and on nothing else. That, I think, is all I need say, except to remind you that you are not in the position of a jury at a criminal trial, who are bound to decide yes or no, guilty or not guilty. If, having considered the evidence, you find it insufficient to enable you to decide between the alternatives of murder and suicide, you are at liberty to say so."

When the coroner had finished speaking, the members of the jury drew together and engaged in earnest and anxious consultation. It was a difficult question that they had to settle and they very properly took their time in debating it. At length the foreman announced that they had agreed on their verdict, and in reply to the coroner's question stated:

"We find that deceased died from the effects of a poison injected into his body with a syringe, but whether the injection was administered by himself or by some other person there is no evidence to show."

"Yes," said the coroner, "I don't see that you could have found otherwise. I shall record an open verdict and any further inquiries that may be necessary or possible will be conducted by the police."

The proceedings having now come to an end, the audience and the witnesses rose and filed out into the street; and as I took my way back to the bank I reflected a little uncomfortably on what I had heard. It was a horrible affair and profoundly mysterious. If I had been a member of the jury my verdict would have been the same as that which had been recorded. But it would not have expressed my inward convictions. The doctor's convincing exposition, which still rang in my ears, had but confirmed in my mind an already formed belief. Every circumstance of the tragedy seemed to whisper "Murder"; and as I entered Ball Court (instinctively avoiding the neighbourhood of the fatal passage) and threaded the maze of alleys into George Yard and Lombard Street, I looked about me with a shuddering interest, speculating on the way that poor Webb had gone to his death and wondering whether the callous murderer – with the charged syringe ready in his pocket – had walked at his side or had waylaid him in the covered passage.

CHAPTER FIVE

Clifford's Inn

The events of the evening which I had spent with John Gillum, though they threw a good deal of light on his financial affairs, by no means diminished my interest in, or curiosity concerning, those affairs. On the contrary, having now clearly established the principal channel through which his money flowed – virtually into the gutter – I found myself the more concerned with the question whether that was the sole channel or whether he might perchance be dropping money in ways even less desirable than gambling. I have mentioned that at intervals of about a month he was accustomed to present a "self" cheque for a considerable amount, never less, though usually more, than five hundred pounds. It might be that this represented merely "the sinews of war" for the month's gambling. But to my eye it looked like something different, something suggesting a definite periodic payment; and this view was strengthened by the fact that other drafts, often for large sums, were presented at irregular intervals. These, from their irregularity in time and amount, seemed much more likely to represent his gaming losses.

The periodic cheque was usually drawn about the fourteenth day of the month (rather suggesting a payment on the fifteenth) and it was Gillum's custom to notify the bank a day in advance of the amount of cash that he intended to withdraw. Accordingly, as the day drew near, I awaited the notification with some

51

expectancy; and sure enough, on the morning of the thirteenth – two days after the inquest – it was delivered at the bank and shown to me by the manager, as Gillum usually elected to transact his business with me. This time the amount was six hundred and fifty pounds; and as Gillum had a preference for notes that had been in circulation, some sorting out of the stock was necessary.

On the morning of the fourteenth, soon after the bank had opened, he made his appearance, and coming straight over to my "pitch," laid his cheque on the counter.

"I'm afraid I'm the bane of your life, Mortimer," said he, "with my big cash drafts. You ought to have a note-counting machine – turn a handle, shoot 'em out by the dozen and show the number on a dial."

"It would be a convenience," I admitted, "though I doubt whether a court of law would accept the reading of the machine as evidence. But it is no great trouble to count a few hundred notes, and at any rate, it is what I am here for."

I brought out the bundles of notes that I had prepared in readiness for the payment and having recounted them, passed the bundles across to him.

"You had better check them," said I as he picked them up and stuffed them into his pocket.

"No need," he replied. "I'll take them as read. I'm not equal to your lightning manipulation, and if we differed I should be sure to be wrong."

He paused to distribute the seven bundles more evenly and then, as there were no customers waiting at the moment, lingered to gossip.

"I hope," said he, "you were none the worse for our little dissipation."

"Thank you, no," I replied. "A little sleepy the next morning, but I am quite convalescent now."

"Good," said he. "We must have another outing soon, not quite so boisterous. We might go and hear some music."

"That is quite a good idea," said I, "and it reminds me that an opportunity presents itself this very day. Do you care for organ music?"

"I like it in church," he replied; "not so much in a concert hall. The appropriate atmosphere seems to be lacking."

"Then," said I, "perhaps you would like to come with me this evening to St Peter's, Cornhill. There is to be an organ recital from six to seven by Dr Dyer. I am going, and if you can manage it, I can promise you a musical treat."

He considered for a few moments and then replied:

"It sounds rather alluring and I've got the evening free. So I accept subject to conditions; which are that after the recital you come along to my chambers and join me in a little rough bachelor dinner. I can't do you in Giamborini's style but you won't starve. When we have fed, we can either smoke a pipe and yarn or go out somewhere. What do you say?"

I accepted promptly, for the proposed entertainment was much more to my taste than a restaurant dinner; and when we had made the necessary arrangements he took his leave and I reverted to my duties.

At half-past five he reappeared at the bank and found me waiting outside, and we strolled together up Gracechurch Street, looking in at Leadenhall Market on our way, and took our seats in the church at five minutes to the hour. The fame of the organist had drawn a surprisingly large number of men and women to the recital, and it was evident by the instant hush that fell as soon as the music began, that Dr Dyer had a genuinely appreciative audience. And I was interested, and a little surprised, to note that Gillum not only enjoyed but – as I gathered from his whispered comments in the intervals – followed the rather austere and technical works that were played with manifest sympathy and understanding. One would hardly have associated the gambling den and the racecourse with a refined taste for music. But Gillum was a rather queer creature in many respects.

When the recital came to an end, we set forth on foot to stretch our legs and sharpen our appetites with the walk of a little over a mile from Cornhill to Clifford's Inn, beguiling the short journey with a discussion of the music that we had been listening to, and comments on objects of interest that we observed by the way. In Fleet Street Gillum gave me another mild surprise by halting me opposite Anderton's Hotel and bidding me note the fine silhouette that St Dunstan's Church and the Law Courts made against the sunset sky.

"I always stop here to look at the view," said he, "and although the shapes are always the same, the picture is different every time I see it. There is a lot of fine scenery of a kind in the streets of London."

Once more, as we walked on, I reflected on the strange contradictions and inconsistencies of my companion's temperament. Somehow, he managed to combine a sensitiveness to the picturesque and beautiful with a singular tolerance of the sordid and unlovely.

A few yards farther on we turned up Fetter Lane, and crossing the road, made for an iron gate set in a row of railings and now standing wide open. Entering, we found ourselves in the precincts of Clifford's Inn and seemed in a moment to have passed out of the clamorous twentieth century into the quiet and dignified repose of a bygone age. I knew the place slightly from having occasionally ventured in to explore and I now looked round with friendly recognition of the pleasant old red brick houses and the slightly faded grass and trees in the garden.

"This is my lair," said Gillum, indicating an arched doorway lighted by a hanging lantern and surmounted by a tablet bearing the inscription "P.R.G. 1682." Within the deep portal a shadowy flight of stairs faded away into profound obscurity, and when Gillum led the way in and up the stairs, he too faded into the darkness and became a mere black shape against the dim light from the landing above. I groped my way up after him (for the lamp at the entry was not yet lit) and presently emerged on to the landing where I found my host inserting a key into a massive iron-bound door above which was painted in black letters on a faded white ground, "Mr John Gillum." The forbidding, gaol-like door swung open heavily disclosing a lighter inner door garnished with an ordinary handle and a small brass knocker. Gillum turned the handle, and throwing open the door, invited me to enter; and as soon as I was inside, he pulled to the outer door, which closed with the snap of a spring latch and a resounding clang suggestive of the door of a prison cell.

"Just as well to sport the oak," said Gillum. "Not that anyone ever comes after business hours, but it is more pleasant to feel that you can't be interrupted."

He switched on the light and I was instantly impressed by the contrast of the cheerful, cosy interior with the rather grim approach. A fire – well banked and enclosed by a guard – was burning in the grate, a couple of easy chairs faced each other companionably, and the table, covered with a spotless white cloth, was laid with all the necessary appointments for a meal.

Gillum was a good host. This was a simple, informal "feed" and I was not a guest but a pal who had dropped in. He established the position at once by setting me to work at decanting the bottle of claret that had been stood on the mantel-shelf to get the chill off, while he attended to the fire.

"May as well make a bit of a blaze," said he, "though it isn't a cold evening. But a fire is a companionable thing."

He tipped the remaining contents of the scuttle into the grate and then, after a hesitating glance at the empty receptacle, put it down.

"Where do you keep your coal?" I asked, with a view to replenishment.

"In the larder, or cellar or store-room," he replied. "It's that door across the landing, and a most excellent larder it makes; perfectly cool even in the height of summer. And that reminds me that we shall want the butter and cheese and perhaps we might as well get out a bottle of chablis to go with the lobster – and, by the way, the lobster is in there, too."

He went to the door and I followed to give assistance in carrying the goods. Not unnecessarily, as it turned out, for the door across the landing was fitted, not only with a night latch, but also with a rather strong spring, fixed to the inside of the door, as the latter opened outwards. I stood with my back against the open door and received the butter and the lobster, holding them until Gillum collected the cheese and the wine and came out, when I moved away and the door closed with a slam and a click of the lock.

"Now, Mortimer," said Gillum, when he had deposited our burdens on the table, "you are the wine waiter. Just open the chablis while I go into the kitchen and hot up the soup."

He retired through one of two small doorways which faced each other at the farther side of the room and I began operations on the capsule of the bottle. But at this moment the empty coal-scuttle caught my eye, and at the same time it occurred to me that we must have left the key in the larder door, since we had both come away with our hands full. With the double purpose of retrieving the key and replenishing the scuttle, I picked up the latter and carried it out to the landing; and, sure enough, there was the key in the door. I turned it, and bearing the spring in mind, when I had pulled the door open I set the scuttle against it while I went in and switched on the light. Then I took up the scuttle, carefully easing the door to, so that it remained unlatched (though there was a knob on the inside by which I could have let myself out), and proceeded to prospect. There was no difficulty in locating the coal, for a large bin or locker that extended right along the farther wall was so well filled that its lid gaped and displayed its contents.

I threw up the lid of the locker, and, taking the scoop from the scuttle, began rapidly to shovel out the coal, my movements rather accelerated by the unpleasant cellar-like atmosphere, which struck an uncomfortable chill in contrast with the warm dining-room. I soon had the scuttle filled, but in my haste let a few lumps of coal fall on the floor. Having put the scoop back in its socket, I stooped to pick up the stray lumps with my fingers. And at that moment I was conscious of a sudden feeling of giddiness and a loud ringing noise in my ears. Whether it was due to my position or to the abrupt change of temperature I cannot say; but as the place seemed to whirl around me and I felt myself swaying as if I were about to fall, I hastily grabbed the edge of the locker, pulled myself upright and staggered out on to the landing.

As I emerged from the larder, letting the door slam behind me, Gillum appeared at the door of the living-room and stared at me in dismay.

"Good God, Mortimer!" he exclaimed. "What on earth is the matter?"

Without waiting for an explanation, he hustled me into the living-room, threw up the window, and dragging a chair towards it, sat me down in the full draught.

"What was it?" he asked.

"I don't know," I replied. "I just stooped to pick up a lump of coal and then I suddenly turned giddy."

"Strange," said he, looking at me anxiously. "Have you ever had any attacks like this before?"

"Never," I answered; "and I can't imagine what brought it on now. I suppose it was the sudden stooping."

"But that won't do, Mortimer," said he. "You've no business to get giddy from stooping at your age. I don't believe you take proper care of yourself. You'd better let me get you a nip of whisky."

"No, thank you," said I. "The fresh air has done the business. I am all right now excepting a slight headache, and I expect that will go off in a few minutes. By the way, I left the light on in the larder."

"I'll go and switch off and get the coal-scuttle," said he, "and then we will have some grub. That will complete the cure, with a glass of wine."

He went out and presently returned with the scuttle, shutting the "oak" behind him. Then he fetched the soup from the kitchen and we drew our chairs up to the table and proceeded to business.

It was a pleasant little dinner, and not so very little, for when we had disposed of the lobster, the raising of a couple of covers revealed a cold roast fowl and a pile of sliced ham, the produce, as I learned, of an invaluable shop in Fetter Lane. Moreover, as the food was cold it lent itself to leisurely consumption and the free flow of conversation. And conversation with Gillum naturally tended to drift in the direction of betting and play.

"How is the infallible system progressing?" I asked.

"Slowly," he admitted, "but still, I think the thing is possible. I don't make much of it from the mathematical direction, so I am falling back on the excellent method of trial and error. I have got a miniature roulette box and I find it invaluable for trying out schemes of chances. I'll show it to you."

He produced a beautifully made little wooden box, and placing it on the table, affectionately twisted the ivory spindle.

"Yes," I agreed, "it is an excellent contraption, for you can play any odds you like against yourself and win in any event. I should advise you to stick to it. Do your gambling at home – and let the Foucaults have a rest."

He laughed, rather grimly I thought.

"Perhaps," said he, "it might rather be a question of their letting me have a rest. But your advice is futile, as you know perfectly well. Solo roulette is well enough for experimental purposes, but it isn't sport and it isn't gambling. You can't gamble if you don't stand to win or lose."

Of course, I knew this and his reply left me with nothing to say; so I reverted to the roast fowl and inwardly speculated on the possibility of a connection between the Foucaults and the morning's transaction at the bank. He had spoken as if they gave him more attention than he cared for, but obviously the subject was one that I could not even approach. Then, searching for some new topic, I suddenly remembered the circumstances of our first meeting and their later developments, in which Gillum might probably be interested.

"I intended," said I, "to bring you a copy of the *Telegraph* which I kept for you. It contains a full report of the inquest on that poor fellow whose body I discovered. But perhaps you have seen it."

"I have," he replied. "I saw a pretty full account of it in an evening paper. Extraordinary affair. Rather horrible, too. I liked the way in which that doctor fellow let out. He knew his own mind."

"Yes, he was remarkably outspoken for a medical witness. But I certainly agreed with him, and so, I think, did the jury. If he hadn't been so downright I suspect the verdict would have been suicide while temporarily insane."

"Very likely. But what was there to suggest insanity?

"Nothing that I know of," I replied. "I was only repeating the usual formula. When a man commits suicide it is generally assumed that he was temporarily insane when he did it."

"I know," said Gillum. "But it is just a convention, and a silly convention which ought to be dropped. Really, it is a theological survival. The pretence of insanity is for the purpose of proving that deceased was not aware of the nature of his act and that therefore he was not guilty of *felo de se* and did not die in a state of mortal sin. It was quite well meant, but it was always a false pretence; and now that we have outgrown theological crudities of that sort, the formula ought to be abolished excepting in cases where there is actual evidence of insanity."

He spoke with an amount of feeling that rather surprised me. For it did not appear to me that the point was of any importance. Nor did I entirely agree with his view of the matter, and accordingly proceeded to contest it.

"I don't think that is quite the position, Gillum," I objected. "No doubt there is a theological factor, but the usual verdict is based on the assumption that the very act of suicide constitutes evidence of mental unsoundness; and I think it is quite a reasonable assumption."

"Why do you think so?" he demanded.

"Because," I replied, "the impulse of self-preservation – the preservation of one's own life – is so universal and so deep-seated as to amount to one of the fundamental instincts of intelligent living beings. But an act which is in opposition to a natural instinct is an abnormal act and affords evidence of an abnormal state of mind."

"I admit the instinct," he rejoined. "But man is a reasoning animal and is not completely dominated by his instincts. If in a particular case he is convinced that the following of those instincts is to his disadvantage, surely it will be reasonable for him to disregard them and adopt the action which he knows is to his advantage. Let us take an instance. Suppose a man to be suffering from a painful and incurable form of malignant disease. He knows that it is going to kill him within a measurable time. He knows that until death releases him he will suffer continual pain. Is he going to drag on a miserable existence, waiting for the inevitable death, or will he not, if he is a reasonable man, anticipate that death and cut short his sufferings?"

He had put his case with such cogency that I was rather at a loss. Nevertheless, I objected, somewhat weakly:

"The instance you give is a very exceptional one. The conditions are quite abnormal."

"Exactly," he rejoined. "That is my point. The conditions being abnormal, the common rules of normal conduct do not apply. The conduct is adjusted to the conditions and consequently is rational conduct. But that is true, I think, in a large proportion of suicides. If you consider them in detail with an open mind you must come to the conclusion that the act is a reasonable response to the existing conditions."

"I doubt that," said I. "The case that you have cited I should be disposed to admit, but I can think of no other."

"The point is," said he, "whether the conduct is or is not adapted to the existing conditions. If it is, it is rational conduct. And a man is entitled to estimate those conditions for himself, to decide whether they are or are not acceptable; whether, in those conditions, he would rather be alive or not. Whether, in short, life is or is not worth living. If he decides that it is not, then it is reasonable for him to bring it to an end."

"My point is," I rejoined, "that a normal man would always rather be alive than not."

"Then, Mortimer," said he, "I think you are mistaken. Let us take a concrete case. Suppose a man, like yourself, an employee of a bank, tied down to a particular place. Suppose he has a quarrelsome wife who makes his life a misery and perhaps gets him into debt, and a family who are a constant trouble and disgrace to him. What is he to do? He can't escape because he is tied to his job. If he finds life intolerably unpleasant under these conditions, which he cannot alter, what could be more reasonable than for him to bring it to an end? Or again, take the case of a man who has inherited a fortune and has had a roaring good time enjoying all sorts of expensive pleasures. The natural result is that he steadily gets through his money. Now when he comes down to his last shilling what is the prospect before him? What is the natural thing for him to do?"

"The most reasonable thing," I replied, "would be to turn over a new leaf; to get a job, work hard at it and live within his means."

Gillum shook his head. "No, Mortimer," said he. "That would not be possible to the type of man that I am describing. He couldn't do it, and he wouldn't try. If he was absolutely broke, he could try to live by sponging, by borrowing, by fraud or by some other form of crime, but either method would bring him, sooner or later, to disaster; and almost certainly, in the end, to suicide. But I contend that the more reasonable plan would be to anticipate and avoid all these troubles. When once his money was gone and the only kind of life that he cared for had become impossible, I say that the sane and sensible thing for him to do would be to recognise the facts and make his quietus – though not with a bare bodkin."

"But," I exclaimed, "do you mean to tell me seriously that is what you would do, as a considered act, in the circumstances that you mention?"

He laughed and shook a finger at me in mock reproof.

"Now, Mortimer," said he, "you know that is quite an improper question. We are considering a hypothetical case, and in effect, a certain question of principle. But you immediately – and quite irrelevantly – turn it into a personal question. What I, personally, might do is beside the mark."

"I don't see that it is," I objected. "If you really mean what you say, I understand that if ever you should go stony broke with no possible chance of recovery you would proceed at once, as a matter of considered policy, to hang yourself or cut your throat."

"No, no, Mortimer," he protested, "I said nothing about hanging or throat-cutting. That would be temporary insanity with a vengeance. No, pray do me the justice of believing that, if the occasion arose, I should perform the coil-shuffling operation with decency, dignity, and the maximum of personal comfort. The rope and the carving knife are the wretched resources of the mere lunatic or moron. There is no excuse for such barbarities when, as we know, there are certain medicinal substances which are perfectly efficient for the purpose and which are not only painless but rather agreeable in their operation."

To this I made no reply, for there had come on me a sudden dislike to the turn that the discussion had taken. He had spoken semi-facetiously, but yet there was an underlying seriousness that gave his words a rather gruesome quality. So I let the discussion drop and, after a short silence, directed our talk into a fresh channel.

After dinner Gillum brewed a pot of excellent coffee and we then adjourned to the easy chairs to smoke our pipes and talk; and as I listened to my host's comments and observations on the various topics that we discussed, I was surprised – having regard to the outrageous folly of his conduct – not only at the range of his knowledge and general information but especially at the shrewdness and sanity of his outlook. Moreover, he was a man of some culture. I had already noticed his interest in the more serious forms of music and his lively appreciation of the fine grouping and skyline of the buildings of Fleet Street, and it now appeared that he shared my affection for the quaint nooks and corners and antique survivals of the older parts of London and seemed to have a quite extensive acquaintance with them. Indeed, so pleasant and sympathetic was our gossip and so agreeably did the time slip away that I was quite taken aback when St Dunstan's clock, reinforced by the more distant bells of St Clement's, announced the hour of eleven and bade me set forth on my journey homewards.

"I will pilot you out as far as Fleet Street," said Gillum, as he helped me into my overcoat. "Next time you will know your way; and I hope the next will be quite soon."

"You have given me every inducement to repeat the offence," I replied. "It has been a jolly evening. Quite a red-letter day for me."

We sallied forth from the dark entry – but it was dark no longer now that the lamp was alight – and, crossing the courtyard, plunged into the tunnel which passes the Hall, and, crossing the little courtyard, entered Clifford's Inn Passage. The main gate was shut and the night porter sat on a chair by the wicket, holding a newspaper and conversing with a spectacled gentleman who was formally arrayed in a frock coat and tall hat and supported himself on an umbrella.

"That is Mr Weech," said Gillum, "the Inn porter; a queer old bird, quite a character in his way and a complete Victorian survival. I'll introduce you as you like antiques."

As we approached, Mr Weech opened the wicket for us and gave my companion "good evening."

"Good evening, Mr Weech," said Gillum. "Taking a last look round to see that we are all safe before you turn in?"

"That is so," replied Mr Weech. "It is my custom to conclude the day's duty with a perambulation of the precincts to see that everything is in order."

"A very wise precaution," said Gillum. "It's of no use to have a locked gate if the doubtful characters are lurking inside. Let me introduce my friend, Mr Mortimer, who has been spending the evening with me, so that you may know him in future as an accredited visitor. This is Mr Weech, the custodian of the Inn and the faithful guardian of our security. As you see, he carries an umbrella as a symbol of his protective functions. Isn't that so, Mr Weech? I notice that you are never without it."

Mr Weech chuckled and glanced fondly at the "symbol."

"I suppose I am not," he admitted. "When I put on my hat I take up the umbrella automatically. It has become a habit and I do it without thinking. *Consuetudo alterus naturum*, as the saying is."

"Well," said I, as I stepped through the wicket, it is a wise habit in a fickle climate like ours. Goodnight, Mr Weech."

He raised his hat with an old-fashioned flourish as he returned my valediction, and Gillum and I walked slowly down the passage to Fleet Street.

"An odd fish is Mr Weech," Gillum remarked. "Quite a good sort but odd. I believe he takes that umbrella to bed with him. And he's a devil for Latin. I suspect he keeps a book of quotations and primes himself with them for conversation. Well, goodnight, Mortimer. Take care of yourself and come again soon."

As I made my way homewards to my lodgings I turned over the events of the evening. It had been a pleasant experience and Gillum had been a most agreeable companion. Indeed, I had been rather surprised at the way in which he had improved on better acquaintance and I was still puzzled by the contrast between his obvious intelligence and culture and the idiotic manner in which he was wasting his life and his substance. But as I recalled our conversation there was one item that jarred on me badly. Gillum's defence of suicide may have been partly playful. Evidently, he rather inclined to the role of the Devil's Advocate and took a perverse pleasure in arguing and defending a paradox. But still, I had an unpleasant feeling that the views that he had expressed really represented his convictions. And what made the recollection of his argument especially disturbing to me was the fact that one of the cases that he had cited in illustration was alarmingly like what his own case might be. At present, it is true, his wild expenditure was balanced by his very ample income. He never overdrew; and as long as his income continued at its present rate, he would remain solvent and merely waste his possessions.

But suppose, some day, his source of income should dry up. Then he would soon be penniless and would quite possibly fall into debt. And if he did, the very conditions that he had postulated as justifying suicide would be brought into being. It was a profoundly disturbing thought; and though I tried to put it away, it recurred again and again, not only during my journey home, but at intervals in the days that followed.

CHAPTER SIX

The Passing of John Gillum

Hitherto I have followed in rather close detail the circumstances of my association with John Gillum. This I have done advisedly; since the purpose of this narrative is to present as clear a picture as I am able of his personality and manner of life. But, having done this, I shall now pass more lightly over the events that occurred during the remainder of our association. That association, which extended over a period of about ten months, was fairly intimate and tended to become more so as the time ran on. Gillum was an entirely acceptable companion; cheerful, lively, humorous, and extremely well-informed. And, apparently, he liked my society, for he took every opportunity of cultivating it. The result was that we met as frequently as could be expected in the case of two rather self-contained men, each of whom had his own particular interests and occupations.

Sometimes he would call for me at the bank, but more commonly our rendezvous was Clifford's Inn, where we would take tea and then sally forth to spend the evening at a concert or a play or in a voyage of discovery into the lesser-known parts of the London in which we were both so much interested. Once, on an off day, I accompanied him to a race meeting, where he narrowly missed winning a considerable sum but actually – as I learned later – dropped about a hundred pounds. But this was the only occasion on which I came into contact with his gambling activities. He had, in his tactful, accommodating way, accepted the fact that betting and games of chance were outside the sphere of my interests and such evidence as came to me of his exploits at the tables or on the turf was in the nature of hearsay. But the books of the bank furnished direct evidence that, whatever those exploits may have been, the net result was displayed on the debit side of his account.

As the period of our friendship lengthened I began to be aware of a rather curious fact; which was that, intimate as we seemed to be, I really knew nothing about him. It was rather remarkable. In respect of his present mode of life and his daily doings he was, or, at least, appeared to be open even to expansiveness. But of his past life or his antecedents, not a word was ever dropped. Gradually I came to realise that, under this appearance of free and frank confidence, lay a profound secretiveness. It was not a pleasing trait; and it occasioned a certain amount of reflection on my part. And when I came to consider it, I began to perceive that the secretiveness was not limited to the past; for, with all his expansiveness, he never made the slightest references to those periodical drafts on which I had looked – and still looked – with so much suspicion. In short, it began gradually to dawn on me that the confidences that he made with so much apparent openness were in fact limited to what I, in my capacity as his banker, already knew.

Of course, I asked no questions. But, naturally, as I reflected on this secretive habit, amounting virtually to concealment, it aroused some curiosity. I am not in general an inquisitive person. But when I came to consider that this man, with whom I was on terms of daily intimacy, was an absolute stranger to me; that I knew nothing whatever of his past, of his relations, of the places where he had lived, of his profession or calling, if he had any, or of how he passed his time or whether he had any occupation other than gambling; it could not but appear very remarkable. And these reflections inevitably led to others. If his past life was never referred to, could there be any reason for this reticence? Was there anything in his past that made concealment necessary?

The question was not entirely without relevance. The periodical drafts, which had always seemed to me to suggest periodical payments, had raised a suspicion that he was being blackmailed; and as time went on, this suspicion tended to grow. But how should he come to be blackmailed? There is no smoke without fire. It is usually impossible to blackmail a man unless there is something in his life that he is unwilling to disclose. Could it be that his past was in some respects unpresentable? Or could it be that, even now he was engaged in some activities that would not bear the light of day?

These questions presented themselves unsought and unwelcomed. For I liked the man and was unwilling to think ill of him or to harbour suspicions concerning him. Still, there were the facts, and I had to recognise them though the process of recognition cost me some mental discomfort. But presently I began to have anxieties of a different kind. I had always assumed that Gillum's income was derived from a permanent source. The large sums that he had paid in at approximately regular intervals had appeared to represent something in the nature of dividends or an annuity. But in the last month of my acquaintance with him this regularity had become suddenly disturbed. One or two large cheques – unusually large ones – had been paid in, but the balance created by them had begun immediately to melt away. I waited in expectation of the usual credit payment. But the time when it should have become due passed and no such payment was made; and Gillum's account began to show an uncomfortably small balance. It looked rather alarmingly like a failure of the source of supply.

Now, so long as his income was regular, his ridiculous expenditure merely kept him poor when he should have been rich. But with the failure of the supply and the continuance of the expenditure, a very different situation was created. As I scanned his account in our books and noted the growing tendency for the debit to overgrow the credit, I felt that – unless there were some change in the conditions – sooner or later, and probably sooner rather than later, some sort of crash was to be looked for; and, knowing what his ideas were as to the way to meet a crash, I had already dimly envisaged the kind of disaster which actually occurred, and of which I shall now proceed to relate the circumstances.

It was in the early afternoon of a rather sultry day in July that a tall, sunburnt, athletic-looking man came to the bank and asked to see the manager, explaining that he had been sent by Mr Penfield and that his business was connected with the affairs of our customer, Mr John Gillum. On this I pricked up my ears, and when he had been ushered into the manager's room, I waited expectantly for the summons which seemed almost inevitable, having regard to my known intimacy with Gillum; and sure enough, in a few minutes, the bell rang and the clerk who went in to answer it returned to inform me that the manager wished to speak to me. Accordingly I went in and found the manager and the visitor seated on opposite sides of a small table.

"This," said the former, introducing me, "is Mr Arthur Benson, a cousin of Mr Gillum's, who has called to make some enquiries; and as you know Mr Gillum personally as well as officially, you will probably be able to give him more information than I can. Mr Mortimer is, I think I may say, a fairly intimate friend of your cousin's, Mr Benson, and may be able to tell you what you want to know."

Mr Benson shook hands heartily and proceeded at once with his enquiries.

"I am in rather a difficulty, Mr Mortimer," said he, "and I may add, a little puzzled and worried by the way in which my cousin is behaving. But I had better begin by explaining the circumstances. I have just come from Australia, where I run a sheep farm in which my cousin, Gillum, is to some extent interested. I have been in regular correspondence with him about our affairs and have sent him cheques from time to time, which have been

R AUSTIN FREEMAN

duly acknowledged. Now, as the business which has brought me to
England arose quite unexpectedly, I wrote to him from Sydney
telling him that I should be coming on by the next boat, and
asking him either to meet me at Tilbury or to send a letter to the
ship there telling me where and when I should find him. Well, he
didn't meet me at Tilbury, but he sent a letter which was handed
to me as soon as the ship brought up in the river. In this he asked
me to come straight on to his chambers in Clifford's Inn.

"Accordingly, I did so; but when I called at his chambers, I
could not get any answer to my knock. The place was all shut up,
and though I hammered at the iron-bound door with my stick for
some time, nothing happened. It was evident that he was not
at home."

"This seemed a bit queer and not at all what I should have
expected of him. However, I went off and got fixed up at an hotel,
and then I came back to the Inn and made another attack on the
door. But still there was no sign of life; so I gave it up for the time
and went back to my hotel and spent the night there. Next day, I
went to the Inn again and had another try. But still there was no
result. The place was as still as the grave.

"It was really very extraordinary and I began to wonder
whether there could be anything amiss. So I went on to Mr
Penfield, who acted for us in our business transactions, and asked
him if he knew anything about Gillum's movements. But he knew
nothing at all, not having seen my cousin for some months, but he
recommended me to come along here and see whether you knew
anything about him or could give me any advice. So here I am; and
the question is, can you give me any sort of help or tell me where
I may be likely to find him?"

The manager looked at me. "What do you say, Mortimer? You
know Mr Gillum's haunts pretty well, I think. Have you any idea
where he is likely to be found?"

"Not the least," I replied. "I should have expected him to be at
his chambers, especially as he had made an appointment with Mr

Benson. That is where he lives, and I had always supposed that he, at least, spent the night there."

"When did you see him last?" the manager asked.

"I haven't seen him for nearly a fortnight," I replied. "The last time that I saw him was when he came to the bank last Friday week to cash a cheque. I had a few words with him then but he did not say anything about his intended movements; and, in fact, he could not have had any intention of going away as he had made this appointment with Mr Benson."

The manager looked thoughtful and rather puzzled. "It really does seem a little queer," said he, "and I think we ought to try to help Mr Benson as he is a stranger in London. What do you suggest, Mortimer?"

"I hardly know what to suggest," I replied. "It is certainly an odd affair. Perhaps it might be worth while for me to run round with Mr Benson to Clifford's Inn and try the door again and if we still can't get any answer we might drop in at the lodge and see if we can get any information from Mr Weech, the porter of the Inn. He might be able to tell us something."

"Yes," said the manager, "that seems about the best thing to do. At any rate, it is worth trying. So perhaps you will kindly take Mr Benson in tow and see what you can do for him."

With this he stood up and shook hands with Benson, and the latter then accompanied me into the outer office, and when I had got my hat and stick we sallied forth together.

It is no great distance from Gracechurch Street to Clifford's Inn and we agreed to walk; Benson for the advantage of seeing the town and I for the opportunity to think things over and possibly get a little additional information. For, as I have hinted, I was more disturbed by the strange state of affairs than I had admitted either to the manager or to our visitor. I had not mentioned to them the amount of the cheque which had been cashed less than a fortnight ago, but it came to my mind now with a slightly ominous suggestiveness. The amount had been two hundred pounds, which I had paid in one-pound notes; and that payment had not only cleared out the balance but had left the account a few pounds overdrawn.

Reflecting on this, I ventured to make one or two discreet enquiries though avoiding direct questions.

"Your name is fairly familiar to me," I began as a cautious lead off.

"I suppose it is," he replied. "You must have had a good many of my cheques through your hands."

"Yes," said I. "They have come in at pretty regular intervals until just lately. But I don't think I have seen one for over three months. However, the last one was quite a big cheque, if I remember rightly."

"It was," said he; "eleven hundred pounds. That was the final payment."

"Indeed!" said I, rather startled. "Then it was not a continuing transaction?"

"No," he replied. "The payments were instalments of purchase money. The sheep farm that I run originally belonged to Gillum. But he had a fancy to come to England and I was connected with a meat-exporting establishment; so he proposed that I should take over the farm and pay for it by instalments out of income while he should buy with the proceeds, or part of them, a partnership in a firm of meat importers in London. He thought that we could work things to our mutual advantage, and so did I. So I fixed up the deal with him and he came to England and arranged the partnership; and I paid off my debt as well as I could out of income. But after nearly two years I thought that it had gone on for long enough, so I raised a loan and paid off the final instalment in one sum."

"By the way," said I, "did it not occur to you to go round to his firm and ask if he had been there?"

"It did," he replied. "I went there before I went to Mr Penfield. And then I got another surprise. It seemed that he didn't take to the meat importing trade and about six months ago he sold his interest in the concern to the other partner and they have not seen anything of him since. It is curious that he should not have said anything about it to me in his letters."

"Very curious," I agreed. And it certainly was very remarkable. But it was not the oddity of his behaviour that principally impressed me. What instantly struck me with devastating force was the appalling fact that, at this moment, John Gillum must be absolutely penniless. Those big cheques had been paid in to my knowledge and had produced a most impressive balance; but that balance had been dribbling away ever faster and faster as the "self" cheques were turned into cash to provide the means for his insane expenditure. And now, as I have said, he had not only drawn out the last penny of his balance but was actually in debt to the bank.

It was a terrible position; and when I reflected on it by the light of his expressed views on the appropriate way to meet a financial crash, the behaviour disclosed by Benson's experiences assumed an undeniably sinister aspect. I said nothing to my companion as to what was in my mind, but, as we approached the neighbourhood of Clifford's Inn, my forebodings became so profound as to engender a very definite distaste for the errand on which I was bent.

We entered the Inn by the postern gate in Fetter Lane, and, crossing the little quadrangle which I knew so well, made our way straight to the rather forbidding entry. As we plunged into the shadow which enclosed the staircase, I could hear the typewriters in the ground-floor office ticking away, conveying a sense of human life and activity which seemed to contrast almost uncannily with the silence and aloofness of the – presumably – empty room upstairs.

We groped our way up the dim staircase and came out on the rather sordid and ill-lighted landing where the empty dust-bin confirmed the suggestion of an absent tenant. But we did not stop to examine the landing. Walking up to the grim iron-bound door, above which the name of Mr J. Gillum could be read on a painted label, now rather faded and dirt-stained, we listened for a few moments and then tapped on the massive oak panel. Perhaps the word "tapped" is inadequate, for Benson, who carried a stout stick of some hard and heavy wood, applied it in the manner of a battering-ram with such effect that the place resounded with the blows and I expected some protest from the office below.

"Well," said Benson, after banging away for a couple of minutes, "I think we may take it that there is no one at home. Shall we go round and hear what your porter man has got to tell us?"

"I think we had better," I replied; and forthwith led the way down the steep stairs, my state of mind by no means improved by the unpleasant fashion in which the noise of Benson's hammerings had echoed through the building. In fact, I found myself growing distinctly nervous and, as we made our way towards the passage in which the porter's lodge was situated, I began to consider what we had better do if we could get no more satisfactory tidings of the missing man. But I still had some hopes that the porter might be able to resolve the mystery or at least give us a hint of some kind.

A hearty pull at the pendent handle outside the lodge door elicited a cheerful jangle from within; and in a few moments the door opened and Mr Weech appeared, fully attired as usual in his long frock coat and tall silk hat. Whether he slept in that hat I cannot guess, but it seemed that he wore it constantly from the time when he arose in the morning until he retired at night. At least, that was my impression, for I never saw him without it. He now regarded me benevolently through his spectacles and then cast an enquiring glance at my companion.

"We have called, Mr Weech," said I, "to make one or two enquiries and see if you can help us. A rather unaccountable thing has happened. My friend, Mr Gillum, seems to be absent from his chambers. We have hammered at his door and can't get any answer, and my friend here, Mr Benson, tried yesterday and the day before, but he also could not make anybody hear."

Mr Weech retired for a few moments, apparently to fetch an umbrella, for he reappeared with one in his hand; and thus fortified, he again inspected me, first through his spectacles and then over them and replied in a tone of mild protest:

"But what about it, Mr Mortimer? A gentleman is not bound to stay in his chambers if he doesn't want to. He isn't under any contract to be in residence excepting at his own convenience and by his own choice. Probably he has gone out of town for a few days. Gentlemen frequently do; and they are not under any obligation to give notice of their intentions. That is the advantage of living in chambers."

"Yes," I replied, "but that is not quite the position. Mr Gillum had an appointment with Mr Benson at his chambers and it was a rather special one, definitely made by letter. Mr Gillum could hardly have gone away for a holiday and ignored this engagement."

Here I gave Mr Weech a slight sketch of the circumstances to which he listened with interest and growing attention.

"M'yes," he agreed, when I had finished, "it does sound a little remarkable, the way you put it. Of course, he might have overlooked the matter, but that doesn't seem likely. Still, I certainly have not seen him about the Inn for the last day or two."

"When did you last see him?" Benson asked.

Mr Weech considered for a few moments. "Now, let me see," said he. "I met him one evening just outside the Hall. He was coming down towards Fleet Street. Now, when would that be? I should say it would be about ten days ago. He reflected again and then confirmed his estimate with the definite statement: "Yes. Ten days ago it was. I can fix it by the fact that one of our tenants, who was a bit in arrears with his rent, came to the lodge to settle up. And very glad I was. The Court don't like rents to get behind-hand."

"Very well, Mr Weech," said I. "You haven't seen him for ten days. Now is that at all unusual?"

Mr Weech, having duly considered the question, decided that it was slightly unusual. "You see," he explained, "I am pretty constantly up and down the Inn and I tend to run up against the resident tenants, particularly if they are fairly regular in their habits, as Mr Gillum is. I should think I must have met him nearly every day since he came here. And he is a rather sociable man and likes to stop for a bit of a chat."

"Then," said I, "that seems to confirm our idea that there is something unusual about this affair. I suppose you don't happen to have a duplicate key of his chambers?"

Mr Weech seemed to stiffen at my suggestion.

"We don't usually keep duplicate keys of gentlemen's chambers," he replied. "The agreements stipulate that the tenants shall have full use and enjoyment of their premises, which would not be the case if we reserved either the right or the means of entry. But, as a matter of fact, I have a duplicate key of Mr Gillum's chambers. I offered it to him, but he said that he had no use for a second key, and he thought that it might be as well for me to keep it in case he might lose his or in the event of some emergency arising. But why do you ask?"

"Well," I said a little diffidently, "it occurred to me that it might be as well, if you had a key, just to look in and see that all is as it should be."

Mr Weech shook his head decidedly. "No, sir," said he, "I have no right to enter the chambers of any of our tenants without his express permission and authority."

I realised Mr Weech's point of view and fully agreed as to its propriety. But, having ascertained that a key was available, I made up my mind quite definitely that those chambers had got to be entered.

"That is true enough in ordinary circumstances," said I. "But the circumstances are not ordinary. You must see that something unusual has happened, and I may say that Mr Benson and I are extremely uneasy. Supposing Mr Gillum should have been taken ill or had some sort of accident."

Mr Weech was visibly impressed though he made no reply, and I proceeded to press my advantage.

"What would people say if it should become known that he had been left in his chambers without help simply because of a mere scruple of official etiquette."

"Yes," Mr Weech admitted, "there is something in that. It would be very awkward for him, shut up there, *solus cum soli,* if he was seriously ill. But we don't know that he is."

"We don't," I agreed, "but we can easily find out. Come, now, Mr Weech, don't stand on mere pedantic ceremony. Do the reasonable thing. Mr Gillum may be, at this moment, lying in there, helpless, waiting for someone to succour him. We ought to go and see whether he is or not. And I am not suggesting anything irregular. Mr Benson is his cousin and I am a responsible friend. I am only asking you to do what he would have expected you to do. You say that he left the key in your custody in case any emergency should arise. Well, an emergency has arisen and you have got the key."

"I should hardly call it an emergency," Mr Weech objected, "but still I don't want to be obstinate. You have shown cause why a visit of inspection might reasonably be made, and, if you and Mr Benson will take the responsibility, I will get the key and go round with you to the chambers. Then you will be able to see for yourselves whether there is or is not any foundation for your anxieties."

With this he went back into the lodge and presently returned carrying on his finger a couple of keys on a string loop to which was attached a wooden label.

Together we passed up the outer passage, across the small courtyard, through the covered way (not to call it a tunnel) on which the door of the Hall opened, and, crossing the inner courtyard, approached Gillum's entry. Our previous visit with its very audible accompaniments had evidently not passed unnoticed, for, as we walked into the entry, the door of the typewriting office opened slightly and a face appertaining to an elderly woman appeared, surveying us with an interest that was not entirely benevolent.

On arriving at the landing, Mr Weech transferred his umbrella from his right hand to the left, the better to manipulate the keys, the larger of which he inserted into the lock. It was not a very good fit, but, after a few tentative turns, he succeeded in shooting back the bolt; having done which, he drew the door outwards a couple of inches and sniffed audibly. Taking the key out of the door, he drew the latter wide open and was preparing to insert the key into the lock of the inner door when he observed that the latter was slightly ajar; whereupon he pushed it open and stepped into the room.

But he took only one or two steps, and then, as he passed the open door, he stopped short, and ejaculating, "God save us!" hastily backed out. And, at the same moment, I became aware of a strange, musty, cadaverous odour.

With all my forebodings intensified and a feeling of extreme distaste, I nevertheless ventured to step in at the open door to see what it was that had given such a shock to Mr Weech. But my stay was little longer than his, though in that instant my eyes took in a tableau that rises vividly before me as I write. As I cleared the edge of the door, I came into view of a couch drawn up by the window, whereon reclined a pyjama-clad figure whose aspect confirmed the worst of my fears.

It was a horrible spectacle, that motionless figure, half strange and half familiar, with its discoloured face and the open mouth from which the two gold teeth seemed to stare out as they gleamed in the bright afternoon sunlight. I stood, as I have said, gazing at it for but a few seconds and then, sick with the horror of the sight and the vile effluvium that filled the room, I hurried out and joined Mr Weech, who stood at the head of the stairs holding a handkerchief to his nose.

As I came out, Benson looked at me, but he asked no question. I suppose he guessed what we had seen, but his nerves were evidently stronger than ours for he strode into the room without hesitation, and pushing the door right back, opened the view into the room so far that I could see him stooping over that dreadful figure, regardless of the foul atmosphere and the obscene flies that buzzed around. He made a long and critical examination of the corpse and then turned to a small table that was placed beside the couch. This, I now noticed, bore a decanter, apparently containing whisky, a siphon, a tumbler, and a small corked bottle; and each of these objects Benson scrutinised minutely.

At length he came out, shutting the inner door after him, and looking very grim and solemn. Evidently he was deeply moved, but, though he was a shade pale, he was quite calm and self-possessed, in striking contrast to Weech and me, whose nerves were quite unstrung by the horrid experience. He closed the outer door, and, taking the key out of the lock, silently handed it to Mr Weech.

"Well," he said, "what is to be done now?"

"I suppose," said Weech, "I had better communicate with the police. They have a telephone in the office below and I dare say they will let me use it."

"Yes," Benson agreed, "that will be the best thing to do; and you had better ask the police how soon they can send someone up. We shall have to wait here and see them, as they will want some particulars and we may as well get the business over at once."

We went down to the ground floor and once more were the objects of interested scrutiny from the half-opened door. Then Mr Weech made his request and was admitted forthwith while Benson and I went out into the quadrangle to wait for him. Presently he came out and joined us, with the information that an officer was being sent up and would be at the Inn in the course of a few minutes. Then he invited us to come to the lodge to await the officer's arrival; an offer which Benson promptly declined, explaining that he wanted to talk things over with me before the officer should arrive. Accordingly, Mr Weech excused himself and went off in the direction of the lodge, and Benson and I turned into the quiet alley between a row of ancient houses and the garden railings.

"This is a very astounding affair, Mortimer," said Benson, when Mr Weech was out of earshot. "Doesn't it seem so to you?"

I hesitated for a moment, but as there was no reason for secrecy, and as I should certainly have to make a statement to the police, or at the inquest, I replied:

"It is a very dreadful business, but I can't say that I am so greatly surprised."

"Aren't you?" he exclaimed. "Now, I should have said that Jack Gillum was the very last person I should have expected to take his life. Why do you say that you are not surprised?"

"Well," I replied, "I have known a good deal about his way of living and the muddle that he has got his affairs into; and, of course, I have certain special knowledge which it would not be permissible for me to refer to."

"If you mean knowledge that you have obtained in your capacity as an employee of his bank," said Benson, there is nothing in it. He was your customer and you had to keep his affairs secret. But now that he is dead, his executor is your customer."

"He made a will, then?" said I, somewhat surprised.

"Yes, by special arrangement. Mr Penfield is his executor and I am the sole beneficiary under the will. So I am, in effect, your customer and am entitled to know how his affairs stand."

I was not at all satisfied that this view was technically correct. But, as it was certain that poor Gillum's affairs would have to be more or less completely disclosed at the inquest, I felt it to be unreasonable to withhold the information from one who was so clearly entitled to know all the facts. Accordingly I replied:

"I am not sure that you are right, but I am prepared to waive the strict letter of the law if you will promise to regard as absolutely confidential anything that I may tell you about Gillum's financial position."

"Certainly I will," said he. "But surely his financial position was perfectly satisfactory?"

"On the contrary," said I, "it was profoundly unsatisfactory; in fact, I don't think I am exaggerating if I say that he was absolutely penniless."

Benson stopped and gazed at me with a frown of astonishment.

"Penniless!" he exclaimed. "But he should have been a rich man, comparatively speaking. When he came to England, he had his very substantial savings, which I know he sent to Mr Penfield to be deposited in a bank – your bank, I suppose."

"Yes," said I. "Mr Penfield opened the account in Gillum's name with a deposit of three thousand pounds."

"Very well. Then he had payments from me from time to time, including the eleven hundred pounds that I sent him a little over three months ago. And he must have got something from the business, to say nothing of the purchase price of his partnership, whatever that may have been. But, of course, you know all about that."

"Yes," said I. "All those big cheques have been paid in, and the amounts have gone out nearly as fast as they have come in, and the position now is that there is not only no balance, but the account is a pound or two overdrawn."

Benson continued to stare at me with the utmost amazement.

"But," he exclaimed, "where the devil has the money gone? Do you suppose he has been playing the fool on the Stock Exchange?"

"I don't," I replied. "I know where, the bulk of the money has gone. It has been frittered away in gambling; some of it on the turf and a good deal on cards and roulette and various other fooleries. I have sometimes suspected that there might be a blackmailer in the background, but I have no knowledge to that effect. I only know that the bulk of the money was drawn out in cash and that he usually asked to have his 'self' cheques cashed in notes of small denomination – preferably in Treasury notes. It looked as if he wanted to secure himself against the possibility of the notes being traced."

Benson reflected on this statement in silence for a few moments, still looking at me with an expression of angry incredulity. At length he rejoined:

"We shall have to go into this in more detail later on. Obviously, as you are in possession of the actual facts, what you tell me must be true. But yet I find it beyond belief. The whole affair, including this suicide – for that is evidently what it is – is so utterly opposed to all that I know of Jack Gillum – and I have known him since he was a boy – that I can make nothing of it."

"Then," I suggested, "he was not always a gambler?"

"No," Benson replied, though without much emphasis. "No, I wouldn't call him a gambler. He liked a game of cards, and he liked to play rather higher than I cared about, and he had a way of betting in a small way and making wagers. But his play was never on a great scale, and his ordinary management of his financial affairs was perfectly reasonable. The amount that he had saved speaks for itself, and you can be sure that I should not have been willing to enter into the arrangements that existed between us if he had been a spendthrift and a wild gambler."

Benson's account of his cousin did not very greatly surprise me. It had been obvious to me that his habits could not always have been such as those that were known to me, or he would never have had any money at all. The gambling habit must have grown on him by frequent indulgence. So it appeared to me, and I answered to that effect.

"My acquaintance with your cousin," said I, "extends only to a short time, only about a year, or rather less. And when I first met him these new habits were already formed, so I never knew him otherwise. But even so, it has been a matter of surprise to me that a man, in other respects so sensible and capable, should have behaved in this idiotic manner. But what you have just told me makes it even more surprising. We can only suppose that the new surroundings, when he came to live in London, must have exerted some peculiar influence over him. And it may be that he fell into the society of people who had a bad effect on him. I happen to know that he was acquainted with some pretty shady characters, though how he came to know them I have no idea."

"There may be something in what you say," said Benson, "in fact, there must be. But the gambling alone doesn't seem to be a satisfactory explanation. I am inclined to suspect that you are right in your suggestion of a possible blackmailer. The way in which the money was drawn out in untraceable notes seems to support that view very strongly. There is no reason why a simple, straightforward gambler should take precautions against having his payments traced. However, we shall have to adjourn this discussion. That gentleman looks like the police officer."

As he spoke, Mr Weech appeared emerging from the covered way in company with a tall, brisk-looking man in civilian clothes who carried a largish attaché case. The two men approached us and Mr Weech effected a concise introduction.

"There is no need for you two gentlemen to come up with me," said the officer; "in fact it would be better for me to go alone so that I can make my observations undisturbed. But I will ask you to be good enough to wait here until I have seen what there is to see. I shall want to take a few particulars for the purposes of the inquest."

With this he departed under Mr Weech's guidance in the direction of Gillum's entry, the approach of the pair closely observed from the window of the typewriting office. When they had gone, I rather expected Benson to resume our conversation. But apparently what had been said already gave him sufficient food for thought, for he paced up and down the alley at my side uttering no word and evidently deep in his own reflections, which, to judge by his stern, gloomy expression, were of a highly disagreeable kind.

The officer's observations took rather longer than I had expected. At each turn of our walk when we came to the end of the alley and in view of Gillum's chambers, I could see Mr Weech at the open landing window, gazing out discontentedly across the quadrangle, and at the office window below watchful heads appeared from time to time over the wire blind. But the officer remained hidden from our sight.

At length, at about the twentieth turn, as we came to the corner of the alley, I observed that Mr Weech had disappeared from his post at the window, and a moment later he came into view in the obscurity of the staircase and then emerged into the open, followed closely by the officer, whereupon Benson and I walked forward to meet them.

"Well, gentlemen," said the officer, "it seems quite a straightforward case from my point of view, but I may as well have a few particulars for the guidance of the coroner's officer in preparing the details of the inquest. I will begin by taking your names and addresses and your relations with deceased."

He looked from one of us to the other, and Benson, as an actual relative, opened the proceedings by giving his name and address and stating his relationship.

"Ah," said the officer, "you are deceased's cousin. Then you will be the proper person to identify the body. Not that it is of any importance as there is no question as to who he is. But you have seen the body. Can you identify it positively?"

"Yes," replied Benson. "It is the body of my cousin, John Gillum."

"Exactly," said the officer. "Now, is there anything that you can tell us that would throw any light on the suicide – assuming it to be a suicide?"

"No," replied Benson. "I can't account for it at all. But I haven't seen deceased for about two years, so I haven't any very recent information about him. This gentleman, Mr Mortimer, knows a good deal more about his affairs than I do."

Thereupon the officer turned to me and asked me to give him any information that might guide him as to the kind of evidence that would be required at the inquest and the names of any witnesses who might have to be called. Accordingly I told him who I was but pointed out that, as an employee of deceased's bank, I was not at liberty to give any information as to his financial affairs.

"No," he agreed, "not in the ordinary way. But the customer's death releases the bank from its obligations of secrecy. However, I won't press you. Any information that the bank may be able to supply will have to be given at the inquest if it is relevant. Should you say that it would be relevant? I mean in relation to the motive for the suicide – assuming it to be a suicide?"

"Yes," I replied, "I think I may say that much. But perhaps you had better see the manager. He knows the ropes better than I do."

"Or Mr Penfield," Benson suggested. "He is Gillum's executor and was his man of business and as he is a lawyer he will know exactly what information he ought to give."

The officer agreed to this and took down the addresses of the manager and Mr Penfield. "And that," said he, "is all for the present. Now I must see about getting the body removed to the mortuary. I had better keep the keys until the inquest is over as we don't want the rooms disturbed, and there may be some letters or papers which ought to be examined either by me or by Mr Penfield. I will hear what he has to say about that. So I will wish you gentlemen good afternoon."

With this he bustled away and Benson and Weech and I walked down to the lodge where, declining an invitation to go in and rest a few minutes, Benson and I left the porter and made our way out into Fleet Street. My companion was still silent and gloomy, uttering scarcely a word as we walked down towards Ludgate Circus. Only just before we parted at the corner did he make any observation on the tragedy. Then, in a tone of almost passionate grief, he exclaimed:

"It is a miserable business, and what makes it more awful to me is the feeling that I have been, in a manner, the cause of the disaster. It looks very much as if poor Gillum had funked meeting me."

I could not but admit that the same idea had occurred to me. It would certainly have been a very awkward meeting, involving some exceedingly uncomfortable explanations.

"But he needn't have funked it," said Benson. "Of course, I should have been pretty sick. But I shouldn't have reproached him and I should not have let him down. He could have come back with me and helped me to run the farm and got back to his natural way of life. However, it is no use thinking now of what might have been. Good-bye, Mortimer. You know where to find me if you should want me."

He shook my hand heartily and turned away down Farringdon Street, and, as it was now too late to go back to the bank, I made my way towards my own place of abode.

CHAPTER SEVEN

The Coroner's Inquest

The facts which were disclosed by the evidence of witnesses at the inquest on the body of John Gillum were mostly new to me only to the extent that they were facts, for most of them had already existed in my mind in the form of suspicions. Nevertheless, the grim proceedings had for me the melancholy interest that now, when all the contributory circumstances of the final catastrophe were assembled, I was able to realise the enormity of that catastrophe. It was really beyond belief. That a man who had seemed to have been the especial favourite of fortune should have mismanaged his affairs so unutterably as to bring himself to actual destitution and to a pauper suicide's grave, appeared, and was, an incredible instance of human folly and perversity. But I need not moralise on the tragedy, the facts deposed to in evidence tell their own tale.

The first witness was Mr Weech, who gave a slightly verbose but very impressive description of the discovery. When he had finished and in answer to a question, had stated the date on which he had last seen deceased alive, he was dismissed and his place taken by Arthur Benson.

"You were present with Mr Weech when the body was discovered," said the coroner. "Were you able to identify the body?"

"Yes," was the reply, "it was the body of my cousin, John Gillum."

"The identity of the body is not in question," said the coroner, "but may we take it that you are certain that it was the body of your cousin?"

"I am quite certain," replied Benson. "The circumstances were so remarkable that I had at first some doubt whether it could really be John Gillum, so I examined it closely and carefully. There is no doubt whatever that it was John Gillum's body."

"Naturally," said the coroner, "you were greatly shocked at what had happened, but were you surprised?"

"I was astounded," replied Benson. "John Gillum was the last man in the world whom I should have expected to have committed suicide. But I had not seen him for nearly two years, when he was leaving Australia to come to England. Up to that time he had been working on a sheep farm and had seemed to be a happy, capable, well-balanced man. But I learn that since he came to this country his habits and even his character seem to have undergone a radical change. Of that, of course, I know nothing."

Here the coroner put one or two questions concerning Gillum's antecedents, to which Benson answered in much the same terms as those in which he had replied to mine, as recorded in the last chapter. And these details of Gillum's pecuniary position formed the remainder of his evidence.

The next witness was Detective-Sergeant Edmund Waters, who stepped up to the place appointed for witnesses and gave his evidence with professional readiness and precision.

"On Wednesday the eighteenth of July, I was informed that a telephone message had been received reporting the finding of the dead body of a man in a room at 64, Clifford's Inn. I proceeded there forthwith, going first to the porter's lodge where I met Mr Weech, who had sent the message, Mr Benson and Mr Mortimer. Mr Weech conducted me to the room, which was in a set of chambers on the first floor, and unlocked the door to admit me.

"On entering the room, I saw the dead body of a man lying on a couch close to a window. From the appearance of the body and a very foul odour which pervaded the air of the room, I judged that the man had been dead several days. I inspected the body without disturbing it but could see no injuries or any sign of violence or any indication of a struggle. The man was lying on the couch in an easy posture, as if he had fallen asleep there and nothing in the room appeared to be disturbed. By the side of the couch was a small table on which was a decanter containing whisky, a siphon of soda-water, a tumbler, and a small bottle labelled 'Tablets of morphine hydrochloride; gr.$^1/_2$.' and containing a number of white tablets. The description on the label was written with a pen in block capital letters.

"I took possession of the bottle and then I examined the tumbler. There were quite a large number of fingerprints on it and most of them were perfectly distinct. There were also fingerprints on the bottle, but these were not so distinct and I had to develop some of them up, especially those on the label, before I could be sure of the pattern. As I had my fingerprint apparatus with me, I proceeded very carefully to take a set of the fingerprints of the body to compare with those on the tumbler and the bottle. When I made the comparison, it became perfectly clear that all the prints on both vessels were made by deceased. Those on the tumbler were prints of the fingers of deceased's right hand and those on the bottle were principally prints of the left hand with one or two of the right."

"You are sure," said the coroner, "that there were no other fingerprints?"

"Quite sure," replied the sergeant. "The prints were all recognisable and I compared each one separately with the prints that I had taken from the body."

"That is very important," said the coroner, "and it seems quite conclusive. Did you make any examination of the room?"

"Not a minute examination. I just looked round to see if there were any signs of anything unusual, but there were not. Everything looked perfectly normal."

"Have you made any further investigation since then?"

"Yes. I went to the chambers with Mr Bateman, who was acting for the executors, to see if there were any papers or documents that might throw any light on the affair. We found the keys in the pockets of deceased's clothes and with them we opened the drawers of the writing-table. In one of the drawers we found several letters in their envelopes tied up in a bundle. We read these letters and we both formed the opinion that they were blackmailer's letters. Mr Bateman took possession of them and I believe he has them still."

"Then," said the coroner, "as Mr Bateman is here and will be giving evidence, we need not go into the question of the letters now. Is there anything else that you have to tell us?"

"No," replied the sergeant, "excepting that I notified the coroner – yourself – that I had the bottle of tablets and, in accordance with instructions, handed it to Dr Sidney."

"Then," said the coroner., "we need not trouble you further unless any member of the jury wishes to ask any questions. No questions? Then we had better next take the medical evidence."

Accordingly, the medical witness, Dr Thomas Winsford, was called and, having given his name and qualifications, deposed, in answer to the coroner's question:

"I have made a careful examination of the body of deceased. It is that of a man about forty years of age, well-developed and muscular and free from any signs of disease. I examined it in relation to the questions of the date of death and its cause. With regard to the first, there was a slight difficulty owing to the condition of the body, which was definitely in a state of incipient putrefaction. But, taking into account the temperature of the room in which it had been lying, I should say that deceased had been dead from six to eight days."

"You speak of the heat of the room. Had you any personal knowledge of the conditions in that room?"

"Yes. I obtained the key of the chambers from Sergeant Waters and went there in the afternoon. The sun was shining in at the window and the room was very hot. I took the temperature with a thermometer and found it to be eighty-one degrees Fahrenheit. That would account for the rather advanced state of putrefaction in the time that I have mentioned, and I am inclined to the opinion that deceased had not been dead more than six or seven days."

"Yes," the coroner remarked, "that seems to agree with what Mr Weech has told us. He saw deceased alive ten days before the discovery of the body. And what do you say as to the cause of death?"

"From the inspection of the body, it was difficult to assign any cause of death. There were no injuries or external marks of any kind or any abnormal appearances whatever. But I had been informed of the finding of the bottle of morphine tablets and I examined the body for signs of morphine poisoning."

"And did you find any such traces?"

"Morphine does not ordinarily leave very pronounced traces, and the condition of the body was not favourable for discovering the more minute signs. But I found a somewhat contracted state of the pupils, and this with the absence of any other signs indicating death from any other cause, confirmed the suggestion that death was due to poisoning with morphine. But I can only say that all the appearances were consistent with morphine poisoning and that I could not discover any other cause of death."

"Did you take any measure, to settle this question?"

"Yes. I removed from the body certain of the internal organs and put them in chemically clean jars which I closed and sealed and affixed to each a label on which I wrote the particulars and the date, and signed my name. These jars, in accordance with instructions, I handed personally to Dr Walter Sidney for analysis."

This concluded the doctor's evidence. He was followed by Dr Walter Sidney, who deposed that he was a pathologist and an analytical chemist, and that he had received from the preceding witness certain jars containing various organs from a human body which he was informed had been removed from the body of deceased. He had also received from Sergeant Waters a bottle containing a number of white tablets and labelled with a written label: "Morphine hydrochloride, gr. $1/2$." He had analysed four of the tablets and found that they were composed of morphine hydrochloride and that each tablet contained half a grain of the drug. He had also made a chemical examination of the organs from the jars and had obtained from them a little over two and a quarter grains of morphine. He estimated the amount of morphine present in the whole body at, at least, four grains, but probably more.

"What do you consider a poisonous dose of morphine?" the coroner asked.

"It varies considerably in different persons," the witness replied. "Half a grain has been known to cause death, but that is very unusual. One grain would be very likely to cause death in a person who was not accustomed to the drug, and two grains would ordinarily be a lethal dose."

"Then four grains is definitely a lethal dose?

"Yes. It would almost certainly cause death in a person who was not in the habit of taking the drug."

"Did your examination enable you to form any opinion as to whether deceased had been in the habit of taking morphine?"

"I should not like to give a very definite opinion. All the organs, including the liver, were quite healthy; which would hardly have been the case if deceased had been in the habit of dosing himself with morphine. I can only say that I found no signs that suggested the habitual taking of the drug. And Dr Winsford's evidence, in which he stated that deceased appeared to be a strong, healthy man, is quite inconsistent with the idea that deceased was a morphine addict."

"As a result of your examination, can you make any suggestion as to the cause of death?"

"Inasmuch as a lethal dose of morphine was found in the body, and as no other cause of death was discoverable, I should say that there is no doubt that deceased died from poisoning by morphine."

"Thank you," said the coroner; "that is what we want to know; and I think that, if you have nothing more to tell us, we need not detain you any longer."

He glanced enquiringly at the jury, and, as neither the jury nor the witness volunteered any remark, the latter withdrew to his seat.

The next witness was Mr Alfred Bateman, a gentleman of typically legal aspect whose acquaintance I had already made. Having been sworn, he deposed that he was the managing clerk of Mr Penfield, a solicitor and executor of the will of deceased, for whom he also acted as man of business.

"Are you in possession of any facts that explain, or have any bearing on, the death of deceased?" the coroner asked.

"I am in possession of certain facts which seem to me to be relevant to the subject of this inquiry," the witness replied. "In the first place, deceased had, in less than two years, got through a fortune, and was, at the time of his death, so far as I can ascertain, absolutely penniless and in debt. In the second place, he was, at the time of his death, being harassed by blackmailers."

"Yes," said the coroner, "those facts certainly seem to be relevant to the subject of this inquiry. Perhaps you might give us a few particulars without going into unnecessary detail."

"As to the financial question," said Bateman, "the facts, in outline, are these: Nearly two years ago – on the sixteenth of April, 1928, to be exact – deceased wrote to Mr Penfield stating that he was coming to England to live and remitting a sum of three thousand pounds which he asked Mr Penfield to deposit in a suitable bank in his, deceased's, name, five hundred to be placed to the current account and the remainder on deposit. I dealt with this matter myself, under Mr Penfield's instructions, and placed the

93

money in Perkins' Bank. Three months after the receipt of this
letter, that is, on the eighteenth of September, the deceased called
at our office to announce his arrival. There were certain business
transactions connected with the purchase of a partnership which I
think I need not describe in detail as they seem to have no bearing
on recent events. When these were concluded, and deceased had
deposited his will with Mr Penfield, I accompanied him to the
bank and introduced him to the manager. Thereafter our contact
with him practically ceased. He came to the office once or twice
afterwards, and then, as we had finished with his affairs and he had
kept the partnership deed in his own possession, we lost sight of
him; and, excepting that his address in Clifford's Inn was known to
us – he having given Mr Penfield as a reference when he applied
for the chambers – we knew nothing of what he was doing or how
he lived.

"He next came into view, so to speak, when his cousin, Mr
Benson, called at our office to ask if we could give him any
information as to where he could find deceased. That was on the
seventeenth of this month. As we knew nothing, we referred him
to deceased's bank, and, as he has deposed, he went there. On the
evening of the eighteenth, Mr Benson called at the office and
informed me – as Mr Penfield had already left – of the discovery
of the body in the chambers. He also informed me that the
keys of the chambers were in the possession of Sergeant Waters.
Thereupon, as I knew that Mr Penfield was the executor of
deceased's will, I thought it best to see the sergeant without delay
and accordingly went forthwith to the police station where I was
fortunate enough to find the sergeant. He suggested that we had
better go to the chambers and see if there were any letters or
papers which might throw any light on the motives for the
assumed suicide.

"I agreed that it was desirable and we accordingly went together
to the chambers and made the search. In a drawer in the writing-
table we found a considerable number of letters and other
documents, all neatly tied into bundles and docketed. There was

one bundle tied with red tape and labelled 'Horse-leech' and this we examined first. It consisted of eleven letters, each enclosed in its envelope. They were all in a similar, and apparently disguised, handwriting, none of them bore any signature or contained any reference to any person by name, and none of them was dated, though the date could be inferred from the postmark on the envelope.

"On reading them, we came to the conclusion that they were undoubtedly from a blackmailer. Ten of them were quite short and were simply reminders that a payment was due. The other one, which appeared to be the first of the series, plainly demanded money with menaces. I produce the letters for your inspection."

Here the witness drew from his pocket a bundle of letters tied together with red tape and laid them on the table before the coroner.

"I think," said the latter, that it would be better for you to read them to us, or, at least, the first letter and one of the others. The jury can inspect them afterwards if they wish to."

Accordingly, Mr Bateman untied the bundle, and, taking the two outside letters, opened one of them and read its contents aloud:

" 'With reference to our little friendly talk last night, as you did not seem able to make up your mind, I will see if I can help you. To put the matter in a nutshell, I want £500 from you as a first instalment. The others we can arrange later, but I must have this at once; and I warn you that I am not going to stand any nonsense. If this is not handed over by Sunday night at the latest, the consequences which I mentioned to you will follow without further notice.

" 'The money is to be paid in pound notes (not new ones) and the parcel is to be handed personally either to me or to the party whom you know and whose name I mentioned to you.

" 'This is the final offer and I advise you to take it. You will be sorry if you don't.' "

"I agree with you," said the coroner, "as to the character of that letter. It is a typical blackmailer's letter. What is the date on the envelope?"

"The postmark is dated the sixteenth of September, 1929. Shall I read the last letter?"

"If you please," the coroner replied, whereupon the witness drew the other letter from its envelope, and, glancing at the latter, said:

"This is dated by the post-mark the fourth of this present month of July and the contents are as follows:

" 'In case you should forget to look at your calendar, as you did last time, I am sending you this little reminder. And don't forget that the notes must be old ones which have seen some service. There were several brand new notes in the last instalment which had to be kept for use on the turf. Don't let that happen again.' "

As he finished reading, Bateman laid the two letters on the table and the coroner, after glancing through them, passed them to the foreman of the jury.

"Beyond these blackmailing letters," said he, addressing the witness, "did you find anything that might throw light on what has happened?"

"Not in the way of letters," Bateman replied. "All the others were just normal business correspondence and letters from his cousin, Mr Benson, sent from Australia. But we found also in that drawer the passbook from deceased's bank, and the entries in that were very significant. We began by looking up the entries corresponding to the dates of the blackmailing letters, and, from what we could see, it appeared that deceased had been paying out £500 every quarter, excepting the last. On the date corresponding to the last letter the amount drawn out was only £200. But when we looked through the entries other than those corresponding to the dates of the blackmailing letters, it was clear that a large number of sums of money had been drawn out in the form of cash, for what purpose we were, of course, unable to guess."

"You found no evidence of any other blackmailers?" the coroner asked.

"No evidence," Bateman replied, "but it looked highly suspicious. The 'self' cheques appeared at very frequent intervals and some of them were for considerable amounts. However, we could not make very much of the passbook, but, from what we could see, it looked as if deceased had spent his money as fast as he received it; and the cheques that were entered to his credit were for quite large amounts.

"But it was on the following day, the nineteenth, that I learned the full enormity of the affair. On that day I accompanied Mr Penfield to the bank, where we had an interview with the manager. He presented us with a statement of his transactions with deceased and showed us how the account stood. I need not trouble you with details, but the position amounted to this; that deceased had drawn out every penny that he possessed and was actually in debt to the bank, though to only a small amount."

"You say that deceased had received considerable sums of money. We don't want details, but, roughly speaking, about how much had he spent and how long had he been in spending it?"

"The total amount that he had held to his credit, including the original deposit, was just over £13,000. And he had got through the whole of this between the end of September, 1928, and the middle of this present month; a period of one year and ten months."

"Did you learn at the bank whether he appeared to have been operating on the Stock Exchange?"

"I think we may definitely infer that he had not. Settlements on the Stock Exchange are made by cheque, and there were no records of any cheques payable to stockbrokers. The comparatively few cheques that appeared in the ledger were mostly small in amount and appeared to have been payable to tradesmen or other persons concerned with the ordinary, normal expenditure. What had exhausted the account was the large number of cheques payable to himself in cash."

"Well," said the coroner, addressing the jury, "there is no object in our enquiring further into the details of this astonishing instance of reckless prodigality. We have the material fact that in less than two years this unfortunate man flung away what most of us would have regarded as a fortune. We also know that, at the time of his death, he was penniless and in debt, and that he was the victim of a particularly rapacious set of blackmailers. I think Mr Bateman has given us some most illuminating information and that we might now thank him for the clear and lucid way in which he has given his evidence and not detain him any longer. Unless any member of the jury wishes for any further information."

One member of the jury, apparently thrilled by the vast sums that had been mentioned, would have sought further details, but was politely suppressed by the coroner; whereupon Bateman was released and retired to his seat. There was a short interval during which the coroner glanced through the depositions, and then, as I had expected, my name was called.

"You have heard Mr Bateman's evidence," said the coroner, when the preliminaries had been disposed of. "As a member of the staff of the bank, you will probably consider yourself prohibited from giving any particulars of deceased's financial affairs. But can you tell us if you endorse what the last witness has stated?"

"I endorse it completely," I replied. "I was present with the manager when the particulars were given to him. And I may say that I am fully authorised by the executor – whom the account is now vested – and the manager, to give any information that may be required as to our late customer's dealings with the bank."

"Then," said the coroner, "as you, in your capacity of cashier, knew exactly what monies deceased received and what he drew out, and in what form, perhaps you can tell us what opinions you held as to his very unusual manner of conducting his affairs. Did you ever suspect that he was being blackmailed?"

"I did."

"What circumstances in particular led you to form that suspicion?"

"In the first place, there were the very large sums which he drew out in cash. It is very unusual for customers to draw out in cash more than quite modest amounts and these large drafts in cash were, in themselves, rather suggestive of some slightly irregular transactions. But what specially tended to arouse my suspicions was the fact that deceased usually asked expressly for old notes; notes that had been in circulation and were more or less soiled."

"What did you infer from that?"

"As the only possible advantage of a note that has been used is that it cannot be traced, I inferred that the notes were to be used for making payments of a secret, and possibly unlawful, character."

"Is it unusual for customers to ask for used notes?"

"It is rather unusual, though some customers prefer the used notes because they are less liable to stick together than the new. But usually, customers express a marked preference for new, clean notes."

"But the new notes are more easy to trace?"

"They are quite easy to trace. Usually, when a customer presents a bearer cheque for a considerable amount, he is paid in notes which have been newly issued and supplied direct to the bank. Such an issue is in the form of a series of notes of which the numbers are consecutive, and the numbers of the series are entered, not only in our own books but in the books of the bank of issue. Moreover, the numbers of the notes paid to the customer are also recorded; so that, if any question arises, it is possible to say with certainty that a particular note was paid to a particular person on a known date."

"You inferred, then, that these notes were being used to make payments of a questionable kind? What led you to suspect blackmail in particular?"

"It is common knowledge that blackmailers always refuse cheques and insist on being paid in cash; and their objection to cheques would equally apply to a series of newly issued notes. The only other kind of persons known to me who demand payment in untraceable cash are either thieves or receivers of stolen goods. But in the case of deceased, blackmailers were more probable than thieves or receivers. And there was another circumstance that strongly suggested a blackmailer. In addition to the smaller drafts which were presented at irregular intervals, there were certain larger drafts which were presented periodically and pretty regularly at intervals of three months. This suggested that someone was being paid a quarterly allowance; and, having regard to the mode of payment, I felt very little doubt that that person was a blackmailer."

"You speak of a blackmailer. It has been suggested that there may have been more than one. What do you say to that?"

"I can only say that I think it highly probable. I have always, from the first, suspected a blackmailer in the background, simply by reason of the large cash withdrawals. But I had nothing more definite than that to go on until the large periodical drafts began last September. If there were any other blackmailers they must have been paid at irregular intervals, and, I should say, in smaller amounts. But it is possible that the irregular cash drafts merely represented what deceased spent on gambling. I know that his expenditure on betting and play was very large."

"But would he have needed used notes for that purpose? Gambling is a foolish pursuit, but it is not usually unlawful."

"No; but it may be associated with other acts which are unlawful. This was certainly the case in the one instance in which I accompanied him to one of his gambling resorts. It was a most disreputable place and the persons present seemed to me to be of the shadiest type. And drink was being sold freely on unlicensed premises and during prohibited hours. The place might have been, at any moment, raided by the police, and, in that case, deceased would not have wished that any evidence should exist that he had been associated with it, if he had happened not to be there at the time of the raid."

"Is it actually known to you that the deceased gambled to a really serious extent?"

"Yes. I was present on two occasions; the one that I have mentioned and another at a horse-race. On the first occasion he played very little as he was merely showing me the place and the people. But at the race he plunged rather heavily and lost – as he informed me – about a hundred pounds. But he was quite unconcerned about it. He seemed to consider the dropping of a hundred pounds as quite a negligible loss."

"Did he know that you were aware of the extent to which he gambled?

"Oh, yes. He made no secret of it. I spoke to him very seriously on several occasions and pointed out to him how his capital was wasting. But he was incorrigible. He took my lectures quite amiably, but he would promise no reform. He was quite confident that he would get all his losses back presently."

The coroner reflected for a few moments on this statement. Then, in a grave and emphatic tone, he said:

"As you were a friend of deceased's and the only person who appears to know much of his affairs, I am going to ask you two questions. The first is: Have you any inkling as to the identity of the person who was blackmailing him?"

Now I had expected this question and had carefully considered the reply that I ought to make. I had a very definite suspicion as to who the blackmailer was. But it was only a guess; and a guess is not an inkling in the sense intended. I was prepared to communicate my suspicions to the police, but I had no intention of making guesses in sworn testimony with the certainty of publicity. Accordingly, I replied with strict truth:

"I have no knowledge whatsoever. Deceased made no confidences to me, and I never hinted to him what I suspected."

The coroner, whatever he may have thought, accepted this answer without comment and wrote it down. Then he put his second question.

"Had you ever any reason to think it possible that deceased might take his life?"

"Yes," I replied, "I have had that possibility in mind for some time, and, as soon as I heard that he was missing, I suspected what had happened."

"What led you to that belief?"

"It was something that deceased himself had said. On a certain occasion we happened to be speaking of suicide and I remarked that, to me, it seemed that the fact of suicide was in itself evidence of an unsound state of mind. With this he disagreed emphatically. He contended that suicide was a perfectly rational proceeding in appropriate circumstances; and when I asked him what he considered appropriate circumstances, he mentioned as an example, total and irremediable financial ruin. From that time, since his affairs were obviously tending in that direction, I have always had an uneasy expectation that, when the crash came, he would take that course for solving his difficulties."

"You had that expectation," said the coroner, "but was it based on the mere opinion that he had expressed or on some more definite indication of intention? I mean, did he ever convey to you that he actually contemplated suicide as an act possible to himself?"

"He conveyed to me quite definitely the view that, if he were reduced to abject poverty, life would not be worth living, and that he would take measures to bring it to an end. He seemed to consider that it was the natural and reasonable thing to do."

The coroner pondered this statement for a while. Then he looked towards the jury.

"Are there any further questions that you would like to ask this witness?" he enquired. "It seems to me that he has given us all the material facts."

That was apparently the view of the jury, for no further questions were suggested. Accordingly, when the depositions had been completed, I was released and returned to my seat, and, as there were no other witnesses, the coroner proceeded to sum up briefly but quite adequately.

"You have now heard all the evidence," he began, "and you will have noticed that it all seems to establish a single conclusion. The medical evidence is quite dear. Deceased died from the effects of a large dose of morphine, or morphia, as it is more commonly called. On the question whether the poison was administered by himself or some other person, we have the evidence of the sergeant that the fingerprints on the drinking-vessel and on the poison bottle were those of deceased himself, and that there were no signs of the presence of any other person. Then we have the clear evidence of Mr Mortimer that deceased had contemplated suicide as a means of escape from the consequences of financial ruin; and we have the evidence of both Mr Bateman and Mr Mortimer that financial ruin had actually occurred on a scale that almost takes one's breath away. So you see that the drift of the evidence is all in the same direction; and I will leave you to consider it with the feeling that you will have no difficulty in finding your verdict."

Apparently the coroner's feeling was a just one, for the jury, after a very brief consultation, communicated their verdict through the foreman. It was to the effect that deceased died from the effects of a large dose of morphine, administered by himself.

"That," said the coroner, "is a verdict of suicide. What do you say as to the state of deceased's mind at the time of the act?"

The decision of the jury, in direct contradiction of poor Gillum's own view, was that he was insane at the time when the act was committed. And when this finding had been recorded the proceedings came to an end.

I lingered after the court had risen to exchange a few words with Benson, to whom I had taken a rather strong liking, and presently we were joined by Mr Bateman, who apparently wanted to learn how his client had been affected by the incidents of the inquiry.

"A most amazing story," he commented, "the evidence in this case has brought to light. I have never heard anything more astonishing. The finding of the jury as to the state of mind of deceased at the time of the act might fairly be extended to all his other acts. The conduct that the evidence has disclosed is the conduct of a sheer lunatic. Don't you agree with me, Mr Benson?"

"I do indeed," Benson admitted gloomily.

"And I think," pursued Bateman, "that you will also agree that, however incomprehensible poor Gillum's conduct may seem to a sane man, the fact that he did act in that insane manner has been established beyond any possible doubt. A consistent story has been elicited and established on an undeniable basis of ascertained fact."

He looked a little anxiously, as I thought, at Benson, who reflected a few moments before replying, but, at length, gave a qualified assent to Bateman's proposition.

"As to the facts which were proved in evidence," said he, "they seem to admit of no doubt or denial. But I still have the feeling that there is something behind all this that I don't understand. The whole affair is too abnormal."

"As to its abnormality," said Bateman, "I am entirely with you. But, abnormal as it is, I think we have got to accept it as a sequence of events that actually happened. Surprise is natural enough, but doubt would seem to be unreasonable."

He paused and looked questioningly at Benson, and as the latter did not reply immediately, he asked:

"You are not contemplating any further action in the matter, are you? Any sort of private or unofficial inquiry? I hope not, "for I feel that nothing could come of it; nothing, that is to say, but the dredging up of a quantity of unprofitable and unsavoury details. And inquiries of this kind are apt to prove costly out of all proportion to their value."

"It would certainly be proper," Benson replied, "for me to give very respectful consideration to your advice, seeing that your experience is so much greater than mine. But I must confess that I am not satisfied. Still, I will not take any decision without earnest consideration of what you have said. I will think things over for a day or two and I will let you know whether I decide to accept this mysterious affair at its face value or to see if any sort of unravelment is possible."

"Very well," rejoined Bateman. "We will leave it at that. If, in the end, you decide to open the matter further, we have the material. Mr Penfield has carried out your instructions. We had, as you may have noticed, our Mr James – a very skilful shorthand reporter – in court today to make a complete verbatim report of everything that was said, in evidence or otherwise. So that we are independent of the newspaper reports and we shall have no need to ask for access to the depositions. But I hope that neither will be required."

With this, Mr Bateman took his leave and bustled away; and, as Benson appeared more disposed for reflection than conversation, and I had my own business to attend to, I parted from him at the entrance to the building and we went our respective ways.

And here my narrative comes to its natural end. Its purpose was to give an account of my association with John Gillum, and this I have done; and if my story is not without an epilogue, that epilogue will issue from a pen other than mine.

PART TWO

THE CASE OF JOHN GILLUM, DECEASED

Narrated by Christopher Jervis, MD

CHAPTER EIGHT

Is there a Case?

The George and Vulture Inn has always been associated in my mind with the historic case of Bardell and Pickwick and those extremely astute gentlemen, Messrs. Dodson and Fogg of Freeman's Court hard by. But nowadays that venerable tavern associates itself more especially with the very queer case of John Gillum, deceased, and a less famous but much more respectable practitioner of the law. For it was at the George and Vulture that I – together with my colleague, John Thorndyke – became introduced to the queer case aforesaid, and the introducer was no less a person than Mr Joseph Penfield.

There was nothing surprising in our encounter there at lunchtime with Mr Penfield, for his office in George Yard was but a few doors from the tavern. Probably it was his daily resort; at any rate, as we entered the grill-room, there he was, seated at a table gravely contemplating a grilled chop which the waiter had just set before him. He observed us as we entered and immediately indicated a couple of vacant chairs at his table.

"This is an unexpected pleasure," said he as we took possession of the chairs. "Isn't the City of London rather outside your radius?"

"No place is outside our radius," replied Thorndyke. "But we have just come from the Griffin Life Office where we have been conferring with our old friend, Mr Stalker. The Griffin retains me permanently."

"As medical referee, I suppose?" Mr Penfield ventured.

"No," replied Thorndyke. "As medico–legal adviser; I might almost say as adviser in doubtful cases of suicide, for that is the kind of problem that is usually submitted to me."

"Ha!" said Penfield; "and I presume that Mr Stalker's bias is usually towards an affirmative view."

"Naturally," Thorndyke agreed, "but he doesn't expect me to share that bias. On the contrary, my usual function is rather to shatter his hopes and to convince him of all the things that he doesn't want to believe."

"Yes," said Penfield, "and a very useful function, too. If more people would seek the services of an expert destructive critic, there would be a good deal less litigation."

With this he returned to the consideration of his lunch while I, having secured the waiter's attention, communicated to him our joint requirements. Meanwhile, Mr Penfield proceeded methodically with his meal, dropping an occasional remark but chiefly leaving the conversational initiative to Thorndyke and me. But as I watched him skilfully dissecting his chop and noted his reflective expression, I had the feeling that he was cogitating some matter arising out of Thorndyke's explanation and his own rejoinder, and I waited expectantly for it to rise to the surface. And at length (as Pepys would have expressed it) "out it come."

"Your description," said he, "of your connection with the Griffin has brought to my mind a matter that is causing me some embarrassment. In short, to be quite honest, it has raised the hope that I may be able to transfer the burden of it from my shoulders to yours. You may consider the case as being within your province. It certainly isn't within mine."

"That suggests to me," said Thorndyke, "that it is a criminal case."

"Yes," replied Penfield, "it is. Highly criminal. A nasty, unsavoury, disreputable affair, and, legally, quite impossible at that.

I will just indicate its nature, though I expect you know something of it already from the newspapers. Probably you heard of a case of suicide that occurred in Clifford's Inn about a month ago."

"I remember it quite well," said Thorndyke, "and I recall that you were the dead man's solicitor."

"Then," said Penfield, "you will remember that the dead man, John Gillum by name, having wasted his substance in riotous living, to wit, in gambling, and having – presumably by his own folly – become the victim of blackmailers, proceeded to overdraw his account at the bank and then to commit suicide."

"Yes," said Thorndyke, "I remember that."

"Very well," said Penfield. "Now deceased had a cousin who was much too good for him; a most estimable Australian gentleman named Benson. I speak of him with sympathy and respect although he is now the bane of my life. He was present when Gillum's body was discovered and he at once formed the opinion that there was something abnormal about the affair; something more than met the eye. And so there may have been. However, he asked me to send a shorthand writer to attend the inquest and make a verbatim report of the proceedings, which I did; and I can let you have a transcript of that report if it is of any use. But I must admit that, on reading it, I was utterly unable to see anything in the case that was not perfectly normal, the circumstances being what they were. And that is still my position, and I have tried to impart that view to Benson. But he is still unsatisfied and he continues to stir me up from time to time with demands that some kind of action shall be taken."

"What does he want you to do?" Thorndyke asked.

"To tell you the truth," replied Penfield, "I am not quite clear. But, primarily, he wants the blood of those blackmailers."

"Naturally," said Thorndyke, "and very properly. But is there any clue to their identity?"

"Not the slightest," replied Penfield. "He expects me, in some mysterious manner, by employing private detectives or other agents, to discover who the blackmailers are and to drag them forth from their lairs and bring them to justice."

"You say that he has nothing to go on. Nothing at all?"

"Nothing," replied Penfield, "but a few letters in a disguised hand, dated only by the postmarks, unsigned, of course, and mentioning nobody by name nor hinting at any locality."

"And have you no letters or documents that might be of assistance?"

"I have Gillum's will. Benson is the sole beneficiary; and the sole benefit that he has enjoyed has been a small debt to the bank, which he has insisted on paying. I have also one or two of Gillum's letters to me, but they are simple business letters making no reference to his private affairs."

"And what do you want me to do?" Thorndyke asked.

"I should like," replied Penfield, "to bring him to you and let him state his case and say what he wants. If you think that it is possible to do anything for him, well and good; and if you think otherwise, I should suggest that you give him some of the medicine that you tell me you administer to Mr Stalker for the cure of unreasonable optimism."

Thorndyke did not reply immediately, but I could see that the case, unpromising as it looked, was not without its attractions for him. For, unlike Penfield, he was stimulated rather than discouraged by apparent difficulties. Still, even Thorndyke could not embark on a case without data of some sort. Eventually, he replied without committing himself to any definite course of action:

"I think it would be worth while to hear what Mr Benson has to say. He may know more than he is aware of; and I recall that at the inquest a friend of Gillum's gave evidence, a man named Mortimer. He seemed to know more about deceased's affairs than anybody else. Perhaps we might get some information from him."

"Excellent!" exclaimed Penfield, obviously delighted at the prospect of shifting his burden on to Thorndyke's shoulders. "Excellent. I can put you into touch with Mr Mortimer, and I am sure he will give you any assistance that he can. And now, as we seem to have finished our lunch, perhaps you will walk down to my office with me and I will hand you the report. It contains all the positive information that I think you are likely to get."

Accordingly, when we had settled our score, we set forth from the tavern down George Yard to Mr Penfield's office. There we observed a rack of deed-boxes the lids of which were decorated, rather like coffin-plates, with the names of Mr Penfield's clients. One of these, bearing the name of "John Gillum Esq.," our friend let down, when he had unlocked the box, displaying a small collection of documents within. From these he selected a large envelope, and having opened it and verified its contents, handed it to Thorndyke.

"That," said he, "is the report. If you decide to undertake the case, I shall, if you wish it and Mr Benson agrees, transfer the deed-box with its contents to you. And now, perhaps we can make an appointment for your meeting with Mr Benson. Will you come here, or shall I bring him to your chambers?"

"I don't see why you should bring him," said Thorndyke, "unless you would prefer to. I suggest that he calls on me one evening by appointment, for an informal talk, and if he can bring Mr Mortimer with him, we shall be able to see exactly how we stand."

"Thank you," said Mr Penfield. "It will suit me much better to send him than to bring him, so, if you will give me a date, I will make the appointment."

"I will give you two dates," said Thorndyke, "and you can notify me when to expect the visit. One will be the day after tomorrow at eight o'clock in the evening, if that will suit you, Jervis, and the other two days later."

"Both these dates will do for me," said I; on which Mr Penfield entered them in his book with undissembled satisfaction.

"I must thank you again," said he, accompanying us out into George Yard. "You have really rendered me a great service."

He shook hands cordially with us both and even stood watching us as we walked away up the court towards Cornhill. And thus was set rolling the ball whose revolutions I was to watch with so much interest during the next few months. None of Thorndyke's cases ever started less hopefully, and few developed in a more surprising fashion.

Mr Benson chose the earlier of the two dates and arrived at our chambers punctually at eight in the evening thereof; so punctually that the Temple clock was actually striking the hour as the knock on our door was heard. He was accompanied by another gentleman, and when I let him in, mutual introductions were effected and followed by mutual inspection. Like Mr Penfield, we were pleasantly impressed by our visitor, indeed by both our visitors. Benson was a typical Australian; tall, well set up and athletic looking, with a fresh, weather-tanned face and a frank, agreeable manner. His companion, Mr Mortimer, was of a quite different type; a quiet, sedate man with something rather studious and bookish in his appearance.

"I suppose," said Benson, when the conversational preliminaries had been disposed of, "Mr Penfield has given you a general outline of the business?"

"He has given me the report of the inquest," replied Thorndyke, "and I and my colleague, Dr Jervis, have read it most carefully. So now we probably know as much as to the facts of the case as you do, and are in a position to discuss them. Mr Penfield informs me that you wish some action to be taken, and the first question is what kind of action you contemplate."

This very definite question seemed rather to disconcert Benson, for he answered in a somewhat hesitating manner:

"Well, you see, I have had all along the feeling that this dreadful affair was perfectly unnatural and that there was something behind it that was never brought out by the inquest. In the first place, my cousin, Gillum, was the very last person whom I should have expected to commit suicide."

"That," said Thorndyke, "is frequently said by witnesses at inquests and probably quite truly. But let us be definite. There are only two possibilities in the case of your cousin's death. Either he committed suicide or he was murdered. The jury decided that he killed himself. Do you contest the fact of the suicide?"

"Well, no," replied Benson. "I don't see how I can. I heard all the evidence; and, unwilling as I am to believe that he killed himself, I don't see that there is any escape from the facts."

"No," Thorndyke agreed, "that is how it appears to me. Then, if we accept, as we seem bound to do, the fact that John Gillum died by his own hand, we can pass on to the next point. What is the further question that you want to raise?"

"The further question," replied Benson, "is, why did he commit suicide? Mortimer thinks that he killed himself because he had gambled away all his money, but I don't believe that. It isn't a sufficient reason. And we know that he was being harassed by blackmailers. Now, my feeling is that it was not the loss of his money that drove him to suicide, but the agony of mind that he was suffering on account of these blackmailing devils."

"That," said Thorndyke, "is a perfectly reasonable view, and I am inclined to agree with you. But what practical effect do you propose to give to your belief?"

"If John Gillum was driven to his death by these wretches," Benson replied with some heat, "they are virtually his murderers. I know that, in law, they are not chargeable with murder. But, even legally, they are guilty of a very serious crime, and I want them found and brought to justice."

"That, again," said Thorndyke, "is a perfectly reasonable position, and I view your desire very sympathetically. But there are two points that I think it necessary to put to you. The first is that what you propose is as nearly as may be an impossibility. So far as I know at present, there is no clue whatever to the identity of these people, nor — so far as I am aware — is anything known as to the circumstances in which the payments were made."

"I think," said Benson, "Mortimer can tell us something about that, and I believe he has some suspicions as to who these people are."

"We will hear what Mr Mortimer has to tell us presently," said Thorndyke. "Meanwhile let us consider the second point. That raises the question whether it is, in fact, expedient to take any action, even with a chance of success."

"Expedient?" Benson repeated. "Is there anything against it besides the difficulty?"

"I think," said Thorndyke, "that if we consider the circumstances as they are known to us, we shall see certain objections to taking the kind of action that you contemplate. May I ask whether your cousin was at all a nervous or timorous man? A man easily intimidated?"

"Most certainly not," replied Benson. "He was a decidedly bold, self-reliant man."

"Very well," said Thorndyke, "then consider his position at the time of his death. He was being blackmailed by at least one person, and that at the rate of two thousand pounds a year. Now, you know, Mr Benson, it is not usually possible to levy blackmail on a person who has nothing to conceal unless that person is more than ordinarily easily frightened. But your cousin was not easily frightened; and yet he was paying this enormous amount. Moreover, as you believe, he was so distressed by his position that he took his life to escape from the persecution. What are we to infer from this? Is it possible to resist the inference that there was something in his life that he was compelled to conceal at any price?"

Benson was evidently a good deal taken aback by Thorndyke's blunt statement of the case. He remained silent for some moments; then he replied:

"It had occurred to me that some mud might be stirred up if we were to bring the blackmailers to justice, but I hadn't put it as strongly as you have."

"It is necessary to face the facts squarely," said Thorndyke, "and those facts suggest very strongly that your cousin was concealing something highly discreditable; and it could have been no trivial scandal. In that case he could have appealed to the police and would have been given ample protection without any inquisition. The amount which he paid suggests something of extreme gravity; something which he dared not allow to come to light. Therefore, I ask you again, would it not be wiser to let sleeping dogs lie?"

Once more Benson reflected before replying, but he was not long in coming to a decision.

"It might be wiser," he admitted, "but it would be against justice and common morality. As to the scandal, poor old Jack is dead, so it won't affect him. And I don't suppose it was anything that would lessen my respect for him. At any rate, I feel strongly that those devils who drove him to a miserable death ought to be dragged out into the light of day and made to pay their debt."

"Yes," Thorndyke agreed, "I think you are right in principle. But I must finally remind you of the difficulties of the case. Remember that, not only are we without any clue as to who these people were – unless Mr Mortimer can supply one – but, even if we could discover them, the principal witness – the vital witness, in fact – is dead, and it might easily turn out to be impossible to make out a case against them, or, at any rate, to prove it. Furthermore, the proceedings, involving the employment of private enquiry agents, might prove to be extremely costly; and in the very probable event of total failure, a vast amount of money would have been wasted."

"I know," said Benson, "and it is very good of you to put the matter so clearly. But my mind is made up. Whatever it costs, if you are prepared to undertake the case, I should like you to get on with it. I am a man of ample means, and I am a bachelor; and if I spend every penny that I have, and even if we fail after all, I shall feel that the money was well spent in trying to bring Jack Gillum's murderers to the punishment that they deserve."

I could see that Benson's attitude had secured Thorndyke's warm sympathy, as, indeed, it had secured mine. But I think both of us rather regretted that he should have embarked on an enterprise that was almost certain to end in disappointment.

"Well, Benson," my colleague said cordially, "I congratulate you on your courage and your very proper desire for justice. I will certainly do what I can to get you satisfaction; but I warn you that, if the case turns out to be quite impossible, I shall not waste my time and your money in pursuing a will-o'-the-wisp."

"Thank you," replied Benson. "I put myself entirely in your hands, and I promise you to abide loyally by your decision."

"Then," said Thorndyke, "as we are agreed on the conditions, we may as well make a start and see exactly what our position is. You said that Mr Mortimer could give us some useful information. Perhaps we had better begin with that."

He looked enquiringly at Mortimer, who, in his turn, looked a little sheepish.

"I am afraid," said he, "that I haven't much to tell. It is only a matter of suspicion."

"Suspicions," remarked Thorndyke, "are of no use as evidence, but they may be quite useful as indicating a line of enquiry. At any rate, let us have them."

"They relate," said Mortimer, "to some people named Foucault who run a gaming house in Gerrard Street. I went there with Gillum on one occasion; on the very night, in fact, when I first made his acquaintance in a social sense. They were an obviously shady lot; but what specially struck me was that Madame Foucault made a dead set at Gillum – flirted with him, or made a show of doing so, in the most ostentatious, almost indecent, manner before the whole roomful of gamesters."

"And was Gillum responsive?" Thorndyke asked.

"Not in the least," replied Mortimer. "But Monsieur Foucault was. He watched them closely the whole of the time that they were together, and his expression as he looked at Gillum was positively murderous. And I gathered that there had been some trouble on previous occasions, for Gillum remarked to me on Foucault's jealousy and made rather a joke of it. And there was no mistaking Foucault's hostility to Gillum. I noticed it when we met in the restaurant before we followed them to the gambling den."

"Have you any further knowledge of these people?" Thorndyke asked.

"No," Mortimer answered. "That was the only occasion on which I met them, and I know nothing more than what I have told you. I must confess that there doesn't seem to be very much in it."

"I am inclined to agree with you," said Thorndyke. "A little made-up scandal of the kind that you suggest might account for an attempt at blackmail on a modest scale. But the one which we are considering seems to have been something much more formidable. Still, I will get you to let me have the names and address of these people so that we may make a few enquiries. And now as we have squeezed Mr Mortimer dry, let us hear what Mr Benson has to tell us."

"I am afraid," said Benson, "that I have nothing at all to tell. You see, it is two years since Gillum left Australia and I know nothing about his doings or way of living since he came to England."

"No," said Thorndyke, "we have to depend on Mr Mortimer for that. But there is his life in Australia. I want you to review that. Blackmail is usually related to the past, and often to a rather remote past. I ask you to try to recall the circumstances of Gillum's life in Australia and consider whether there may not have been some incident which could have been the subject of blackmail."

"I will think that question over," said Benson, "but, at the moment, I can recall nothing that could possibly have been used against him to extort money. He had no enemies, he never, to my knowledge, had any troubles with women, and I never heard of any sort of scandal."

"Well," said Thorndyke, "turn the question over at your leisure. Now, as we seem to have drawn a blank in Australia, let us take the next stage, his voyage to England. Do you know anything of the incidents of that voyage?"

"Not in much detail," replied Benson; "but I came to England in the same ship, and I had some talk about him with the captain and the first officer."

"Then," said Thorndyke, "try to recall what you learned from them and consider whether there was anything – in his relations with the other passengers, for instance – that might be worth enquiring into."

"I don't think he had much to do with the other passengers. There were only a few of them – the ship was chiefly a cargo ship – and they were mostly men in the meat trade. I gathered that Gillum spent most of his time playing cards with the doctor and the purser in their cabins, particularly in the purser's room. Those two men were his special cronies, and, by all accounts, he struck up a very close friendship with them both."

"Then," said Thorndyke, "they ought to be able to tell us all about the voyage and who the other passengers were."

"Why do you suppose anything happened on the ship?" Benson asked.

"I am merely considering it as a possibility," Thorndyke replied. "Remember, Benson, that something happened somewhere. That blackmail was not paid for nothing; and as we have not yet found a starting-point for an inquiry, we must trace Gillum's doings and his contacts with other persons as well as we can. Probably these two men are at present not available for inquiries. I suppose the ship is now outward bound?"

"Yes," replied Benson, "but neither of those men is on board. Both of them left the ship and the service at the end of the voyage. I learned that when I was on board."

"You mean that they both left the ship at the same time as Gillum?" Thorndyke asked.

"Not actually at the same time," Benson replied. "Gillum went ashore at Marseilles and travelled overland, making a leisurely journey across France so as to see something of the country. I think he arrived in England about six weeks or two months after the others. But I know that the doctor and the purser both left the service at the end of the voyage, when they had settled their business with the owners."

"Then," said Thorndyke, "it is possible that their relations with Gillum may have continued during the time of his residence in England, in fact, it is rather likely. You don't, I suppose, know where it would be possible to find them?"

"I asked about them at the shipping office," replied Benson. "As to the doctor, they knew nothing but that he had some idea of going into practice or else getting a job on a different line. But the purser is certainly beyond our reach. He is dead. They told me about him when I called at the office. It seems that he died under rather mysterious circumstances, for there was some uncertainty as to whether he had committed suicide or had been murdered. But I don't know any of the details. As the man was a stranger to me, I didn't go into the matter."

"No," said Thorndyke, "but I think we shall have to find out what the circumstances were. A suicide, and still more a murder, seems to demand investigation. Do you remember the purser's name?"

"Yes," replied Benson, "his name was Abel Webb."

"Abel Webb!" Mortimer exclaimed in a tone of the utmost astonishment. "Why, that was the name of the man whose body I discovered in the porch of St Michael's Church. It is a most astonishing coincidence. And what makes it still more so is the fact that the finding of that body was the occasion of my making Gillum's acquaintance."

"You had better tell us about that," said Thorndyke. "I mean as to Gillum's connection with your discovery. The case itself I remember quite clearly."

"It happened this way," said Mortimer. "I had seen the police carry the body down to the ambulance and was standing there in the crowd waiting to see it move off when someone came up and asked me what the excitement was about and whether it was a motor accident. I turned round to answer, and then I recognised the questioner as one of the bank's customers, Mr Gillum. I told him what had happened, and I also told him, and he could see for himself, that I was a good deal upset by the affair. He was extremely kind and sympathetic and eventually insisted on taking me off in a taxi to dine with him at a restaurant. And it was that same evening, after dinner, that I went with him to the gaming house that I told you about."

"I take it," said Thorndyke, "that you did not know at the time who the dead man was."

"No," answered Mortimer. "I learned that first at the inquest."

"Did Gillum come forward to give any evidence as to deceased at the inquest or afterwards?"

"He couldn't have come forward before the inquest because the identity of the deceased had not been disclosed. But I should say that he never did."

"Do you know whether Gillum ever learned who the dead man was?"

"I know he did, for I discussed the case with him. He had read a very full report of the inquest and seemed to remember all about the evidence. And the report contained not only the name of the deceased but his description as a former purser of one of the Dominion Line ships."

"Did he tell you much about his relations with Webb?"

"No," replied Mortimer, "the astonishing thing is that he never let drop the faintest hint that he had ever heard of the man before. In our talk about the inquest, he spoke of the dead man as if he had been a complete stranger."

"That is very extraordinary," exclaimed Benson.

"It is," Mortimer agreed, "though Gillum's reticence in this case is less remarkable than another man's would have been, for he was reticent about everything; I might almost say, secretive. He never told me anything about himself – excepting his gambling exploits. He was confidential enough about those. But he was extraordinarily close respecting his private affairs. You will hardly believe it, but until after his death I never knew that he had been in Australia."

When Mortimer had finished speaking, a rather curious silence fell on us all. Benson looked puzzled, but he made no remark and put no question to Mortimer. But I could see that the latter's statement had made a deep impression on Thorndyke, as it had on me; and when the discussion was resumed, the drift of his questions made it clear to me that what had struck me had also struck him.

"I think," said he, "that Webb's death occurred about a year ago. Do you happen to remember the approximate date, Mortimer?"

"I remember the exact date," was the reply. "It was the ninth of last September."

Thorndyke made a note of the date and then remarked:

"The fact that Abel Webb met a violent death makes it necessary to look rather more closely into the incidents of the voyage to England. Of course, there may be no connection; but it is an abnormal circumstance and we are bound to take note of it. And as Abel Webb has gone out of our ken, the only person left from whom we could get any information is the doctor. Benson can't tell us where he is to be found, but a doctor is usually easy to trace, as he is bound to keep the Registrar informed as to changes of address. What was his name?"

"His name was Peck," replied Benson. "Augustus Peck."

"I will look him up in the directory," said Thorndyke, "or at the Registrar's office and see if we can get into touch with him. And now, Mortimer, to return to the evidences of blackmail. Apart from the large drafts that you have mentioned, evidently connected with the letters that were found, is there any positive suggestion of other payments, earlier in date? It is important that we should fix, if possible, the time when the blackmailing began. Can you tell us anything definite about that?"

"Yes," replied Mortimer, "I think I can. Quite recently I have gone into the question afresh. Benson has kindly lent me Gillum's pass-book so that I could study it at home. I have gone through it very carefully, and it occurred to me that if I made a graph of the dates and amounts, any small periodic fluctuations would be made visible."

"Excellent," said Thorndyke. "And what did your graph show?"

"It showed a small periodic rise corresponding roughly with the ordinary quarter days. This began quite early, within a month of the opening of the account, and it went on until the big drafts began."

"Do you say," Thorndyke asked, "that the small rises ceased when the large drafts began, or were you unable to ascertain that?"

"I am disposed to think that the small rises ceased when the large quarterly payments began, though they might have become merged in higher rises of the curve due to the big payments. But, allowing for the possibility of this confusion, the smaller payments ceased and were replaced by the larger."

"What were the amounts of the smaller payments?"

"So far as I could judge, the excess above the ordinary withdrawals would be about two hundred pounds a quarter."

"What did you infer from this? Did it seem to you to suggest that there was more than one blackmailer?"

"No," replied Mortimer. "My reading of it was that there was only one; that for about a year he had been satisfied with a payment of something like eight hundred a year, and that he had then suddenly increased his demands. That would account for the smaller payments ceasing when the larger ones began."

"Yes," Thorndyke agreed, "that appears to be a reasonable inference. But it is difficult to judge. We really want to know more about Gillum's private life and habits; but I don't see where we are to gain the knowledge."

"I think," said Benson, "that Mortimer may be able to help you in that. He is writing some sort of account of his connection with my cousin. How are you getting on with it, Mortimer?"

"I have finished it" Mortimer replied, "but I don't think it would be of much use to Dr Thorndyke. You see," he continued in
 an enquiring glance from my colleague, "it occurred to
he inquest that it would be rather interesting to put on

record, while the facts were still fresh in my memory, the whole incident of my acquaintance with John Gillum; and I have found it quite interesting to write, but I don't think it would be very thrilling to read. And I doubt whether it would be of any use to you, for I wrote it without any thought of an inquiry such as you are engaged in."

"But, my dear fellow," said Thorndyke, "that is precisely its most valuable quality. A man writing an account with the conscious intention of throwing light on some question tends unconsciously to select the facts which appear to him to be important and to ignore other facts which seem to have no bearing. But his selection may be all wrong. He may omit something of vital importance through having failed to realise its significance. Whereas your little history gives the facts impartially without selection. Would it be possible for us to have the privilege of reading it?"

Mortimer smiled rather shyly. "It is a poor performance in a literary sense," said he, "but, of course, you can see it if you wish to. I rattled it off on the typewriter, and, as I did it in duplicate, you can have one copy to keep as long as you like. I will post it off to you tonight."

"Thank you," said Thorndyke. "I shall read it with interest even if it throws no further light on the case. And there are two other matters that may be mentioned before we adjourn this meeting. Who has the blackmailer's letters?"

"They are in Penfield's custody at present," replied Benson. "He has all the documents."

"The other matter," said Thorndyke, "refers to Gillum's chambers. Who has possession of them? You, I suppose, are the nominal tenant."

"Yes, I am the tenant until Michaelmas or until they are let. Why do you ask?"

"I merely wanted to know whether they would be available if it should seem desirable to make an inspection."

"What use would an inspection be?" Benson asked.

"It is impossible to say," replied Thorndyke. "Probably none. But some point may arise from the reading of Mortimer's manuscript which may be elucidated by looking over the premises."

"Well, you know best," said Benson. "At any rate, I will send you the keys in case you should want them. And I think that finishes our business for the present. It is very good of you to have given us so much of your time; but, before we go, there is one question that I should like to ask. You have gone very patiently into the case tonight. From what you have learned from us, do you think you will be disposed to do what I am hoping you will; to prosecute a search for those wretches who are responsible for poor Jack Gillum's death?"

"I am prepared to look into the case," Thorndyke replied. "If I find that we come to an absolute dead end, I shall advise you to abandon the inquiry. But if I see any prospect whatever of bringing it to a successful conclusion, I shall place my services unreservedly at your disposal. Will that satisfy you?"

"It will more than satisfy me," replied Benson, "and, for my part, I promise to be guided by your advice, whatever you may decide."

With this, the two men rose, and, when we had escorted them to the landing and seen them safely launched on the stairs, we wished them good-night and re-entered our chambers.

CHAPTER NINE

The Empty Nest

"Well, Thorndyke," I said when we had re entered and closed the door, "this has been quite an entertaining interview. I fancy that your drag net brought up rather more than you expected. A mightily queer catch, in fact."

"Yes," he agreed, as he dug out his pipe with a thoughtful air, "a decidedly queer catch. And it will need some sorting out. What do you make of it?"

"It seems to me," I replied, "that we have identified one of the blackmailers and accounted for the other."

"That is the result in a nutshell," said he. "But I should like to hear how you arrived at it."

"The argument," I replied, "consists in stating the facts in their natural sequence. To begin with Abel Webb. I remember the case quite clearly. It was that cyanide injection case; and when we discussed it, we agreed that suicide could not be entertained. It was a blatant case of murder."

"Yes," Thorndyke agreed. "I accept that."

"Then we agree that Abel Webb was murdered. He was murdered on the ninth of September. At that time Gillum was being blackmailed at the rate of eight hundred a year. But exactly a week after the murder, on the sixteenth of September, the blackmail suddenly jumped up to the rate of two thousand a year.

127

"At, or about, the time of the murder, Gillum is known to have been in the neighbourhood, within a few yards of the place where it was committed; and, after the murder, although he and Mortimer discussed it in detail, he concealed from Mortimer the fact that he had been acquainted with Webb. You agree to that?"

"Yes," Thorndyke replied. "Mortimer referred to it as reticence, but reticence to that extent amounts to concealment."

"Those, then," said I, "are the facts, and my interpretation of them is this: Abel Webb was blackmailing Gillum to the tune of eight hundred a year. Possibly he was also becoming troublesome. At any rate, Gillum got tired of it and took an opportunity to kill Abel Webb. For that I don't blame him, although his methods were not pretty. But then Gillum had bad luck. Somebody knew more than he was aware of, and promptly put on the screw; and put it on so forcibly that when Gillum came to the end of his resources, he committed suicide rather than face the consequences of not being able to pay. That is my reading of the case, and I rather think it is yours too."

"Yes," Thorndyke agreed, "that is what the facts seem to suggest, and I am prepared to accept your theory as a working hypothesis. Without prejudice, however, as our friend Penfield would say. I mean that, while adopting it as a working hypothesis, we must not lose sight of its hypothetical nature. Fresh facts may lead us to modify our views."

"Yes, that is true," I admitted; "but you speak of a working hypothesis. But how does it work? The problem is to find the principal blackmailer. But I don't see that what we have learned gets us any more forward on that quest."

"There," said Thorndyke, "I disagree entirely. Assuming your interpretation of the facts to be correct, we have a most important clue to the identity of the chief blackmailer. You have said it yourself. 'Somebody knew more than he was aware of.' But what did that somebody know? He must have known, not only of the connection between Gillum and Webb, but that Webb was blackmailing Gillum. That implies that the blackmailer must have known Webb pretty intimately; but if Webb was really a blackmailer, the suggestion is that the matter which supported the blackmail was something connected with the voyage from Australia to England. But that, in its turn, seems to connect the unknown blackmailer with the voyage; and if we are right in inferring such a connection, we have a very valuable hint as to where to look for further information."

"You mean the ship's doctor?"

"Yes. If the blackmail arose out of any incident that occurred on board ship, and still more if the blackmailer should have been one of the other passengers, the doctor could hardly fail to have some knowledge of the matter, or some knowledge of the circumstances out of which the blackmail arose. Even if he had no suspicion of the blackmailing transaction, he must know what the general conditions were on the voyage. There isn't much privacy on board ship, especially on a long voyage."

"Yes," I agreed, "the doctor should be a useful witness. Benson's knowledge of the matter is based on hearsay, but Dr Peck's is first-hand, so that we could cross-examine him in detail. But the question is, how are we to get into touch with him? He may be in India or China by this time."

"That is a possibility," said Thorndyke, "but we had better begin by finding out his permanent address from the Medical Directory."

He went into the office and returned with the volume in his hand. Laying it down on the table, he turned over the leaves until he found the entry, which he read out.

"Augustus Peck, MRCS, LRCP, LDS, Surgeon, Commonwealth and Dominions Line. Permanent address, 87, Staple Inn."

"Staple Inn," I repeated. "It is rather odd that this case should be connected with the only two remaining inns of Chancery. And I notice that he has the dental as well as the medical qualification."

"Yes," said Thorndyke, "and quite a useful combination for a ship's surgeon. I suppose our next move must be to call at Staple

Inn and see if we can discover his present whereabouts. But there is no hurry. We shall have Mortimer's manuscript in the morning and it may be that we shall pick up some hint from that."

This ended our discussion for the time being; and if it had not carried us far, it, and the preceding interview, had yielded more matter for investigation than Penfield's dismal account of the case had led us to expect.

On the following morning, Mortimer's manuscript arrived, and the same post brought a package from Benson containing two keys tied together and bearing a parchment label inscribed, "64, Clifford's Inn, 1st floor." As Thorndyke was occupied during the morning and I was free, I took possession of the manuscript and read through the seven chapters of which it consisted with close attention and growing disappointment. For I had expected that Mortimer's story would furnish us with some new facts; whereas it seemed to me merely to repeat at greater length what he had already told us or what we had gathered from the report of the inquest.

But in this, as appeared later, I was mistaken; and as Mortimer's history contained practically all that we ever knew of the period that it described, I have attached it as a preface to this record and shall henceforth assume that the reader is fully acquainted with its contents. And it may be that he, or she, more discerning than I, will already have noted certain points the significance of which I failed to appreciate.

Certain suspicions did, indeed, cross my mind on the subject, especially when I noted the deep interest and attention with which Thorndyke studied the document. But then my colleague was a man who habitually gave his whole attention to even the simplest matters; and I could see that this case, with all its obscurities and ambiguities, had taken a strong hold on him. It was the kind of puzzle that he really enjoyed; and he was going to spare no pains in seeking out the solution.

About a week after the arrival of the manuscript I ventured to ask his views on it, with the above suspicions in mind.

"What do you make of Mortimer's history?" said I. "To me it seems rather barren of matter. I have not extracted from it anything that I did not already know."

"Nor have I," he replied, "in the sense of new facts of a fundamental order. I hardly expected to. But the story has its value in that it gives us a lively picture of the man, Gillum. It shows us a shrewd, ingenious, rather subtle man, with a distinctly casuistical type of mind; and it enables us to contrast his apparent intelligence with his amazingly foolish conduct."

"But we were able to do that already," I objected; "and as to the main problem, the identity of the principal blackmailer, it gives us not the faintest hint."

"That is true," said Thorndyke. "But perhaps the immediate problem is rather the occasion of the blackmail; what it was that Gillum had done to render him susceptible to blackmail. Mortimer throws no light on that question either. Whatever we are to learn from his story must be gathered by reading between the lines and considering the possible significance of apparently trivial things and events."

"You mean, in relation to our working hypothesis?" I suggested.

"Yes," he replied. "But let us not be obsessed by our hypothesis. It may be entirely erroneous; and while we are using it as the only instrument of investigation which we possess, we should scrutinise every new fact, as well as the old ones, to see whether any alternative hypothesis is suggested. Read Mortimer's history again, Jervis, and ask yourself, in respect of Gillum's sayings and doings and the little trivial occurrences which Mortimer chronicles, whether they support our hypothesis or whether they seem to be consistent with some different meaning."

As this implied that Thorndyke had already taken his own prescription, I decided to study the manuscript afresh. Meanwhile, by way of "getting some of my own back," I remarked with a grin:

"There is one thing that I have been expecting ever since Mortimer's document turned up; and I'm still expecting it."

"What is that?" he asked, regarding me suspiciously.

"I have been expecting that you would want to go across to Clifford's Inn and nose round the empty chambers."

"And why not?" said he. "I think it is an excellent suggestion. It would be quite interesting to fill in Mortimer's picture with its appropriate background; and as we have the afternoon free, I propose that we put your idea into execution forthwith. We will go over as soon as we have had lunch."

Of course, I agreed (noting that Thorndyke, according to his habit, had planted his "idea" on me); and, when we had dispatched our meal, and Thorndyke had provided himself with his invaluable research-case and his graduated walking-stick, we went forth, and passing out of the Inner Temple gate, crossed Fleet Street, and walking up Clifford's Inn Passage, came out into the courtyard by the garden.

"*Sic transit,*" Thorndyke remarked, regretfully, as he cast a disparaging eye on the garish new buildings that were beginning to replace the pleasant old houses. "John Penhallow's chambers have gone and soon all the others will follow; and then all that will remain to show posterity the quiet sumptuousness and dignity of London chambers in the seventeenth century will be Penhallow's rooms in the Victoria and Albert Museum."

He stood for a few moments running a reflective eye over the exterior of Number 64, observed by a pair of inquisitive eyes from the window of the typewriting office on the ground floor; then he plunged into the dim entry and I followed him up the stairs until we emerged into the daylight of the first-floor landing.

"This is rather gruesome," said I, as we threw open the inner door and looked into the room. "With the exception of the corpse, the place is just the same as it appeared to Mortimer when he and Benson and Weech discovered the body. Nothing seems to have been moved."

"No," Thorndyke agreed. "We have only to imagine the body lying on the couch and we have the tableau that Mortimer described."

We went in and looked curiously at the couch, the pillow of which still bore the impression of the dead man's head, and the little table by its side with the siphon, the tumbler, and the decanter, all bearing the very distinct prints of the dead man's fingers.

"We may as well preserve these," said Thorndyke, slipping on a pair of loose gloves. "They are not likely to help us, but you never know. It is a good rule never to destroy evidence."

"I don't see what evidence they could furnish," said I, "seeing that they were proved to be Gillum's own fingerprints."

"But that is evidence," he replied. " 'Prints like these are Gillum's; and prints unlike them are those of somebody else. As we are seeking an unknown person, that kind of evidence may be quite material. And you notice that there is a nearly complete set of both hands."

He looked about the room, and observing a built-in cupboard by the fireplace, turned the key which was in the lock, and opened the door. One of the shelves was nearly empty, and as the height was sufficient to take the siphon, he transferred that and the tumbler and the smooth, patternless decanter from the table to the vacant space and closed the door.

"We will lock the cupboard and take the key when we go," said he. "Meanwhile, we may find some other things which we may think fit to put in it."

He went back to the couch and ran his eye over the cushions and the pillow, stooping over the latter and examining it more closely.

"This is worth noticing," said he. "The man's head could have rested on this pillow only a few hours while he was alive and capable of movement, but yet there are no less than three hairs sticking to the fabric."

"He may have used the pillow on other occasions," I suggested; to which Thorndyke assented.

"At any rate," he added, "we may as well collect these hairs, as we can assume them to be authentic samples of Gillum's hair."

"I suppose so," I agreed, though without enthusiasm; for it would have been more to the point if they had been authentic samples of the blackmailer's hair. Thorndyke noted the tone of my remark and smiled as he opened his research case, which he had deposited on the table.

"You think," said he, "that we are collecting all the things that don't matter. Probably you are right; but it is better to provide yourself with useless material than to throw away things that may later be badly needed."

He took out of the case a pair of forceps and one of his invaluable seed envelopes, and with the former picked out the three hairs – two black and one white – and transferred them to the envelope, on which he wrote a brief description, before returning it to the case. Then he began a leisurely perambulation of the room, inspecting its various contents and making occasional remarks on them. The bookcase seemed to interest him, for he stood before it running his eye along the rows of volumes and apparently reading their titles.

"In general," said he, "the books seem to confirm Mortimer's estimate of Gillum's character and tastes. There are six works on London topography, catalogues of the National Gallery, the Tate, and the Wallace Collection, a book on games of chance, and one on the theory of probability. Those are according to expectation and so is the book on Modern Organ Music; but Staunton's Chess is not. I don't think that chess-players are usually interested in games of chance."

He turned away from the bookcase and resumed his travels round the room, halting presently before a rather elegantly turned roulette box.

"This," said he, "is the box that Mortimer speaks of. Apparently, Gillum used it for experiments in connection with his projected system. But it is possible that he may have used it for actual play with some of his visitors. Perhaps it would be as well to put it away with the other specimens."

He took it up in his gloved hands and carried it over to the cupboard where he placed it on the shelf with the objects from the table. Then, having exhausted the interest of the living-room, he passed through into the bedroom.

It was a small room, simply and rather barely furnished, but clean and orderly with the tidiness of a ship's cabin, a fact which attracted Thorndyke's attention as well as mine, for he remarked:

"The late Gillum seems to have been a tidy, methodical man. You noticed evidences of that in the living-room, and it is still more striking here. The bed, you observe, has been carefully made; and presumably he made it himself, though he must have known that he was never going to sleep in it. And no cast-off clothes lying about or even hanging on the pegs. I suppose, when he undressed, he put them into the wardrobe."

He verified the surmise by opening the doors of the wardrobe; which showed, in the one division, the clothes that Gillum must have taken off hanging on the side pegs, while, in the other division, which was fitted with shelves, were stored clean shirts, collars, handkerchiefs, several pairs of shoes and three hats. These things he considered attentively, and especially the cast-off clothes, which he took down from the pegs and, having looked them over, turned out the pockets, returning the contents of each after having examined them. But Gillum seemed to have carried few things in his pockets, and of those which we found none appeared to be of any interest. A bank-note case – empty – a handful of silver and bronze coins, a pocket-knife and a set of well-worn dice formed the principal items.

"Not much to be learned from those," Thorndyke remarked as he closed the wardrobe, "excepting that he respected his clothes and avoided bulging pockets."

He walked across the room to the large chest of drawers that stood in the corner near the bed, lifting the valance of the latter and revealing a sponge bath underneath. As we reached the chest, I observed in the dark corner between it and the wall a good-sized cylindrical basket which had apparently served as a rubbish dump, and drew Thorndyke's attention to it as a possible mine of evidential wealth. He ignored the irony of my tone and, promptly adopting my suggestion, picked up the basket and turned out its contents on to the bed. It was certainly a very miscellaneous collection and as I regarded it with a faint grin I wondered what Mr Penfield would have thought if he could have seen my colleague systematically sorting it out and placing each article after inspection at the foot of the bed. Over some of these, such as three obviously superannuated socks and a couple of slightly frayed collars, he passed lightly with a single glance; but most of the things he inspected attentively, little as they seemed to merit his attention, evidently considering what inferences they suggested. I watched him curiously, my tendency to be amused by the apparent triviality of the proceedings restrained by the recollection of the surprising results of similar examinations in the past; and, as I looked on, I made a mental inventory of the collection with a view to possible results in the future.

Besides the socks and collars, a pair of worn fabric gloves and a broken shoe-lace, the "find" included an empty tin which had once contained an antiseptic toothpowder, which Thorndyke opened, and sniffed at the pinch of powder which still clung to the box; two empty "Milk of Magnesia" bottles, a worn-out toothbrush (which Thorndyke examined closely and also smelt), an empty bottle labelled "Bromidia," which seemed to suggest that Gillum had suffered from insomnia, another empty bottle labelled "Cawley's Cleansing Fluid," from which Thorndyke drew out the cork in order to smell at what remained of the contents, several crumpled-up tradesmen's bills, and a small, heavy object wrapped up in a sheet of writing-paper. This Thorndyke took up and carefully opening out the paper displayed a small bolt with a fly nut attached.

"Now," said be, "I wonder what that might have belonged to. A one-inch, square-headed eighth-inch bolt with what looks like a Whitworth thread and a fly nut. Apparently part of some mechanism; but we have not come across any mechanism to which it corresponds."

He smoothed out the paper and examined it on both sides, but there was no writing on it to give any clue to the use of the bolt. Finally he wrapped the latter up again in its paper and dropped it into his pocket, presumably for further consideration at his leisure. And having thus exhausted the material from the basket, he gathered the derelicts together and returned them to their receptacle.

The chest of drawers had apparently served the purpose of a dressing-table in conjunction with a good-sized looking-glass which hung on the wall beside the window. Like the rest of the room, it was quite tidy though now covered with dust, and the objects set out on it represented the bare necessaries for the toilet. On a china tray were two toothbrushes and a small tin of "Odonto" dentifrice, and beside the tray were a pair of nail scissors, a button-hook, and a turned wooden box containing spare collar-studs − one gold and several ivory − and a pair of cheap rolled gold links. There was also an earthenware bowl and a pair of hairbrushes. The latter Thorndyke took up, and, separating them, looked them over in his queer, inquisitive way. They were good brushes, though old and much worn as to the bristles, with ebony backs in which the initials "JG" had been inlaid in silver, but they appeared not to have been cleaned very lately, for the bristles held a considerable quantity of hair.

"I think," said Thorndyke, "we will take these and sort out the hairs. Probably they are all Gillum's but it is possible that the brushes may have been used by some of his visitors, if he ever had any, and we may learn something about them."

He put the brushes in his coat pocket and then took up the bowl, which was of red earthenware, fitted with a cover bearing a highly coloured label with the inscription: "Dux Super-fatted Shaving Soap."

"Rather a nice bowl," said Thorndyke, holding it out at arm's length to view it; "a pleasant shape and very suitable to the plain earthen body. But I am surprised that Gillum didn't soak off that label."

He lifted the lid of the bowl, and finding it empty save for a few drops of moisture at the bottom, sniffed at it and passed it to me.

"It smells to me," said I, "like chlorine, or perhaps chlorinated soda; some lotion of the Eusol type."

"Yes," he agreed, "something of that kind. Apparently it came from the bottle of antiseptic cleansing solution that we found in the tidy."

He put the bowl back in its place and then pulled out the drawers of the chest in succession. All of them seemed to be filled with articles of clothing, neatly folded and smelling slightly of camphor. These he glanced at but without disturbing them, and, when he had pushed in the last of the drawers, he turned away and stood a while, looking thoughtfully around the room, apparently memorising its contents and their arrangement. There was not very much to see. The mantelpiece was bare save for a couple of candlesticks carrying rather large stearine candles. There remained only the large porcelain sink in the corner; a deep, rectangular sink of the kind used in chemical laboratories, but which here seemed, by the bracket over it bearing a soap dish, a nail-brush, and a bath sponge, to have served the purpose of a lavatory basin as well as a means of emptying the bath.

When we had inspected the sink, Thorndyke drew my attention to a mouse-hole in the corner beneath it which had been very neatly and effectively filled with Portland cement.

"That," said he, "suggests a man with a practical and efficient mind. Some people will go on for ever setting traps, regardless of the rate at which rodents increase. But in old buildings the only effective method is to stop the holes with Portland cement, preferably mixed with an "aggregate" of sand or powdered glass. That is Polton's plan, and it keeps our chambers practically free from mice."

From the bedroom we passed through a narrow doorway into the kitchen, and here we noticed the same appearance of order and tidiness as in the other rooms. It was a small place, but very completely equipped. There was a little gas cooker mounted on a stand and bearing a large aluminium kettle, a range of shelves on which the china was neatly disposed, the plates on edge and the cups inverted and all spotlessly clean; another shelf bore a row of covered jars and tins, each labelled with the name of its contents; several dish covers of wire gauze or aluminium hung from nails on the wall with a frying-pan and a couple of small saucepans, and a carpet-sweeper in the corner accounted for the conspicuous cleanness of the floor. And here, too, I noticed a couple of neatly stopped mouse-holes.

The kitchen communicated with another room by a narrow doorway. The door was locked, but as the key was in the lock we were able to open it and pass through into the adjoining room, which I recognised as the larder that Mortimer had described.

It was smaller even than the kitchen, being only about eight feet by six; and this small space was further reduced by the great coal-bin, which occupied the whole of the longer side of the room. But like the kitchen it was admirably arranged. There were two shelves on one of which lay three bottles of claret and one of sauternes, while the other was occupied by one or two dishes protected by wire covers through which could be seen – and smelt – some mouldy remains of food. In addition to the open shelves there was a tall, narrow, meat-safe through the wire gauze panels of which a mouldy, cadaverous odour exhaled. I opened the door and looked in, but as the odour then became more pronounced, I was about to shut it when Thorndyke stooped to examine the bottom shelf and then, reaching in, brought out from the back of the shelf a basin which was thickly encrusted with Portland cement and in which a rough bone spatula still stuck.

"I see," said Thorndyke, "that he used the same 'aggregate' that Polton favours – powdered glass. It is more effective than sand."

"Yes," said I, "and I notice that he has infringed another of Polton's copyrights – the utilisation of worn-out toothbrushes by shaving off the bristles."

I broke the spatula off the cement and scraped it clean with my pocket-knife, when it revealed itself as a bone-handled dental-plate brush from which the bristles had been cleanly shaved off leaving a broad, blunt blade perfectly suited for the purpose for which it had been used.

"It is really remarkable," I commented, "that a man of so much common sense and capacity in small things should have been such a fool in the things that seriously matter."

"It is," he agreed, "but Gillum's case is by no means unique in that respect."

He turned away from the safe and transferred his attention to the coal-bin.

"I think," he remarked, "that this is the largest bin that I have ever seen in a set of chambers. Coal storage is not usually their strong point."

He measured the principal dimensions roughly with his graduated stick and then continued: "Eight feet long by thirty inches wide and twenty-nine inches deep – roughly fifty cubic feet. I don't know what that represents in coal, but it would seem to be a fairly liberal allowance for a man living alone and cooking by gas."

"Yes," I agreed. "Nearly a year's supply, I should think. And it seems," I added, as I lifted the lid and found the bin nearly full, "as if he had replenished his stock shortly before his death. Which appears an odd proceeding when we remember what the weather was like at that time. But perhaps he took advantage of the low summer prices to lay in his year's supply."

"Possibly," Thorndyke agreed, "that is to say, if it is really all coal. The quantity seems rather incredible."

He thrust his stick down into the loose coal, and at a few inches of depth found it stopped by an obviously solid obstruction.

"There seems to be a false bottom," I remarked. Convenient enough for keeping the coal within easy reach, but rather a waste of space."

"Perhaps he didn't waste the space," said Thorndyke. Let us see."

With the scoop that lay on top of the coal, he began to shovel the latter away from the right-hand end, piling it in a heap at the left end. This soon brought the false bottom into view, and with it an iron ring sunk into the board near the right-hand end. Further shovelling disclosed a crack across the bottom near the middle, that divided it into two halves. Taking down a brush that hung from a nail on the wall, and that had manifest traces of coal dust on its hair, Thorndyke proceeded to brush away the small coal and dust until the surface of the false bottom was comparatively clean. Then he slipped his finger through the ring and lifted the right half of the bottom out bodily.

"The space wasn't wasted, you see," he said. "It seems to have been used as a store for things that were only occasionally wanted."

As he spoke, he threw the light of his pocket-lamp into the dark cavity, revealing a number of tins of various sizes, apparently containing tongue and other preserved foods, and seven or eight bottles of port and sherry.

"There was a good deal of space wasted nevertheless," said I. "The cavity looks about eighteen inches deep, and only four or five have been used."

Thorndyke dipped his stick into the cavity and read off the measurement.

"Nineteen inches from the top of the supporting blocks to the floor. It would have held a good deal more than he put into it, but it was not a very handy container as the coal had to be moved every time it was opened. But it looks as if the contrivance had been put in by Gillum, himself. The bin is obviously old, perhaps as old as the house, but the false bottom and the blocks that support it look quite fresh and new. Evidently, they were a recent addition."

He put the false bottom back in its place and then, taking a last look round, stepped up to the window. Apparently, a sash cord had broken and not been repaired, for the lower half of the sash was held up as far as it would go by a piece of wood on either side, which had been jammed into the groove and fixed with screws. It looked a makeshift arrangement, but as Thorndyke pointed out, it had been adopted deliberately, for the little wooden props had been neatly planed and fitted their place exactly, and the holes for the screws had been properly countersunk.

"I think," he said, "that there is no need to assume a broken sash line. It looks like an arrangement to fix the window open permanently so as to make sure of constant ventilation. You notice the row of holes at the foot of the door evidently bored for the same purpose, and apparently by Gillum, himself, to judge by the fresh, unstained wood inside them."

We let ourselves out by the door which opened on to the landing and which, presumably for that reason, had been fitted with a Yale night-latch and a spring. When we had come out and closed the door, Thorndyke stood for a few moments hesitating.

"I suppose," he said, "that is all, excepting the key of the cupboard." He unlocked the living-room door and re-entered, and when he had locked the cupboard and pocketed the key, looked about the room to see if there was anything that we had omitted to examine.

"What about the writing-table?" said I. "Oughtn't we to see what is in the drawers?"

"I expect Bateman took away all the papers," he replied. "Still, we may as well take a glance at them."

We went over to the table and tried the drawers, but they were all locked, excepting the top one, and we had no key; and the top drawer contained nothing but Gillum's stock of note-paper and envelopes, of each of which Thorndyke took a sample before closing the drawer.

"And that," said he as he folded the paper neatly and slipped it into the envelope, "I think completes the inspection, for the time being, at any rate; unless you can suggest anything further."

"I can suggest lots of things," I replied with a grin. "For instance, you might take the legs off the tables and chairs as the police did in Poe's story of 'The Purloined Letter'; and you might go over the walls and furniture for fingerprints. And then there is the floor. You might set Polton to work on it with a vacuum cleaner and examine with the microscope the dust that he collected. This has been quite a superficial inspection."

He smiled indulgently at my rather feeble joke, but the result of it was not quite what I had expected.

"I think," he replied, "that we will leave the furniture intact and reserve the fingerprint hunt for some future occasion. But, really, your suggestion of the vacuum cleaner is an excellent one, though Gillum's sweeper may have left us a rather meagre gleaning. I will get Polton to go over the floors, and hope that Gillum was not too thorough in his use of the sweeper."

This reply to my facetious suggestion took me aback completely. For my knowledge of Thorndyke told me that he was, according to a playful habit of his, crediting me with an idea which was already in his own mind. He had certainly intended to collect the dust from those floors for examination. But I could not imagine why. Considering the nature of our problem, the proceeding seemed to be completely futile and purposeless. Yet I knew that it could not be. And so the old familiar feeling came over me; the feeling that he had seen farther into this case than I had; that he had already some theory and was not groping in the dark as I was, but was even now seeking an answer to some definite question.

Chapter Ten

Mr Weech Disapproves

As we came out of the entry into the courtyard, we became aware of our old acquaintance, Mr Weech, the porter of the Inn, hovering in the background, whence he had probably observed us at the landing window. Mr Weech had always interested me. He was a complete and unabridged survival from the Victorian age, alike in his dress, his habits and in a certain subtle combination of dignity and deference in his bearing towards his social superiors. His costume invariably included a tall silk hat and a formal frock coat. Formerly, perchance, but not in my time, the hat may have borne a gold-laced band, and the coat have been embellished with gilt buttons. But nowadays the hat and coat were distinctive enough in themselves; and even the umbrella which was his constant companion, his sceptre and staff of office, seemed not quite like modern umbrellas.

In speech he was singularly precise and careful in his choice of words, though, unfortunately, his judgement was not always equal to his care. For he loved to interlard his sentences with Latin tags; and, as he obviously had no acquaintance with that language, the results were sometimes a little startling.

As we came into view, then, Mr Weech quickened his pace and advanced towards us with the peculiar splay-footed gait characteristic of men who stand much and walk little, and peering at us inquisitively through his spectacles, essayed cautiously to ascertain what our business was.

"I am afraid," said he, "that you will have found poor Mr Gillum's chambers locked up – if it was his chambers that you wanted."

"Thank you, Mr Weech," Thorndyke replied, but we have the keys. Mr Benson has lent them to us."

"Oh, indeed," said Mr Weech, in a tone of mild surprise and still milder disapproval.

"We just wanted to look over the chambers," Thorndyke explained.

"Did you indeed, sir?" said Mr Weech with rather more definite disapproval. "Not, I venture to hope, for professional reasons?"

"I am sorry, Mr Weech," Thorndyke replied suavely, "but it must be admitted that our interest in the chambers has a slight professional taint. The fact is that Mr Benson has asked me to make certain enquiries concerning his late cousin."

"Oh, dear!" exclaimed Weech, now undisguisedly disapproving. "Has it come to that? I had hoped that we had heard the last of that dreadful business. Don't tell me that these quiet, respectable precincts are to be involved in another scandal."

"I'll tell you all about it," said Thorndyke. "There is no need to be evasive with an old friend like you; and I know that I can trust to your discretion."

"Undoubtedly you can," replied Mr Weech, evidently mollified by Thorndyke's candour (he didn't know my colleague as well as I did).

"Well," said Thorndyke, "the position is this: the evidence at the inquest disclosed the existence of certain blackmailers who had been preying on Mr Gillum. Now, Mr Benson holds those blackmailers accountable for his cousin's death, and he wants them identified and, if possible, brought to justice."

"M'yes," said Mr Weech, clearly sceptical and unsympathetic. "I don't see why. What's the use, even if it were possible? Poor Mr Gillum is beyond their reach now. Your protection of him has come – or would come, if it came at all – too late. It's a case of *post bellum auxilium."*

"I am inclined to agree with you, Mr Weech," Thorndyke replied, "but it is not my choice. Mr Benson wants these rascals found and prosecuted, and he has engaged my professional services to that end; and it is my duty to render those services to the best of my ability."

"Certainly, sir," Mr Weech agreed; "and I don't say that I would not be glad to hear that those wretches had been brought to justice, if it were possible – which I don't believe it is."

"And I am sure," said Thorndyke, "that you would give me any help that you could, as a matter of public policy."

"I would for old acquaintance sake," replied Weech, "though I can't pretend that I am anxious for you to succeed, seeing what a rumpus there would be if you did. And I really don't see how I can help you."

"I think," said Thorndyke, "that you could help me by supplying certain information that I should like to have. For instance, as a rather important point, you could tell me what visitors Mr Gillum received."

"But I don't know," Weech protested. "How should I? Both gates are open all day and strangers pass in and out unquestioned. My impression is that he had very few visitors, but that is only a guess. As far as actual knowledge goes, I can recall only two. One was a Mr Mortimer, who, I think, came to him several times – "

"We know Mr Mortimer," interrupted Thorndyke. "Who was the other?"

"I have no idea," replied Weech. "I know about him because he spoke to me when I was standing at the gate by the lodge. That would be about the beginning of last September. He asked me if a Mr John Gillum lived in the Inn. I replied 'Yes,' and gave him the number of the chambers; whereupon he bustled off. I didn't go with him, as he couldn't make any mistake, there being only the one set of chambers in that building."

"Can you describe him?" Thorndyke asked.

"Yes," was the reply. "Curiously enough, I remember him quite well, perhaps because he was a little out of the ordinary. He was a short, stocky man with a sallow face, a small moustache, waxed at the ends, and bushy black eyebrows. He wore a rather queer kind of single eyeglass. It had no rim and no cord; it was just a plain glass, stuck in his eye with no kind of support. How he kept it there I can't imagine. Then, as he walked off up the passage, I noticed that he had a slight limp and that he used a stick to help himself along; and a most uncommonly fine stick it was; a thick malacca with a silver band and a big ivory knob."

Thorndyke jotted down in his note-book the points of this excellent description and then asked:

"Do you know how long he stayed with Mr Gillum?"

"I don't. I never saw him again; but he might have gone out by the Fetter Lane gate. It couldn't have been a long interview because, about a quarter of an hour later, I saw Mr Gillum come out of his chambers alone, and I thought he looked a little annoyed and upset."

"By the way," said Thorndyke, "you mentioned just now that there is only one set of chambers in that building. But there is a second floor."

"Yes," Mr Weech explained, "but it is not suitable for chambers. We use it as a general lumber room for the Inn, and it is always kept locked."

As the conversation had developed, we had moved away from the window of the typewriting office on the ground floor and began slowly to pace up and down the courtyard, but I noticed that every time that we re-passed the window there happened to be some person looking out of it. Apparently we were being kept under observation.

"I am wondering," Thorndyke said after a pause, "by what chance Mr Gillum, an Australian, strange to England, should have happened to discover such a retired backwater as Clifford's Inn. Did he ever tell you?"

"He did not, because, in fact, he did not discover it. Being a stranger, he very wisely employed an agent to find him rooms."

"Do you mean a regular house-agent?"

"I don't know what he was, but I had an idea that he was a personal friend of Mr Gillum's. At any rate, he not only carried out all the negotiations but he furnished the chambers and got them ready for the tenant by the time he wanted them."

"I wonder," said Thorndyke, "whether you would mind giving us a more circumstantial account of this transaction."

"Well," Mr Weech replied, "let me see. It happened, so far as I can remember, somewhat like this. One morning, towards the end of August, 1928, a man came to the lodge to enquire about some chambers that we had to let at that time. He seemed to think that Number 64, which was empty, might suit him; so I gave him the keys and he went off to have a look at them. Presently he came back and said that they would suit him perfectly and that he would like to take a lease of them. But then he explained that they were not for himself but that he was acting as agent for a gentleman of means, and that he was fully authorised to execute an agreement and to furnish references and to pay whatever deposit I might think necessary. I would rather have dealt direct with the prospective tenant, but he produced a written authority from his principal, Mr Gillum, who, he assured me, was a gentleman of good position and ample means, and he referred me to Mr Gillum's solicitor and his bank; but he did suggest that it would be better not to take up the references until the tenant came and entered into residence."

"Did he give any reason for that suggestion?"

"Yes, and quite a sound one. He said that Mr Gillum had lived abroad for some years and was still abroad and that his relations with both his solicitor and his bank had been conducted by correspondence and that neither of them knew him personally. Well, as he was willing to pay half a year's rent in advance and to sign a provisional agreement *per procurationem*, I closed with him. He paid the money – twenty-five pounds – signed the agreement, and I handed him the keys. He wanted them because Mr Gillum had asked him to get the rooms furnished so far as to be fit for immediate occupation. And that, in fact, is what he did. He took possession and had the chambers furbished up and some odd jobs done, and he ordered in enough furniture to enable Mr Gillum to go into residence at once."

"I am rather surprised that you agreed to the deal," said I.

"I don't see why," he retorted. "It was a slightly unusual transaction, but it was quite straightforward. The man couldn't run away with the chambers. What possible danger of injury was there? *Ad quod damnum*, as the lawyers would say." (He pronounced the last word "damn 'em.") "At any rate, the transaction turned out all right, so my action was justified by the results."

"Yes," I replied, "that has to be admitted. *Finis coronat opus.*"

"Exactly," he rejoined eagerly (and, I suspect, made a mental note of the tag with a view to future use). "The proof of the pudding is in the eating, as the vulgar saying has it."

"When Mr Gillum arrived," said Thorndyke, "was he introduced to you by the agent?"

"No," replied Weech. "As I understood from the night porter, the two gentlemen came to the Inn together at night between nine and ten. He mentioned the matter to me the next morning because the agent had asked him to. When they knocked at the wicket, he opened it, and, as he knew the agent by sight, having seen him once before, he let them pass through, and they went up the passage. Presently the agent came back alone and said: 'By the way, that gentleman is Mr Gillum, the new tenant of Number 64. You might mention to Mr Weech that he has come to take possession.' Which, as I have told you, he did."

"Did he mention to you how long the agent stayed that night?"

"No. But, you see, that was no business of mine."

"And when did you first meet. Mr Gillum?"

"The very next morning. I made it my business to. I looked in at the chambers about eleven in the forenoon, and the door was opened by Mr Gillum himself. I told him who I was and asked him if he acknowledged the agreement signed by his agent. He said 'yes,' but that he would rather have a new agreement signed by himself to put things on a regular footing. I thought he was quite right; and, as I had the agreement with me and some forms in my pocket, we filled in a new form, and, when he had signed it, we tore up the old one. Then he gave me his references and that finished the business."

"By the way," said Thorndyke, "you didn't mention the agent's name."

"I'm not sure that I remember it," replied Weech. "But does it matter?"

"It might matter," Thorndyke replied, "if it should seem desirable to get into touch with him, as I think it may be."

"Well," said Weech, "I seem to remember that it was something like Baker or Barber, or it may have been Barker – something of that sort."

"Of that sort!" I protested. "But there is all the difference in the world between a man who bakes your bread and one who shaves you or barks at you."

Mr Weech smiled deprecatingly. "I was referring to the sound," said he. "They are a good deal alike. And really, his name did not arise, excepting when he signed the agreement; and his signature was not very distinct."

"But," objected Thorndyke, "there was the cheque and the receipt that you gave him."

"There was no cheque," replied Weech. "He paid in five five-pound notes. And the receipt was made out, at his request, to Mr John Gillum. So, you see, his name was never mentioned; and I only saw it once in writing."

"Perhaps," Thorndyke suggested persuasively, "you might give us some idea as to what this gentleman was like. I am rather interested in him because he must know more about Mr Gillum than most of my informants seem to."

"Well," Weech replied musingly, "I don't remember much about him. He was a tallish man – about my height – and he was a fair man, with a light-brown, tawny beard and moustache and blue eyes. He was quite a gentlemanly man with a pleasant, persuasive manner, not to say plausible. And that is really all that I can remember about him. You see, I only saw him once to speak to, and only once or twice at a distance when he was furnishing the chambers; and I have never seen him since. He may have been here to see Mr Gillum on some occasions, but, if so, I never happened to see him."

Thorndyke reflected on this statement for a few moments. Then he asked, apparently apropos of nothing in particular:

"I noticed that some carpenter's work had been done in the rooms at Number 64; some alterations to the coal-bin and the larder door. Do you happen to know whether they were done by Mr Gillum or by the agent?"

"They were done by the agent – Mr Barker, we'll call him. I only heard of it afterwards from Mr Wing, the carpenter, of Fetter Lane, who does most of the odd jobs about the Inn. He ought really to have got permission to have the alterations made, though there isn't much in it. The false bottom to the coal-bin was a distinct improvement, but I did think the holes in the larder door a trifle *ultra vires*." (Mr Weech made "*vires*" rhyme with fires; but we knew what he meant.)

Here there was a brief pause, and, as we passed the window of the typewriting office, I observed a lady in a hat, putting on her gloves. Then Thorndyke resumed the conversation with the question:

"Did you find Mr Gillum a satisfactory tenant?"

"Very," Mr Weech replied. "A model tenant. Paid his rent promptly on quarter day, kept his chambers clean and tidy, and gave no trouble in any way. I greatly regret his loss, and so, I am sure, does Miss Darby, the lady who has the ground floor."

"Why?" I asked, scenting a romance.

"Well, you see," he replied, "the gentleman who had Mr Gillum's chambers before him was terribly untidy, particularly in the matter of food, which is what matters in chambers. He used to leave food uncovered on his table and even in the larder, and the crumbs from his meals all over the floor. The natural consequence was that the place was overrun with mice; and, of course, they overflowed into the ground floor and kept the lady's nerves fairly on edge. But when Mr Gillum took over, the nuisance stopped at once. The mice disappeared like magic. Of course, it was quite simple. Mr Gillum used to sweep up his crumbs after each meal and keep all food in the larder under covers or in tins or jars with lids. There was nothing for the mice to feed on. And what is more, he stopped up all the mouse-holes. Here is Miss Darby, and I am sure she will bear out what I have said."

At this point the lady whom I had seen at the window emerged from her entry and met us on our return march. Mr Weech raised his hat with the kind of flourish which is possible only with a "topper" and accosted her.

"We were just speaking of the way poor Mr Gillum cleared the mice out of his chambers. You remember, I dare say."

"Indeed I do," she replied emphatically. "Before he came, my rooms simply swarmed with the nasty little creatures. The man on the first floor must have lived like a pig – kept a regular restaurant for mice. It was awful. I had great difficulty in getting the young ladies to stay with me. But when Mr Gillum came, the little beasts disappeared completely. We never saw a mouse. I can't tell you how grateful we were."

"Very naturally," said Thorndyke. "Mice are pretty little animals, but they are most unpleasant in their habits. However, I hope that your mice have gone for good. I suppose you are still clear of them?"

"Well, you know," Miss Darby replied with a slight frown, "the rather curious thing is that we are not. Just lately, one or two have made their appearance again. I can't understand it. Of course, we have our teas in the office, and sometimes our lunches. But we used to do that before. And we are most careful to sweep up all crumbs and to leave no food about. It is really rather strange."

"It is," Thorndyke agreed. "But perhaps you would get rid of your uninvited guests if you were to adopt Mr Gillum's plan; stop up the holes with Portland cement mixed with powdered glass. I strongly recommend you to try that remedy."

Miss Darby thanked him for the advice and then, with a smile and a little bow, bustled away and disappeared into the tunnel-like passage that ran past the hall door. And thither we shortly followed her, as it appeared that Thorndyke had squeezed his informant dry — with mighty little result, as it seemed to me. But then you could never tell what was in Thorndyke's mind or what might be the significance to him of trivial facts that seemed to have no significance at all.

Mr Weech walked with us down the passage to Fleet Street and finally dismissed us with another impressive flourish of his hat, which we returned punctiliously and then crossed the road to the Inner Temple gate.

As we walked down the lane past the church I reflected on what we had heard and seen. Presently I remarked:

"Weech's description of the unknown visitor at the Inn seemed to me to correspond pretty closely with that of Abel Webb."

"So I thought," replied Thorndyke; "and, for the present, I am assuming that he was Abel Webb, though we shall have to get confirmation if possible."

"I don't quite see how," said I. "But assuming him to have been Webb, how does that square with what we have been inferring about the relations between him and Gillum? It seems to me to be rather a misfit. If the man was Webb, that must have been his first visit to Gillum as he had to inquire of Weech and was not sure of the address or that Gillum did actually live there. Now that visit was made only a few days before his death. But we inferred — at least, I did — that Webb had been blackmailing Gillum for the best part of a year. There seems to be a radical disagreement. You can hardly blackmail a man whose address you do not know."

"It is not actually impossible," said Thorndyke, "but I agree with you that it is extremely difficult to see how it could be done.

However, we are not certain that this man was Webb, and, before we make any further inferences, we must get more evidence. The whole question of the relations of these two men needs to be elucidated; for if we were wrong in our original inferences we may have to recast our theory of the circumstances of Webb's death. Obviously, the first thing to do is to ascertain, if possible, whether the man who came to the Inn was really Abel Webb."

CHAPTER ELEVEN

A Fresh Puzzle

My colleague's remark that it would be necessary to test our belief as to the identity of the visitor to Gillum's chambers rather puzzled me. For, apparently, Mr Weech was the only person who had seen that visitor, and he had told us all that he had to tell; and I could not think of any means by which we could check his description. But, on the very next day, Thorndyke reopened the subject and disposed of my difficulties.

"I think," said he, "that it is desirable that we should confirm or disprove our assumptions as to the identity of Gillum's visitor at the Inn. At present our belief is founded entirely on Mortimer's not very precise description of the stick and the eyeglass. That is not enough. The question whether Abel Webb did or did not go to Gillum's chambers is a very important one and we ought to settle it more definitely. Indeed, the whole of the Abel Webb incident requires clearing up."

"And how do you propose to set about it?" I asked.

"I propose," he replied, "to go to the place where Webb was employed and get a description of his person. We have an excellent one from Weech with which to compare it. And perhaps, if we are fortunate, we may pick up some additional information. We want it badly enough."

"Yes," I agreed; "the Abel Webb business is rather in the air."

"Very much so," said he. "We have adopted the provisional theory that John Gillum, a most respectable gentleman, murdered Webb. That is a theory that wants clearing up, one way or the other. So, as the matter is of some urgency, I am proposing to devote the afternoon to it as we are both free and I hope that the expedition will interest you. What do you say?"

Of course I agreed, with some enthusiasm; and, as there were no preparations to make, we set forth within a few minutes.

It was characteristic of Thorndyke that, in making his way to Webb's place of business, he should choose the route that carried us over the scene of the tragedy. Leaving the Temple by the Tudor Street gate, we made for the Temple Station and travelled to the bank, whence we started along the south side of Cornhill until we reached the Church of St Michael. Here we turned up the alley, and, in a few paces, came to the arched entrance to the covered passage that Mortimer had described. A few steps along this brought us to the cavern-like south porch of the church; and here we both halted to reconstitute the picture that Mortimer had drawn so vividly, though the appearance of the place, in the bright afternoon light, was not easily reconciled with his description.

"It is an astounding affair," said Thorndyke, as he gazed into the now well-lighted porch. "By whomsoever that murder was committed, it was a remarkable exploit; and the murderer must have been a remarkable man – a man of iron nerve who combined the utmost audacity with caution and sound judgment. Not a man in ten thousand would have dared to take the risk; but yet, apart from that momentary risk, the crime was absolutely safe from detection. The actual murder can have taken but a matter of seconds; and the instant the blow was struck the murderer could slip out into the alley, quietly walk down into Cornhill, and there instantly become merged into the indistinguishable population of the street. For a premeditated murder, which it must have been, it was the boldest and the most skilfully managed crime that I have ever known."

"I don't know," said I, "that I am so much impressed with his judgment. It was a terrific gamble and he took a frightful risk. It doesn't seem to me that he made such a very good choice of the place."

"I am rather assuming," Thorndyke replied, "that he had not much choice. The suggestion to me is that of a desperate man who felt an immediate need to dispose of Webb; who had no time to make suitable arrangements but had to seize the one opportunity that presented itself. It *was* an opportunity, and he took it, and the result justified him in accepting the risk."

I was disposed to smile at Thorndyke's ultra-professional view of this murder, which he was evidently considering purely in terms of efficiency; putting himself, in his queer way, in the murderer's shoes and debating the appropriate technique. But I suppressed my amusement, and, following his own train of thought, asked:

"How do you suppose the murder was actually carried out?"

"I should assume," he replied, "that the murderer knew that Webb would pass through this passage at a certain time and that – greatly favoured by the unusual darkness of the evening – he lurked here, keeping a look-out from either end for possible wayfarers who might be approaching. Then, when Webb appeared at the entrance – the coast being clear at the moment – he made his attack. Probably Webb saw him, and there was a brief struggle, as suggested by the hat in the churchyard. But when they came opposite the porch the murderer thrust in the syringe, pushed his victim down on the steps, and walked away down St Michael's Alley. But the point of interest to us is that the murderer seems to have been familiar with Webb's habits. Perhaps we may get some further light on that point from our enquiries at Cope's."

With this we turned away from the porch, and, stepping up into the churchyard, took our way along the paved walk, out into Castle Court and through the little covered passage into Bell Yard. At the entrance of the yard into Gracechurch Street, Thorndyke paused and ran his eye along the houses on the south side of the street until it rested on a building which bore in large gilded letters the inscription, "The Cope Refrigerating Company," when we crossed the road and bore down on it.

On entering by the main doorway, we found ourselves in a large showroom filled with a bewildering assortment of various types of refrigerators, and were confronted by a member of the staff.

"I think," said Thorndyke, addressing him, "that the late Mr Abel Webb was employed here."

"Yes," was the reply, "but not in this department. We deal here with refrigerating apparatus and plant. Mr Webb was in the solid carbonic acid department. That is next door. You turn to the right as you go out."

Following this direction we entered a small doorway adjoining the main entrance and came into a long narrow shop or warehouse fitted with a counter which ran from end to end. Behind this were two men, one at the farther end, who was delivering one or two large and heavy packages to a carman, and the other, nearer to us, who appeared to be disengaged. To the latter Thorndyke repeated his former question, and thereby immediately captured his attention.

"Yes," he replied, "poor Mr Webb was employed here. He was assistant manager. Most of his time was spent in the manufacturing section, which adjoins this warehouse, and it was there that I knew him. I only came out into the retail department a short time before his death."

"Then," said Thorndyke, "as you knew him fairly well, perhaps you could tell us what sort of a man he was to look at. Would you mind?"

"Certainly not," was the cordial reply. "But may I ask, if it is not an impertinence, whether you two gentlemen are connected with the police?"

"We are not," Thorndyke replied. "My friend and I are lawyers; but I may say that our interest in Mr Webb is a professional interest. We are trying to get some fresh light on the circumstances of his death."

"I am glad to hear that," said the assistant. "It's time someone did. The police came here once or twice after the inquest, but, of course, we couldn't tell them much, and they didn't seem particularly keen. But I don't think the affair ought to have been let drop in the way that it was. Now, as to what Mr Webb was like. He was rather a noticeable man, though short. He was a bit of a dandy, always well-dressed and smartly turned out; waxed the ends of his moustache and wore a single eye-glass. Quite a nut in his way."

"Yes," said Thorndyke, "and to come to particulars; was he dark or fair, fat or thin?"

"He was dark. Sallow face, black moustache and eyebrows – bushy eyebrows like young moustaches; and I wouldn't call him fat. He was just stoutly built, and looked stouter because of his shortness."

"You spoke of an eyeglass. What was that like?"

"It was just an eyeglass. No rim or frame, no cord or ribbon. Just a plain glass. He used to carry it in his waistcoat pocket, and, when he wanted it, he would take it out and fix it in his eye, and there it stuck as if it were glued in."

"When he was out of doors, did he carry an umbrella or a stick?"

"A stick, always. He had just a slight limp – I think one leg was a little shorter than the other. That was why he gave up the sea. Found it a trifle inconvenient on board ship. So he used a stick for a bit of extra support. And a rare fine stick it was; a very thick malacca with a silver band and an ivory knob like a young billiard ball. And that, I think, is all that I can tell you about Mr Webb."

"Thank you," said Thorndyke, "you have given us a very admirable and complete description." He paused for a few moments and appeared to be reflecting. Then he opened a new topic.

"I notice that you seem to reject the idea that Mr Webb committed suicide."

"That I certainly do," was the reply. "Webb was not the man to commit any foolishness of that kind. Besides, it was a plain case of murder. Anyone could see that from the way it was done – and the place, too, for that matter."

"What is the significance of the place?" Thorndyke asked.

"The significance is that anyone waiting at that place at the right time would have been sure of meeting him. He used to get on his bus at the Royal Exchange and he always walked there by the same route; through Bell Yard, Castle Court and the churchyard and out into Cornhill by St Michael's Alley. Always the same way; he told me so, himself, one day when I walked that way with him. He said that he liked the walk through the churchyard. And he was wonderfully punctual, too. He would stay on here finishing up the day's work after the rest of the staff had gone; but at seven-thirty, sharp, he would take his stick and hat and off he would go. Anyone waiting for him in that dark passage could have been certain of him to half a minute. It would have been perfectly easy if there happened to be nobody about."

"Yes," Thorndyke agreed, "that is quite an important point. But you see that the idea of some person lying in wait there suggests the further idea of someone who had an intimate knowledge of Mr Webb's habits. Can you think of any persons who had that knowledge?"

"No. I don't know that anyone besides myself knew what his habits were; and even if any of our people knew, there is none of them that I could possibly suspect."

Thorndyke agreed cordially with the latter statement and again paused with a reflective air, and I got the impression that he was feeling about for a new opening. Apparently he found one, for he proceeded to put a fresh case.

"Looking back on that time – the time just before Mr Webb's death – can you recall any incident that could possibly be, in any way, regarded as suspicious?"

Our friend weighed the question seriously for some seconds but finally concluded that he really did not think that he could.

But yet I seemed to detect a certain hesitancy in his reply as if he did not absolutely reject the suggestion. And this was evidently perceived also by Thorndyke, for he returned to the attack with his customary persistence, tempered by suavity.

"You must forgive me for pressing you, Mr–"

"My name is Small."

"Mr Small. But, looking back by the light of what happened, can you think of any incident – we won't say actually suspicious; perhaps quite trivial and commonplace, but which, considered retrospectively, might conceivably have had some connection with the tragedy. Any strangers, for instance, who might have called to see Mr Webb, or who might have met him by chance. Now, what do you say?"

Mr Small was still hesitant and slightly evasive.

"You see," said he, "when an awful thing like that has happened, it tends to upset your judgment and sense of proportion. You look back on what went before and you are apt to magnify every little simple thing that occurred and think that it might have had something to do with the disaster."

"Exactly," said Thorndyke. "And so it might have had. Don't forget that. It is by the close scrutiny of little simple things that we sometimes get a valuable hint. Now, Mr Small, I can see that there is something in your mind that you have given some thought to, but that you are shy of mentioning because of its apparent triviality. Let us have it. Perhaps it may not appear so trivial to me; and if it does, there will be no harm done."

"Well," Mr Small replied with some reluctance, "it is really a very trivial incident, but yet I have sometimes thought it rather odd. It just amounts to this: One evening, not very long before closing time, a man – a gentleman, I might call him – came here to buy some four-pound blocks of snow – solid carbonic acid, you know – and he had brought a sort of suit-case to carry it away in. Now, I had got the blocks, wrapped in a rough insulated packing, and was just handing them to him when Mr Webb came in through that door and stopped to look up at the shelves, standing about where the other assistant is standing now. Well, what attracted my notice was this; as Mr Webb came through the doorway, the customer glanced at him, and then he looked again very hard with an expression as if he was surprised or startled. And at that moment Mr Webb noticed him, and *he* looked very hard at him. But he couldn't get a very good view of him, for the customer turned away so that his back was towards Mr Webb while he was packing the blocks in his case. And when he had got them in, as he had already paid for them, he said 'good evening' and walked out. When he had gone Mr Webb asked me if I knew who the customer was, and I said I didn't. 'Well,' he said, 'the next time that he comes, find out his name if you can,' and I said I would."

"And did you?" Thorndyke asked.

"No," replied Small, "because he never came again, and I have never seen him since."

"Do you remember, roughly, the date on which this incident occurred?"

"I should say that it was from ten days to a fortnight before Mr Webb's death; and that happened on the ninth of September. That is what has made it stick in my memory. I have often wondered whether it could have had any connection with that dreadful affair."

"Naturally," said Thorndyke; "and it does not appear so very improbable that it had. It might be useful to have a description of that customer if you could remember what he was like."

"I can't remember much about him," said Small, "though I should know him if I met him, but, of course, I didn't notice him particularly. I know that he was a rather tall man, say about five foot ten, and dark; black hair and a smallish black beard with a close-clipped moustache; and that is about all that I do remember."

"You didn't by any chance notice what his teeth were like?"

Mr Small seemed to start, and gazed at Thorndyke in evident surprise.

"Well, now," he exclaimed, "that's curious because, now that you come to mention it, I *did* notice his teeth, when he smiled at something that I said. His upper front teeth had been stopped with gold; pretty extensively, too; and those stoppings were no ornament. I wonder he let the dentist disfigure him in that way. But you seemed to know the man, to judge by your question."

"It was only a shot," replied Thorndyke. "I remembered a man who might have been surprised at seeing Mr Webb here. But, as that man is now dead, there isn't much in it."

As Thorndyke seemed to have elicited the information that he had come for, I ventured to seek a little on my own account.

"What sort of people use those blocks that you were speaking of," I asked, "and what do they use them for?"

"All sorts of people use the solid carbonic acid," replied Small. "The standard twenty-five-pound blocks are mostly used by brewers and mineral water manufacturers. The small four-pound blocks were made in the first place principally for the convenience of the ice-cream tricycles, to keep their stuff cold. But nowadays those blocks are used for a number of purposes. Doctors use them for freezing warts and moles, and engineers and motor repair men use them quite a lot."

"What on earth do engineers want carbonic acid snow for?" I asked.

"Principally," he replied, "for shrinking metal. Say you have got a bush that is just too big to drive into its hole. Well, you can get it in either by expanding the piece with the hole in it by making it hot, which may be a big job, or you can shrink the bush by freezing it with the dioxide snow, which is much more convenient."

Hitherto, fortunately for us, the warehouse had been so nearly empty that the other assistant had been able to deal with the business. But now several customers came in, and their arrival brought our conversation to an end. Mr Small apologised for having to leave us in order to attend to them, and accordingly, when we had thanked him for having given us so much of his time, we wished him good afternoon and retired.

We took our way back by the way we had come, through Bell Yard and the paved walk beside the little grass plot, lingering a while in the quiet and seclusion of the churchyard to discuss the results of the expedition.

"That was a bold shot of yours," I remarked, "with respect to the teeth. What made you think that the man might be Gillum – for there can be no doubt that it was he?"

"Practically none," he replied. "But the reasons that made me chance the suggestion were, first, that the circumstances seemed to make it probable that the man was Gillum, and, second, the description that Small gave fitted Gillum perfectly, so far as it went."

"I don't quite see the probability that you mention," said I; "in fact, I find these new developments rather bewildering. I can't fit them into our scheme. Small's description almost suggests an unexpected meeting, which might be natural enough on Webb's part, but hardly on Gillum's. For, as he was neither an ice-cream vendor nor a doctor nor an engineer, it would seem that the purchase of the blocks was merely a pretext for going to Webb's place of business and getting into touch with him. But that doesn't seem to fit in with our theory at all; and neither does Webb's visit to Clifford's Inn – for that visitor certainly was Webb."

"Yes," Thorndyke agreed, "Small's description corresponds exactly with Weech's. But you are quite right, Jervis. These new facts do not fit our theory in its original form. We shall have to modify it. But you notice that our new discoveries, so far from exonerating Gillum, tend to confirm our suspicion that he was responsible for Webb's death. What we shall have to reconsider is the possible motive for the murder. We assumed that Webb was a blackmailer. We may have been right, but these two meetings, as you say, do not fit comfortably into the group of events that we assumed. We must have another try. But what will be much better than speculating on the possible alternatives, will be the collection of some further data. There are still some unexplored territories in which we may possibly make new discoveries."

"Yes," I agreed; "there is, for instance, Dr Peck. He might be able to give us some useful information. But the question is: where is he? He may be in the middle of the Pacific."

"True," Thorndyke admitted; "but, on the other hand, he may not. I think that your question has to be answered, and I propose that we seek the answer without delay."

Chapter Twelve

The Pursuit of Dr Peck

Thorndyke's decision that an immediate answer must be found to my question, "Where is Dr Peck?" was given effect on the very following morning; when, as our engagements permitted, we set forth together for the pleasant old precinct of Staple Inn. As our business was with the porter, and he was most likely to be found in his lodge by the main gate, we took our way up Fetter Lane and along Holborn until we reached the arched entrance in the ancient timber houses through which the wayfarer in the busy street can get a glimpse of the quiet, secluded quadrangle. And here, passing under the archway, we found the lodge door open and the porter plainly visible within.

Observing that we had halted with an air of business, he came to the door and asked, civilly, what he could do for us.

"I want," said Thorndyke, "to get into communication with one of your tenants; a certain Dr Peck."

"Ah!" the official replied, "then you have made a bull's eye at the first shot; though he is not one of our tenants now. But I can give you his address."

This he proceeded to do, writing it down on a slip of paper which my colleague offered for the purpose. And, with this, it seemed to me that our business had come to an unexpectedly swift conclusion, and that we might forthwith go about "getting into communication" with our quarry. But this was evidently not

Thorndyke's view, for having put the slip of paper in his pocket-book, he developed an unmistakable tendency to open a conversation and to start the porter talking. From which I inferred that he hoped to gather up a few unconsidered trifles of a biographical nature which might be dropped in the course of a properly directed gossip.

"I came here," said he, "because this was given as his address in the Medical Directory; though I hadn't much hope of finding him, as he spends most of his time at sea."

"No," replied the porter, "and if you had come a little earlier you wouldn't have found him or got any news of him either. He seems to have been all over the world this last trip, not on an ordinary voyage out and home, but changing about from one ship to another and going into all sorts of unheard-of places."

"But I suppose," said Thorndyke, "he kept in touch with you so that you could send on his letters?"

"Not a bit," was the reply. "He couldn't. He never knew where he was going to next, and he never stayed long in any place. He meant this to be his last trip at sea, and he was determined to see as much of the world as he could before he settled down ashore. And he did. It must have been a regular Captain Cook's voyage."

"And he never gave you any place to send his letters to all the time that he was away? There must have been a pretty considerable accumulation when he came home."

"I expect there was. But I never collected them from his chambers as I had no place to send them to. In fact, he told me to leave them where they dropped through the letter slit."

"I suppose you heard from him from time to time, when the rent became due, for instance?"

"No, he never wrote. There was nothing to write about. He had always left an order with his banker to pay his rent as it became due, when he was away at sea, and he did the same this time."

"It seems a wasteful arrangement," said Thorndyke, "to have kept a set of chambers empty, month after month while the tenant was wandering about the earth. Don't you think so?"

"I do, and I told him so. But he said that a doctor has to have a permanent address to keep his name on the register; and he liked to have a place to come to when he returned from a voyage. But this last trip did really seem to me out of all reason. He was away close upon two years; and all that time there were the chambers lying empty and the rent going on just the same as if he had been living in them. It happened to be a low rent, because he was an old tenant. He came here years ago when he was a medical student. We used to have a lot of students in those days, mostly from Barts, and when one qualified and gave up his chambers, he was allowed to hand them on to a new student. So Dr Peck had been living here more years than I can remember, and I suppose he didn't like the idea of giving up his old chambers. But still, as you said, two years' rent for unoccupied chambers does seem a wicked waste."

"Perhaps," Thorndyke suggested, "he didn't expect to be away so long."

"Oh yes, he did. He told me that he might be away for as much as a couple of years. He meant to go overland to Marseilles and there pick up some kind of foreign tramp and go with her wherever she might be going, and after a time, change over to another ship and make a voyage somewhere else. And he made mighty preparations so that he should be as comfortable as possible. He got a brand new cabin trunk, in addition to his old ones, and he had a couple of portable bookcases made so that he could have his library with him."

"He must have reckoned that those tramps would have pretty liberal cabin space," I remarked. "You couldn't get many bookcases into an ordinary tramp's cabin, so far as my experience goes."

"Oh, but these were quite small things," the porter explained. "Only about three foot high by a couple of foot wide. And uncommonly cleverly they were planned, too, at least, so I thought. You see, they were intended to travel with the books in them. They had moveable fronts fixed on with a dozen long screws, well greased so that they would come out easily, and lying flush so that there was nothing projecting to catch when they were travelling.

And when you had got them into your cabin, all you had to do was to take out the screws and the front was free. You could just take it off and slip it behind the case out of the way, and there was your bookcase with all your books properly arranged and ready for use. I thought it a mighty neat idea."

"So it was," Thorndyke agreed. "Extremely convenient, not only for use on board ship, but for travelling on land. Did you see the cases?"

"Yes," was the reply, "I saw them in Mr Crow's workshop just before he delivered them, and I complimented him on having made such a good job of them. He had got them stained and varnished so that they looked quite smart, although they were only made of deal, you understand."

"Mr Crow, I take it," said Thorndyke, "is a local craftsman."

"Yes, he lives close by in Baldwin's Gardens, so we give him all the jobs that we want done about the Inn. And a real good tradesman he is. I always recommend him whenever I can. It's a kindness to him and to the customer, too."

"It is, indeed," said Thorndyke, "especially to the customer. Really skilful and dependable tradesmen are getting scarce, and it is no small advantage to know where one can find such a man on occasion. I shall make a note of Mr Crow's address, and perhaps call on him. I am quite impressed by your description of those bookcases."

"Well, I think you would find them handy if you travel much," said the porter, apparently much gratified by the impression he had made. "Dr Peck did, as he told me; and they took the fancy of the captain of his last ship to such an extent that when the doctor left the ship at Marseilles to come home overland, the skipper insisted on buying the cases, books and all."

"Then you have seen Dr Peck since he came home?"

"Lord, yes," the porter chuckled, "and I didn't recognise him at first. You see, he had shaved off his beard; and when a beaver does a clean shave, the results are apt to be surprising. But he was quite right. A beard is the thing on board ship, where shaving isn't very convenient and not at all necessary, but, as he said very truly, when a man is in practice as a doctor, he doesn't want a bunch of hair on his chin to stick in his patient's face. Yes, he came here to give notice and settle up, and to move his things out of the chambers."

"When did he arrive in England?"

"Ah!" was the reply, "that I can't say, exactly. I didn't know that he was back until he turned up here, as I have told you. That was about three weeks ago. But he must have been in England some time before that, seeing that he had taken a house, and perhaps a doctor's business as well."

"Then he never came back here to live?"

"No. Which makes the waste of money seem worse than ever. He appears to have taken his new premises, furniture and all, and settled there at once. So I understood."

"And he is now engaged in medical practice at the address you gave me just now?"

"Well," the porter replied with a faint grin, "that's as may be. If he bought a going concern, I suppose he is. But if he just took the premises without any goodwill, he is probably squatting there and waiting for business to turn up. However, in either case, he has got a brass plate at the address I gave you; and there you'll find him, and he will be better able to give you the particulars about himself than am."

I seemed to detect in the final sentence a subtle hint that our friend thought that he had asked enough questions, and so, apparently, did Thorndyke, for he accepted the hint – the more readily, I suspect, because he had no further questions to ask – and brought the interview to an end by thanking our friend for the address and wishing him good morning.

As this dialogue had proceeded, I had become more and more puzzled. For I had supposed that our mission had the simple purpose of finding out, if possible, the whereabouts of Dr Peck; and I had imagined that our business with Peck was to elicit from him whatever he might be able to tell us about the incidents of the voyage from Australia as affecting John Gillum. But it seemed that neither of these suppositions was true. Thorndyke was not interested only in what Peck might be able and willing to tell us; he was interested in Peck, himself. The apparently trivial conversation to which I had listened was, I felt sure, a carefully conducted examination designed to elicit certain facts. But what facts? I had listened attentively and even curiously; but not a single fact of any apparent significance seemed to have transpired. Yet something had transpired, unperceived by me. Thorndyke's behaviour had convinced me of that. The way in which he had, almost abruptly, closed the conversation, told me that, whatever might be the item of information which he had been seeking, that item was now in his possession. But I could not form the vaguest guess as to what it could be.

My confusion of thought was rather increased by Thorndyke's conduct when we emerged from the Inn; for, halting at the edge of the pavement and looking across the road, he said, meditatively:

"Baldwin's Gardens. I think that turns out of the Gray's Inn Road a little way down on the right, doesn't it?"

"Yes," I replied. "About the third turning. Were you thinking of paying a visit to the ingenious Mr Crow?"

"Why not?" said he. "We may as well look him up now, as we are so near."

"But," I protested, "why look him up at all? Those bookcases were very ingenious and handy for the purpose for which they were made, but you have no use for such things. You don't make sea voyages or even prolonged journeys away from home; and if you did, you would hardly want to take your library with you."

"But they would be useful for carrying other things besides books," he replied; "apparatus and reagents, for instance. At any rate, I should like to get particulars of construction and dimensions."

"With a view," said I, "to pinching Mr Crow's copyright and having a pirated edition turned out by Polton."

"Not at all," he retorted. "If I decided to have one, or a pair, made, I should certainly commission Mr Crow to make them."

As he had evidently got some kind of unreasonable fancy for those bookcases, I said no more. We crossed the road and in two or three minutes found ourselves at the corner of Baldwin's Gardens, whence we began a perambulation of the street. It was some time before we were able to locate Mr Crow's premises, but eventually we discovered, at the corner of a side passage, a painted board inscribed with the name of "William Crow, Carpenter and Joiner" and the intimation that his workshop would be found on the right up the passage. We accordingly followed the direction and, coming to a door on which the description was repeated, pushed it open and entered a spacious, well-lighted workshop in which a tall, elderly man was engaged in planing up the edge of a board. At the sound of our entry, he turned and looked at us over the tops of his spectacles, and then, laying his plane down on the bench, enquired politely what he could do for us.

Thorndyke briefly stated the purpose of our visit, whereupon Mr Crow took off his spectacles to get a better view of us and appeared to meditate on what my colleague had said.

"A pair of bookcases, you say, sir, made for a gentleman in Staple Inn of the name of Peck. Yes, I seem to remember a-making of them, but I can't rightly recollect exactly what they were like. Small cases, I think you said?"

"Yes; about three feet by two."

"Well, sir," said Mr Crow – very reasonably, I thought – "if you will tell me just what you want, I can take down the particulars and make the articles without troubling about those other ones."

But this simple plan apparently did not commend itself to Thorndyke, for he objected:

"I am not sure that I have got the full particulars and I rather wanted to see the construction and dimensions of those that you made for Dr Peck. Don't you keep an account in your books of work that you have in hand?"

"Oh, yes," replied Crow, "I've got the particulars all right if I only knew where to look for them. But you see, it's a longish time ago and my memory ain't what it was. I suppose, now, you couldn't tell me about when those cases were made?"

"I can't give you the exact date," said Thorndyke, "but I should say that it would have been some time in September, 1928, probably the early part of the month. Or it might have been the latter part of August. What do you say, Jervis?"

"I expect you are right," I replied, "though I don't quite see how you arrived at the date."

But however he had arrived at it, the date turned out to be correct; for when Mr Crow, having resumed his spectacles, had picked out from a row of trade books a shabby-looking folio volume and opened it on the bench, the required entry came into view almost at once.

"Ah!" said Crow, "here we are. Twenty-eighth of August, 1928. I see the order is marked 'urgent.' Things wanted as soon as possible. They usually are. So I treated it as urgent and delivered the goods at the Inn on the thirty-first, in the evening, as soon as I had got them finished."

"That was a fairly quick piece of work," I remarked.

"Yes," he replied, "I got a move on with 'em. But there was not a lot of work in 'em, as you can see by the drawings. No dovetails and no gluing up except for the backs. They were just screwed together and stained and brush-varnished. It wasn't a job to take up much time. I have written the dimensions on the drawings, so you can see exactly what the cases were like."

We looked over the drawings, which were quite neatly executed, though rapidly sketched in, with the dimensions marked on them in clear legible figures; notwithstanding which, Mr Crow proceeded to expound them and the details of construction.

"The cases," said he, "were of yellow deal, stained and varnished; three foot three high by twenty inches wide and fourteen inches deep, all outside measurements; and as the stuff was full one-inch board, the inside measurements would be two inches less in height and width and one inch less in depth. There were three shelves in each case, equal distances apart, so you have got four spaces of a little under nine inches each, as the shelves were only half-inch stuff. All the parts were fastened together with screws, excepting the shelves, and they slid freely in grooves. The fronts were the same size as the backs, and they were just laid on and fixed in position by twelve two-and-a-half-inch number eight screws, which had to be well greased with tallow so that they would come out easily. It was quite a handy arrangement for, you see, you just filled the case up with books and then you put on the front and ran in the screws and you'd got a thoroughly secure packing-case with no hinges or other projections to get in the way when it was being stowed. Then, when you had got it in the place where it was to be, such as the cabin, all you had got to do was to draw out the screws, take off the front, and slip it behind the case, and there you were with all your books ready to hand."

"Wouldn't it have been stronger," I suggested, "if the top and bottom had been dovetailed to the sides?"

"Yes, it would," he agreed, "and that is what I wanted to do. But he wouldn't have it. He said that all the parts were to be screwed together with greased screws so that it could be taken to pieces if necessary for stowage or storing."

"I don't see much utility in that," I remarked.

"There isn't," he agreed, "excepting that, if the cases should be out of use at any time, they could be taken apart, and then the pieces would lie flat and take up less room than the assembled cases."

"I certainly think it a good method of construction," said Thorndyke. "The case would be strongly bound together by the back and front when it was travelling, and when it was not travelling, the extra strength would not be wanted."

"Then," said Crow, "you'd like yours made the same way, I suppose. Did you wish me to make one case or two?"

"You may as well make two while you are about it," answered Thorndyke, "and I think you had better make them in every way similar to those that you have in your day book and of the same dimensions. They are quite suitable and I don't think they could be improved on. But I may say that this order is not urgent. You can take your own time over them."

Mr Crow thanked him for his consideration, and when he had booked the order in the current book and taken Thorndyke's name and address, we took our leave and made our way homeward. During our walk along Holborn and down Fetter Lane very little was said by either of us. Thorndyke appeared to be cogitating on the morning's experiences, and my own reflections were principally concerned with speculations on the nature of his. For, as far as I could see, the only tangible result of the expedition was that we had got Peck's address and had secured two bookcases which we did not want. In addition, we had picked up a number of rather trivial personal particulars relating to Peck and his comings and goings, none of which seemed to have the slightest bearing on the problem which we were endeavouring to solve. But I suspected that there was more in it than this; that, out of the porter's trifling reminiscences, Thorndyke had gathered something, the significance of which was evident to him though it had, for the present, escaped me.

We entered the Temple by Mitre Court and, as we emerged into the upper end of King's Bench Walk, we observed a figure advancing up the pavement from the direction of our chambers, which, as we drew nearer, resolved itself into that of our friend Benson. He recognised us at the same moment and quickened his pace to meet us.

"I have taken the liberty," said he, when he had shaken hands heartily, "to drop in at your rooms, as I was in the neighbourhood, not to detain you and waste your time, but just to ask if there were any news of our case."

"There is nothing definite to report," replied Thorndyke. "I am making various enquiries and picking up such facts as I can, but, so far, the result is a rather miscellaneous collection which will want a good deal of sorting out and collation. But I am by no means hopeless. Won't you come back and have a bit of lunch with us? There are one or two questions that I wanted to ask you, and we might discuss them over the lunch table."

Benson looked at his watch. "I should like to,"said he, "but I think I had better not. I have an appointment at half-past two, and I mustn't be late. Could I answer your questions now?"

"I think so," replied Thorndyke. "It is just a matter of personal description. You see, as I never saw John Gillum and have only the vaguest idea as to what he was like, I shall be rather at a loss if I have occasion to trace his movements. I can give no description of him. Could you sketch out a few personal characteristics by which he could be described or identified?"

Benson reflected as we turned to walk slowly down the pavement.

"Let me see," said he. "Now, what do you call personal characteristics? There is his height. He was rather a tall man; about five feet ten. In colour he was a mixture – dark and fair. His hair and beard were black, but his skin was fair and his eyes were blue; you know the type of black-haired blond. But probably the most striking and distinctive characteristic, and the most useful for identification would be the peculiarity of his teeth. You have heard, I think, that his upper front teeth were extensively filled with gold; and as they showed a good deal, they were a very serious disfigurement."

"Yes, I have heard of those teeth," said Thorndyke, "and I have rather wondered why a fairly good-looking man, as I understood him to be, should have allowed himself to be disfigured in that way. Were his other teeth filled extensively in the same way?"

"No," replied Benson, "that was the exasperating feature of the case. He had an exceptionally fine, sound set of teeth; not a stopping among the whole lot, I believe. It was bad luck that the only unsound ones should have happened to be those that were constantly on view. And I have an impression that they were really sound; that the spots of decay on them were started by some kind of blow or injury. But I think the dentist might have done something better for him."

"Yes," I agreed. "A competent man would not have used a gold filling at all. He would have put in a porcelain inlay."

"To return to the hair," said Thorndyke. "You described it as black. Do you mean actually black, or very dark brown?"

"I mean black. There was no tinge of brown in it, to the best of my belief. It seemed to be dead black, with just a tiny sprinkling of grey. But the grey was hardly noticeable, except, perhaps, on the temples above the ears. Otherwise, there was only a white hair here and there; single hairs that you would scarcely notice and that did not interfere with the general effect of black hair."

"Thank you," said Thorndyke, "Your description is quite helpful. But what would be still more helpful would be a portrait. If you can show a portrait and say, 'Is this the man whom you saw?' the identification is much more definite. I suppose you don't happen to have a photograph of your cousin?"

"Not here," Benson answered; and then, as with a sudden afterthought, he said, "Wait, though. I have got something that will possibly answer your purpose. You must know that I am an amateur photographer in a small way. I run a pocket camera, and I have a sort of a book file for the film negatives. That file I have brought with me and it is in one of my trunks. Among the old films are one or two of Gillum, mostly in groups, but I don't suppose that will matter. They are not very good portraits – you know what snapshot portraits are like – and of course, they are rather small. But they could be enlarged. Do you think they would be of any use to you?"

"They would be of the greatest use," Thorndyke replied. "They could not only be enlarged, but they could be retouched to get rid of the exaggerated shadows, which are the principal cause of the bad likeness in outdoor snapshots. Will you let me have one or two of them?"

"Certainly," said Benson. "I will look them over and pick out a few of the best and clearest and send them to you. And I have got a photograph that the first officer gave me, which he took on the former voyage. It is a group of officers and passengers, including a fairly good portrait of Gillum. I will send that too. And now," he added, once more glancing at his watch, "I think I must really be running away. There wasn't anything more that you wanted to ask me, was there?"

"No," replied Thorndyke, "I think that was all. If you send me the photographs and they are reasonably good ones, my difficulties in the matter of identification will be disposed of."

With this we both shook hands with him and stood awhile, watching him as he strode away towards Crown Office Row, the picture of health and strength and energy. Then, as our fancies lightly turned to thoughts of lunch, we walked back to our entry and ascended to our chambers where we found the table already laid and Polton on the look-out for our arrival.

CHAPTER THIRTEEN

Dr Augustus Peck

Of certain men we are apt to say that once seen they are never forgotten. They are not mere samples of the human race, turned out from the common mould, but executed individually as special orders and never repeated. Such were Paganini and the great Duke of Wellington, recognisable by us all from their mere counterfeit presentments after the lapse of a century.

Now Mr Ethelbert Snuper was exactly the reverse. He might have been seen a thousand times and never remembered. So exactly was he like every other ordinary person that he might have come straight out of a text-book of "The Dismal Science" – the Economic Man, now for the first and only time enjoying a concrete existence. Often as I met him, I recognised him with doubt. And the worst of it was that when at last I thought that I had committed his impersonality to memory, behold! the very next time I met him he was somebody else. It was quite confusing. There was a sort of unreality about the man. His very name was incredible, so exactly did it define his status and his "place in Nature," (but one meets with these coincidences in real life. I once knew a ritualist clergyman named Mummery).

For Mr Snuper was a private inquiry agent and, especially, a professed and expert shadower; a vocation to which his personal peculiarities (or should I say, his impersonal unpeculiarities?) adapted him with a degree of perfection usually met with only in

179

the lower creation. Even as the cylindrical body of the mole answers to the form of his burrow, and the flatness of *Cimex lectularius* (Norfolk Howard) favours unostentatious movements beneath a wallpaper, so Mr Snuper's total lack of individual character enabled him to walk the streets a mere unnoticed unit of the population.

I had often met him about our premises, for Thorndyke had employed him from time to time to make such enquiries and observations as were obviously impossible to either of us; and now, the day after our visit to Staple Inn, I met him once more, descending our stairs, and should certainly have passed him if he had not stopped to wish me "good afternoon." As he had evidently just come from our chambers, I assumed that there was something afoot and was a little curious as to what it might be, and the more so as we had no case on hand which seemed to need Mr Snuper's services.

Of course, I could not put any questions to the gentleman himself, but I had no such delicacy with Thorndyke. As soon as I entered our chambers I proceeded to make a few private enquiries on my own account.

"I met Snuper on the stairs," said I. "Is there anything doing in his line?"

"It is just a matter of one or two enquiries," Thorndyke replied. "I have set him to collect a few data concerning Peck."

"What sort of data?" I asked.

"Oh, quite simple data," he replied; "what sort of practice he has, whether he lives on the premises, how he spends his time, what bank he patronises, and so on. You see, Jervis, we know nothing about Peck, and it would be useful to have a few facts in our possession when we call on him."

"I don't see that the kind of facts that you mention have much relevance to our inquiry," I objected.

He admitted the objection. "But," he added, "your experience in cross-examination will have taught you that an irrelevant question, to which you know the answer, may be a valuable means of testing the general truth of a witness' statements."

To this I had to assent, but I was not satisfied. Such extremely vague enquiries would have suggested that Thorndyke was at a loose end, which I did not believe he was.

"You are not connecting Peck with the blackmailing business, are you?" I asked.

"Why not?" he demanded.

"But the thing is impossible," I exclaimed. "The man was absent from England during the whole of the material time."

"Which is a fact worth noting," said he. "But what do you call the material time? When we were discussing Abel Webb, we agreed that the clue to this business was to be sought in the events of the voyage from Australia. Peck was present then."

"But he was on the other side of the world when the great blackmailing took place, after Abel Webb's death and apparently connected with it. However," I concluded, "it is of no use discussing the matter. I expect you have perfectly good reasons for what you are doing and are keeping them to yourself."

He smiled blandly at this suggestion, and the subject dropped; and as we had several court cases which kept us employed during the fortnight which followed, the Gillum mystery fell into abeyance, or, at least, appeared to. Mr Snuper made no further appearances (but then he never did in the course of an inquiry, reports by post being more safe from observation); and the case had nearly faded out of my mind when my interest in it was suddenly revived by Thorndyke's announcement that he proposed to call on Dr Peck on the following day shortly before noon.

"By the way," said I, "where is he carrying on his practice?"

"His premises are in Whitechapel High Street," Thorndyke replied.

"Whitechapel High Street!" I repeated in astonishment. "What an extraordinary place to have pitched upon."

"It does seem a little odd," he admitted, "but somebody must practise in Whitechapel; and there are some advantages in a poor neighbourhood. At any rate, that is where he is, and I hope we shan't find him too busy for an interview. I don't much think we shall, judging from Snuper's reports of the practice."

How far Mr Snuper's estimate was correct I was unable to judge when we arrived at the premises on the following morning. From a brass plate on a jamb of the side door of a tailor's trimming warehouse I learned that Augustus Peck, Physician and Surgeon, had consulting-rooms on the first floor and was to be found in them between the hours of 10.30 a.m. and 1, and in the afternoon from 2 to 6 p.m. Accordingly, it being then about 11.30 a.m., we entered the doorway and ascended a flight of rather shabby stairs to a landing on which two doors opened, one of which bore the doctor's name in painted lettering with the instruction: "Ring and enter"; which we did, and found ourselves in a large room covered with floorcloth and provided with a considerable number of chairs, but otherwise almost unfurnished. However, we had no time to inspect this apartment – of which we were the sole occupants – for, almost as we entered, a communicating door opened and a rather tall, well-dressed man invited us to come through into the consulting-room. We followed him into the sanctuary, and, when he had shut the door and placed a couple of chairs for us, he seated himself at his writing-table, and, having bestowed on us a look of more than ordinary attention, asked:

"Which of you is the patient?"

Thorndyke smiled apologetically as he replied:

"Neither of us is. We have not come for medical advice, but in the hope – rather a forlorn hope, I fear – that you may be able and willing to assist us in some inquiries that we have in hand."

Dr Peck smiled. "I was afraid," said he, "that you were too good to be true. My practice doesn't include many members of the aristocracy. But what kind of inquiries are you referring to? And, if you will pardon me, whom have I the honour of addressing?"

Thorndyke took out his card-case, and, extracting a card, said, as he handed the latter to Peck: "This will introduce me. My friend is Dr Jervis, who is collaborating with me."

Dr Peck took the card from him and glanced at it, at first rather casually; but then he looked at it again with such evidently awakened interest that I felt sure that he had recognised the name. Indeed, he said so when he had pondered over it a while, for, as I offered him my card and he took it from me, laying Thorndyke's down on the table, he asked:

"Are you the Dr Thorndyke who used to lecture at St Margaret's on medical jurisprudence?"

Thorndyke admitted that he was the person referred to. "But," he added, "I don't remember you. Were you ever at St Margaret's?"

"No," replied Peck, "I am a Bart's man. But I remember your name, as our lecturer used to quote you rather freely. And that brings us back to the question of your inquiry. What is its nature, and how do you think I can help you?"

"Our inquiry," said Thorndyke, "is concerned with a man named John Gillum who came from Australia to England about two years ago. Do you remember him?"

"Oh, yes," replied Peck, "I remember him quite well. He was a passenger on the *Port Badmington*, of the Commonwealth and Dominions Line, of which I was medical officer. He came on board, I think, at Perth and travelled with us to Marseilles. What about him?"

"Did you know that he is dead?

"Dead!" exclaimed Peck. "Good Lord, no. When did he die?"

"He was found dead in his chambers in Clifford's Inn nearly three months ago. Apparently, he had committed suicide – at least, that was the verdict of the coroner's jury."

"Dear, dear!" Peck exclaimed in a tone of deep concern. "What a dreadful affair! Poor old Gillum! A most shocking affair, and surprising, too. I can hardly believe it. He was such a cheerful soul, so gay and happy and so full of the high old times that he was going to have when he got to England. I suppose there is no doubt that he really did make away with himself?"

"There seemed to be no doubt whatever," replied Thorndyke; "but I can speak only from hearsay. I had no connection with the case at the time."

"And now that you are connected with the case," said Peck, "what is the nature of your inquiry? What do you want to know?"

"The answer to that question," said Thorndyke, "involves a few explanations. From what transpired at the inquest, it appeared that Gillum had been driven to suicide by the loss of his entire fortune. It was only a modest fortune – about thirteen thousand pounds – but he had got through every penny of it. Part of it he had wasted by betting and other forms of gambling, but a quite considerable portion of what had been lost appeared to have been paid away to blackmailers."

"Blackmailers!" Peck repeated in a tone of the utmost astonishment. "It seems incredible. The gambling I can understand to some extent, though that surprises me. For, though he certainly did like a little flutter at cards, I should hardly have called him a gambler. But blackmail! I can't believe it. Who on earth could have blackmailed Gillum? And what possible chance could he have given them to do it?"

"Precisely," said Thorndyke. "That is our problem. Gillum's relatives are convinced that it was the blackmail, and not the mere gambling losses, that was the determining cause of the suicide; and they have commissioned me to make such inquiries as may establish the identity of the blackmailers and bring them within reach of the law."

"Very proper, too," said Peck, "but it doesn't look a very hopeful job. Have you anything to go on?"

"Not very much," Thorndyke replied. "There is this and there are some other letters, but, as you will see, they are not very helpful."

As he spoke he took from his pocket a little portfolio, from which he drew out a single sheet of paper and handed it to Peck; who read its contents slowly and with deep attention and then asked:

"Is this the original letter?"

"No," Thorndyke replied. "One doesn't hawk original documents about, which may have to be produced in court. This is a copy, but it is certified correct. The attestation is on the back."

Peck turned the sheet over and glanced at the certificate; then he turned it back and once more read through the letter.

"It's an astonishing thing," said he. "The blackmail works out at two thousand a year. Gillum must have had some pretty hefty secrets if he was prepared to pay that. But I don't quite see where I come in."

"You come in," said Thorndyke, "at precisely the point which you, yourself, have indicated: the identity of the blackmailer and the subject of the blackmail."

Peck looked at him in astonishment. "I don't understand what you mean," said he. "This man, Gillum, travelled on my ship from Australia to Europe. He came on board a complete stranger to me; he went ashore at Marseilles, and I never saw him again. Moreover, I have been abroad for nearly two years and I came back only a couple of months ago. How could I know anything about Gillum or his blackmailers?"

"It had occurred to me," Thorndyke replied, "that the blackmailers might have been some of his fellow passengers on that voyage, and that the blackmail might have been based on some incidents that had occurred on board. What do you say to that?"

"It is quite possible," replied Peck, "but I know of nothing to support the idea. Gillum seemed to be on good terms with everybody, and, as to the other passengers, I knew very little about them. A much more likely source of information would be the purser, if you could get into touch with him. He knew Gillum better than I did, and he knew more about the passengers. Get hold of him if you can. His name is Webb. Abel Webb."

"Abel Webb is dead," said Thorndyke. "He was found dead about a week after the date of that letter."

Dr Peck stared at Thorndyke, round-eyed and open-mouthed.

"Good God!" he exclaimed. "Found dead! Don't tell me that he committed suicide, too."

"It was suggested that he did," Thorndyke replied, "but it is more probable that he was murdered. The jury returned an open verdict."

For some seconds Peck sat motionless and silent, his wide-open blue eyes fixed, with an expression of horror, on Thorndyke's face. At length he said in a low tone, as if deeply moved:

"You are making my flesh creep, doctor. Two of the ship's company cut off by violence in a few months! I almost ask myself if it will be my turn next."

There was a long pause, during which Peck and Thorndyke looked at each other in silence and I continued my observation of the former. He was a rather good-looking man, clean-shaved and well-groomed, with close-cropped light-brown hair and clear blue eyes. His manners were easy and pleasant, and he had an undeniably engaging personality. And yet, somehow, I did not very much like him; and I liked him least when he smiled and exposed an unpleasing array of false teeth, mingled with one or two rather discoloured "aboriginals." He had better have kept his moustache.

"Well, doctor," he said, suddenly recovering himself and handing the letter back to Thorndyke – who replaced it in the portfolio "you see what my position is. I should have liked to help you, but I really have no connection with the business at all."

"No," Thorndyke agreed, "that appears to be the case. But I am not greatly disappointed. It was, as I said, only a forlorn hope. Nevertheless," he added, as he rose and pocketed the portfolio, "I am greatly obliged to you for having received us so kindly and given us so much of your time."

"Not at all," Peck replied, opening the side door, which gave access to the landing, "I am only sorry that your time has been occupied to so little purpose. Good morning, doctor. Good morning, Dr Jervis." He bowed and dismissed us with a genial smile, and we retreated down the shabby stairs and out into the busy High Street.

CHAPTER FOURTEEN

Further Explorations

The advantages of modern transport do not include facilities for conversation. The fact was recognised by us both as we sat in the motor omnibus which bore us at lightning speed – when it was not held up by an immovable jam of other lightning speeders – from the cosmopolitan region in which Dr Peck had pitched his tent towards the less picturesque but more respectable west. But even in a motor-bus thought is possible; and thus I was able to beguile the – intermittently – swift journey by cogitating upon our recent interview.

As to the results achieved, they were, so far as I was concerned, exactly what I had expected. The man had been absent from England during the whole of the blackmailing period and had nothing whatever to tell. And if Thorndyke had learned anything of his personality – which I had not – the knowledge could be only curious and irrelevant. For the one fact that had emerged was that, for the purposes of our inquiry, Dr Peck was completely outside the picture.

When the bus delivered us at Holborn Circus and we strode away along the broad pavement, I ventured to present my views as aforesaid, adding:

"It doesn't seem to me that Snuper's inquiries have helped us very much, but, of course, I don't know what discoveries he made."

"They were not very sensational," Thorndyke replied, "and mainly they agree with our own. Peck has just squatted in Whitechapel. His practice consists, at present, of a brass plate and an empty waiting-room, and his arrangements dispense with the inconveniences of a night-bell."

"He doesn't live there, then?"

"No. He lives at Loughton, on the skirts of Epping Forest, quite accessible to East London, and very delightful in the summer but rather bleak and muddy in the winter."

"It is not very obvious why he gave up his chambers," said I. "Staple Inn is nearer to Whitechapel than Loughton. What else did Snuper find out about him?"

"Very little. He ascertained that Peck seems to be a solitary man with no discoverable friends or acquaintances; that he spends his spare time in wandering about the far east of London or in long walks in the forest; and also – which is the most curious discovery – that he, apparently, has three banks, and that he visits each of them regularly twice a week."

"That really is odd," said I. "What on earth can he want with three banks? And for what purpose can he make these regular visits? If he has no practice there can be no cash to pay in, and he can't draw out twice a week, and from three banks, too."

Thorndyke smiled in his exasperating way. "There, Jervis," said he, "is quite a pretty little problem for you to excogitate. Why should a man who has no visible cash income pay in to three banks at once; or, alternatively, why should a man whose visible expenditure is negligible draw out twice a week from three banks?"

"Is there any answer to it?" I asked dismally as we turned into Fetter Lane.

"There must be," he replied. "Probably several, and one of them will be the right one. I strongly recommend the problem for your consideration. Attack it constructively. Think of all possible explanations, and then consider which of them is applicable to the present case. And, meanwhile, I suggest that we drop in at Clifford's Inn and see how Polton is progressing."

"What is Polton doing at Clifford's Inn?" I asked.

"My dear fellow," he replied, "he is carrying out your own suggestion; collecting dust for microscopical examination."

I smiled acidly at this outrageous fiction; for, of course, my suggestion had been made ironically as an example of superlative futility. The idea had been Thorndyke's own; and since there must have been some reasonable purpose behind it, I was now all agog to discover what that purpose was. It was not discoverable, however, from Polton's activities, for they exhibited only the method of procedure, which was, characteristically, orderly and systematic. The vacuum cleaner that he was using consisted of a sort of steel jar, into which the suction tube opened, the latter having a nozzle on which a gauze bag could be fastened. Thus, when the air-tight lid was on the jar and the machine was set working, a stream of dust-laden air was discharged into the bag, which detained the dust and let the air escape through its pores. Polton had provided himself with half a dozen or so of these bags, and, by the time when we arrived – letting ourselves in with a duplicate key of his manufacture – most of them had been filled and now stood in a row on the mantelpiece, each fitted with a label describing the source of its contents and referring to a sketch plan of the premises.

"You see, sir, I have nearly finished," said Polton, as Thorndyke glanced along the row of bags and scanned the labels. "I've done the bedroom, the kitchen and the larder, and now I am going over this room in sections. But," he added gloomily, "I'm afraid it will be a poor harvest. The floors are terribly clean. That carpet-sweeper must have taken off the cream of the really valuable dust, and they seem to have used it to a most unnecessary extent. However," he concluded, "I've got what I could out of that sweeper. I've combed the brushes and vacuumed the inside thoroughly."

"That was a capital idea," said Thorndyke. "The sweeper is probably quite a storehouse of ancient dust, and of the most useful kind for our purpose. By the way, did you have time to make that key?"

"Yes, sir," replied Polton. "I've got it here. It's only a skeleton. There was no use in fiddling about with wards, so I just cut the middle of the bit right out. But it opens the lock all right. I've tried it."

With this, he produced from his pocket a monstrous skeleton key, such as might have been fabricated by Jack Sheppard to open the gates of Newgate, and handed it to Thorndyke, who remarked as he took it that "they liked good, substantial keys in the days when these houses were built."

"What key is it?" I asked.

"It belongs to – or rather, it opens – the door on the landing, which I have assumed to be that of the staircase leading up to the lumber-room above which you heard Mr Weech refer to. I hope there isn't another locked door at the top. Shall we go and see?"

I assented and followed him out to the landing, speculating on his object – if he had one – in surveying the lumber-room. But I asked no question and made no comment. His proceedings in this case were getting out of my depth.

The big key seemed to fit the lock snugly and shot the bolt back with unexpected ease, but the ancient hinges groaned when Thorndyke pulled the door open and exposed the bottom of a flight of rude steps, a sort of compromise between stairs and a ladder. Only the lower steps were visible, for they rapidly faded upward into the total darkness of the chimney-like cavity, but we both noticed that they bore distinct footprints on their dusty treads. Thorndyke went first, lighting our way with the little electric lamp that he always carried, until we were near the top, when a faint glimmer from above mitigated the darkness, and increased as we ascended.

There was no landing at the top, but just a space cut out of the floor to accommodate the steps, so that we came up into the room like a couple of stage demons rising through a trap. When he reached the floor level Thorndyke stepped sideways, clear of the well, and stood motionless, peering into the dim interior. I followed him in the same way, to avoid having the dangerous staircase well behind me, and stood beside him, looking about me with mild curiosity.

It was a rather eerie place; a great, bare room, little lighter than the staircase. For, though there were three large windows, they were all closely shuttered, and what vestiges of light there were filtered in through the cracks and joints at the hinges and folds. But to our accustomed eyes the general features of the place were visible in the dim twilight; the disorderly piles of "junk," ranged along the sides of the room, shadowy forms of chairs, cupboards, baths, tables, rejected and forgotten and probably ruinous, chandeliers, lengths of water-pipe, and multitudinous indistinguishable objects, the accumulations, it might be, of a century or more. But it was not the "junk" that had attracted Thorndyke's attention. Along the clear space in the middle of the room a double row of footprints could be seen, extending from the head of the staircase and fading away into the darkness at the farther end.

"Someone has been up here comparatively recently," said he, "and went directly to the farther end either to fetch or to deposit something. Perhaps we shall be able to judge which. But before we disturb anything I think we had better take a record of these footprints. Polton has the small camera downstairs as there were one or two photographs to take. I'll just go and fetch him up. And, meanwhile, you might open one set of shutters, if you can get at the window."

He handed me his lamp, and, when I had seen him safely on to the steps, I approached the only accessible window and investigated the fastenings of the shutters. They were simple enough, consisting of a thick wooden bar resting in wooden sockets and requiring merely to be lifted out; and when I had done this I was able to pull back the shutters and let in the light of day.

191

And now I could see how the footprints had come to be so surprisingly distinct on the bare floor. In the years during which this room had lain undisturbed, the dust had been settling continuously until it now formed a thick grey mantle on every horizontal surface and the footprints were almost as clear as if they had been in snow or on a sandy shore. In some the very brads in the soles and heels could be seen.

I was still examining them and speculating on Thorndyke's unaccountable interest in them, when the staircase became brightly illuminated and my colleague appeared carrying an inspection lamp and followed by Polton with the camera slung over his shoulder and the tripod under his arm. Apparently he had his instructions, for he proceeded at once to walk along parallel to the tracks, minutely examining each footprint until he found one that satisfied him. Then he opened the tripod, fixed the camera to the attachment specially designed for the purpose, laid a foot-rule down beside the print, and proceeded to focus them both.

When he had made the exposure – carefully timed by his watch – and changed the film, he picked up the rule and moved along a few paces, when he halted by a specially clear impression of a left foot, and, having drawn Thorndyke's attention to its remarkable sharpness, fetched the camera and repeated his former procedure.

"And now," said Thorndyke, as Polton carefully repacked his apparatus, "let us see if we can find out what was the object of this visit; to take something away or to get rid of some unwanted article. The latter seems the more probable."

He followed the double line of footprints to a dark corner at the farther end of the room, where they became confused with various large objects – including a big copper bath – which had evidently been moved, as we could see by the marks on the dusty floor. Behind these, and close to the wall, was a pile of dismembered remains – a small cupboard door, a broken table-top, some odd shelves, pieces of board and fragments of some kind of box or case. A glance at the pile made it evident that the collection had been disturbed, for there were traces of finger-marks on some of the fragments and others seemed to have been wiped, while the heap, as a whole, was free from the thick mantle of dust which shrouded all the untouched objects in the room. Apparently this pile had been the object of the unknown visitor's activities.

"It is evident," said Thorndyke, "that all these things have been moved, and that they were piled up as we see them by the person who made the footprints. Now, the question is: did he take something away or did he add something to the pile? And if he added something, what is it that he added?"

"It is impossible to say," I replied, "whether he took anything away, but some of those pieces of wood at the bottom look newer than the rest, and, if they are, they are probably what he added, though it is curious that they should be at the bottom. What do you say, Polton, as a practical wood-worker?"

"If you mean those bits of a chest or case," he replied, "I should say they are not more than six months old, and the broken edges are quite fresh. Shall I get them out?"

Without waiting for an answer he scrambled over the obstructions and proceeded to lift off the upper members of the pile, handing them to Thorndyke and me as he removed them, until he came down to six pieces of board, the clean surfaces of which contrasted noticeably with the ancient grime of the objects that had been removed. When he had handed these out he scrambled back, and he and Thorndyke began a systematic examination of the fragments – rather to my surprise; for there was nothing remarkable in their appearance. They seemed to be just the remains of a broken box or case of some kind.

"What puzzles me," said Polton, who was keenly interested because he saw that Thorndyke was, "is how these pieces got broken. Sound one-inch board like this takes some breaking. It couldn't have been an accident; yet why should anyone want to break up a good piece of board?"

"What do you suppose it was, originally?" I asked. "Was it some sort of packing-case?"

"No, sir," he replied, "it couldn't have been that. The stuff is too good – prime yellow deal, excepting that bit of American white wood – and so is the workmanship. You see that there are three glued joints and they have all held. It was the wood that broke, not the joints; which means that whoever made it was a proper tradesman who could plane a joint true. Besides, all these pieces were stained on both sides and varnished on one, which must have been the outside. I should say it was a permanent case made to carry some particular thing. You see, there are three grooves in the side piece, so there were three partitions. But whatever it was meant to carry must have been pretty heavy to require one-inch board throughout. And just look at the screw-holes. Number eight screws they will have been, and plenty of them, too."

"I suppose they are all parts of the same thing?" said I.

"They seem to be," he replied, running his foot-rule along one piece and then resting them upright on the floor. "They are all one length – thirty-nine inches – and these three broken pieces fit together to make a complete top or bottom twenty inches wide, while the other two broken ones seem to make two-thirds of a similar top or bottom; and the screw-holes in them correspond to those in what must have been one of the long sides. That's what I make of them, sir."

As he concluded, he looked enquiringly at Thorndyke, who agreed that the reconstruction appeared to be correct. "But," he added, "I think we might consider them more conveniently in our own premises. I suppose you have a bit of string about you, Polton?"

"Do you propose to annex them, then?" I asked, as Polton produced the inevitable hank of string and proceeded to lash the pieces of board together.

"Yes," Thorndyke replied. "It is a little irregular, but I shall call on Weech and explain matters."

But the explanatory call proved unnecessary. For, almost as Thorndyke was speaking, we became aware of sounds from the staircase as of someone ascending the steps, slowly and by no means easily. As the sounds drew nearer we turned to see who the intruder might be, and presently there arose out of the well, first a chimney-pot hat, then a pair of spectacles, and finally the entire person of Mr Weech, complete with umbrella. When he reached the floor level he stood for a few moments gazing at us, steadily. Then he advanced towards us with an expression of something less than his usual cordiality.

"I happened to notice," he said, rather dryly, "as I passed, that the shutters of one window were open; and as the only key of these premises is at this moment hanging on the key-board in the lodge, I concluded that some person, or persons, had obtained access to the said premises without authority and by some irregular means. Apparently I was right."

"You were perfectly right, Mr Weech," said Thorndyke, "as you always are. We are entirely unauthorised intruders. I ought to have applied to you for authority to inspect this room, but as I happened to have a key that fitted the lock, and as I merely wanted to look round, I – well, I waived the formality, thinking that I would mention the matter the next time we met."

"Yes," said Mr Weech, fixing a stony gaze on the pieces of board under Polton's arm. "Quite so. Perhaps it would have been more regular to obtain the authority before the event rather than after. May I ask why you wished to inspect this room?"

Now this was precisely the question that I had been asking myself. But I had not the slightest hope of enlightenment. My learned senior was not in the least addicted to disclosing his motives. Nevertheless, I was curious to see how he would avoid this rather awkward question.

"I wished," he replied, "for certain reasons connected with my inquiries, to ascertain whether this apparently disused room is, in fact, really disused, or whether it is ever visited or made use of."

"I could have told you that if you had asked me," said Weech. "It is not. I could have told you that nobody has entered this room for several years."

"Then, Mr Weech," Thorndyke retorted, "you would have told me what is not true. For I have just ascertained that it has been entered within the last six months; and that it was entered, apparently, for the purpose of depositing these remains of an obviously new box or case."

"Which," said Weech, with a sly smile, "I see you have taken possession of and are carrying away without authority. However," he concluded with a return to his usual geniality, "I raise no objection. The things are of no value, and *de minimis non curat lex*. I don't understand what you want them for, but that is your affair. Have you finished your explorations?"

"Yes," replied Thorndyke, "we were just about to retire; and you had better let me hand you your umbrella when you are safely at the bottom of the steps."

Mr Weech gratefully accepted this offer, and, when he had closed the shutters, he embarked on the perilous descent and we followed. He lingered on the landing to wait for us, and, when Polton had let himself into the chambers, he strolled in and looked round.

"I see you are having a spring clean," said he, glancing at the vacuum cleaner. "Not very necessary, I should think, but perhaps just as well after what has happened."

He wandered through the rooms while Thorndyke retired to the bedroom – where I caught a glimpse of him making a survey of the late John Gillum's shoes – and eventually accompanied us down to the courtyard, when we departed for home and a rather belated lunch, attended by Polton with the camera and the purloined wood. We paused for a minute or so outside the entry to exchange a few final words with Mr Weech, and it was at this moment that a rather curious thing happened.

As we were standing there, almost facing the covered passage that connected the two courtyards, I saw a man come through it and appear at the arched entrance. And there he halted. But only for a moment. For, having taken a single quick glance at us, he turned about, looked at his watch, and hurried away back through the passage. It was but an instantaneous glimpse that I had of him; but yet, in that instant, it seemed to me that the man was extraordinarily like Dr Peck. Obviously, it could be no more than a chance resemblance, for we had left that gentleman established in his consulting-room waiting for the arrival of patients. But yet his was a face that one would remember, and the resemblance had certainly been rather remarkable.

I was still reflecting on the coincidence when another man came up the passage and emerged from the archway. Preoccupied as I was with the first man, I hardly noticed him, for, unlike the other, he was quite undistinctive – he might have been a solicitor's clerk or a superior type of traveller. Subconsciously, I was aware that he wore horn-rimmed spectacles, that he carried a small bag and an umbrella and that he walked with a slight limp. Only as he passed close to us on his way to the Fetter Lane gate did I become conscious of a feeling that I had seen him somewhere before; and that feeling might have been due to the fact that, as he passed us, he gave a quick look at Thorndyke, who seemed to return an instantaneous glance of recognition.

When we had shaken off Mr Weech at the door of the lodge, I raised the question.

"Did you recognise that man who passed us in the Inn?"

"Hardly," Thorndyke replied with a laugh. "Not until he looked at me. Did you?"

"I seemed to have seen him before, but I can't give him a name."

"You weren't meant to," Thorndyke chuckled. "That was our invaluable and Protean friend, Mr Snuper."

"Of course!" I exclaimed. "But I never can spot that fellow. He looks different every time I see him. But there was another man who came up the passage and who produced exactly the opposite effect. I thought I recognised him though I must have been mistaken. Did you notice him?"

"Yes," he replied. "What was your impression of him?"

"I thought he was extraordinarily like Dr Peck."

"So I thought," said Thorndyke.

"Then it was a real resemblance and not a mere illusion. But it is a queer coincidence; for, of course, the man couldn't have been Peck. The thing is impossible."

"It isn't impossible," he replied. "Only wildly improbable. He had no apparent reason for following us as he had our cards and knew where we lived. But if he had wanted to follow us, it was actually possible for him to have done it. Snuper did."

"Snuper!" I exclaimed. "You say that Snuper followed us! How do you know that he did?"

"I saw him in Whitechapel High Street as we came away from Peck's."

CHAPTER FIFTEEN

Sermons in Dust

The appearance of the party that gathered that same evening round the table in our sitting-room to examine Polton's gleanings from John Gillum's chambers struck me at the time as slightly ludicrous. And that is still my impression when I recall the scene. In the middle of the table was a collection of the labelled bags, containing the floor-sweepings, or vacuum-cleanings, from the respective rooms. Before each of the three investigators was a microscope with triple nose-piece, flanked by a large photographic dish, a jar for waste, and a small covered glass pot for "reserved specimens"; and the appointed procedure consisted in scanning the material with a very low magnifying power, examining objects of interest with the higher powers, and the preservation of special "finds" for subsequent consideration.

We began by each taking a bag and turning out its contents on to the dish; the said contents forming an unsavoury heap of the material known to housewives as "flue" – the sort of stuff that you can rake out from under a chest of drawers or a neglected bedstead. From the heap a pinch was taken up with forceps, spread out on the glass plate and rapidly inspected through the microscope. If it contained nothing of interest, it was cast into the waste jar and a fresh pinch taken.

"Are we looking for anything in particular?" I asked as I turned out my mass of flue into the dish; "or do we report everything?"

"You know what is likely to turn up in a floor-sweeping," Thorndyke replied. "We can ignore the inevitable wool fibres from the carpet, and cotton and linen fibres. Everything else had better be noted."

With this we all fell to work, stimulated at first by the hope of turning up something interesting or curious. But, as the things which we were to ignore appeared to be the only things discoverable, the occupation began presently to pall, and I don't mind admitting that I found it rather tedious. By the time that my heap was reduced to a mere handful, I had observed – apart from the ubiquitous fibres – nothing more thrilling than a few minute particles of what looked like broken glass.

"Yes," said Thorndyke, when I mentioned my discovery, "I have found some, too. It isn't quite obvious what they are, but we had better keep them. Possibly we may come on a larger fragment with a more definite character."

Accordingly, I picked out the grains with fine forceps, aided by a pointed sable brush, moistened at the tip, and deposited them in the glass pot. Having done this, I was about to reach for a second bag when Polton announced a discovery.

"I've found a hair," said he. "It looks like a moustache hair, but it must have been a funny sort of moustache. It seems to have been dyed. Must have been. But did you ever see a man with a violet moustache?"

He passed the slide to Thorndyke, who confirmed the discovery.

"Yes," said he, "it is a moustache hair – a rather fair one – dyed black."

"But," protested Polton, "it's violet."

"Hardly violet," said Thorndyke. "A dull, bluish purple, I should call it. That is the appearance of a single hair, seen under the microscope by a strong transmitted light. Seen in a mass by the naked eye and by reflected light, it would appear jet black."

"Would it, now," said Polton. "Think of that. The microscope is a wonderful instrument, but you mustn't believe all that it tells you."

He took back his slide, and picking the hair out daintily with his forceps, deposited it in the glass pot, while I, encouraged by his success, began an attack on a fresh bagful of flue.

This time, I had considerably better luck. At the first cast I struck an object which looked like a coarse and rather irregular thread of glass; and, as I could make nothing more of it than that, I passed the slide to Thorndyke for a "further opinion."

"Ha!" said he, when he had taken a look at it, "now we know what those other particles were. This is undoubtedly a fibre of silicate wool, or slag-wool, as it is sometimes called. It is made from the slag from the smelting furnaces, which is really a kind of crude glass."

"And what is it used for?"

"For a variety of purposes. As it is cheap and incombustible, is unaffected by acids – excepting hydrofluoric acid – or by moisture, and is a bad conductor of heat, it is useful for packing, and especially for packing hot or cold substances."

"I wonder what Gillum used it for," said I.

"We had better defer speculations and inferences," Thorndyke replied, "until we have examined the whole of the material"; and with this he took a fresh bag and resumed his observations.

My good fortune did not stop at the slag-wool fibre. Presently there came into the field of the microscope a hair, obviously a scalp hair and probably from a man's head, though the sex is not so easy to decide in these days of shingling and Eton cropping. At any rate, it was a short hair and had been recently cut; and as it had been dyed the same dull purple colour as Polton's moustache hair, it was reasonable to infer that it came from the same person. Accordingly, I considered it attentively in its bearing on that person's natural characteristics. The dye did not, of course, extend to the root. There was a space of, perhaps, a twelfth of an inch above the neck of the bulb – representing the growth since the last application of the dye – which was of the natural colour; and from this I was able to infer that the man was of a medium complexion, inclining to be fair rather than dark; that the hair had been originally of a somewhat light brown tint. This was also Thorndyke's opinion, based on an inspection of my "find" and of another scalp hair which he had found in his own material.

"So," he concluded, "we now know that this was a rather blond man who wore a moustache. What we don't know is whether he shaved his chin or wore a beard."

"Begging your pardon, sir," Polton interposed, "I think we do. I have just found another hair, a thick, rather wavy one. It isn't a moustache hair and it doesn't look like a hair of the head. I think it must be a beard hair. Will you just take a look at it, sir?"

Thorndyke took the slide from him, and having made a brief examination of the specimen, decided that it was undoubtedly a beard hair; a decision that I confirmed when the slide had been submitted to me.

"So," said I, "we now have a fairly complete picture of this man, and the question is: Who can he have been? Do you think it possible that Benson could have been mistaken? That what he took for natural black hair was really dyed hair?"

"No," Thorndyke replied, decidedly. "That is impossible for two reasons. First, Benson had known Gillum since his boyhood – practically the whole of his life. But the second reason is absolutely conclusive. You remember that Benson described Gillum's hair as being slightly streaked with grey; that is to say, there was a slight sprinkling of white hairs among the black. And he expressly stated that he had examined the hair of the corpse to see whether the proportion of white hairs had increased, and that he found them apparently unchanged. Moreover, there are the hairbrushes that we found in the chambers – apparently Gillum's brushes. I have examined some of the hairs from those brushes and found them to be natural black hairs with a very few white ones. So these dyed hairs are not Gillum's, but those of some other person who had frequented those chambers."

"Yes," I agreed, "that is perfectly clear. I wonder who he can have been. Is it possible that we have struck the actual villain – the blackmailer, himself?"

"It seems quite possible," Thorndyke replied; "but we had better get on with our search and see what the other bags have to tell us."

We worked on steadily for another hour, making no further comments but transferring all new finds to the glass pots. By this time we had dealt with all the bags excepting the two small ones containing the material from the sweeper and the coal-bin; and the net result was, five more dyed hairs, one natural black hair and seven fibres of slag-wool. Of the two small bags, I took the one labelled "coal-bin," while the other was divided between Polton and Thorndyke, the latter taking the extracted dust while Polton was awarded the fibrous mass that he had so industriously combed from the sweeper's brushes.

As for my material, I approached it with no expectation of any discovery, whatever. In a coal-bin one may reasonably anticipate the presence of coal. And coal there certainly was. When I turned the bag out into my dish, the contents presented an undeniable heap of coal-dust, a trial sample of which I took up with the blade of my pocket-knife and sprinkled over the glass plate. But when I applied my eye to the microscope, the appearance of that sprinkling came as a considerable surprise. Undoubtedly there was coal galore; a scattered mass of black, opaque, characterless fragments. But everywhere in the spaces between the particles of coal, the glass surface was covered with a multitude of slag-wool fragments of all sizes from quite considerable lengths of thread down to mere grains of glassy dust. I announced my discovery to Thorndyke and passed the slide to him, but when he had examined it, with evident interest, he handed it back to me with no comment beyond the suggestion that it seemed desirable to preserve the whole of the material from the bin.

His own portion of sweeper dust yielded nothing but a single dyed hair and a few particles of slag-wool, but Polton's combings from the sweeper-brushes were quite rich in material so far as quantity went. But they contained nothing new. There were no less than seven hairs, all dyed, one or two threads of slag-wool, and a number of particles of no interest such as crumbs of bread or biscuit, tobacco ash, a piece of cotton thread and some shavings from a lead pencil. The combings were, in fact, but a sort of condensed epitome of the general "floor-sweep."

"Well, Thorndyke," I said, as I rose and stretched myself, "I think my brilliant and original idea has justified itself by the results. But I'm hanged if I understand them. The gent with the purple hair has deposited well over a dozen samples in different parts of the premises, including the sweeper, whereas John Gillum has dropped only one. But Gillum was the resident. The other fellow could only have been a visitor, even if Gillum put him up. It seems quite inconsistent, unless we assume that the purple chappie was moulting; which I am not prepared to do."

"No," Thorndyke agreed, "we shall have to find some explanation more plausible than that. And now, if you and Polton will clear away the remains while I jot down a few particulars of the evening's work, we shall all be ready for supper. I presume," he added, addressing Polton, "that the contingency has been foreseen."

It had. There could be no doubt of that, though Polton's only reply was a smile which converted his countenance into the likeness of one of good Abbot Mendel's famous wrinkled peas. But even that smile understated the gorgeous reality. A cold boiled fowl and a ham were mere incidents in the Sybaritic menu. As Polton deposited "the goods" on the table with another smile – which left the Mendelian pea nowhere – I was once more impressed by the queer contradictions in his character. For Polton, himself a spare-living, almost ascetic little man, was apt, when Thorndyke was concerned, to manifest his devotion by developing a sort of vicarious gluttony. He would contemplate Thorndyke's robust appreciation of good food and wine with the sympathetic joy of a fond mother administering delicacies to a beloved child.

Of course, we made him join us at the feast. He could not be allowed to go away and feed in the laboratory, as he had proposed; and when he had taken his place at the table and I had filled his glass with Chambertin (I believe he would rather have had ginger beer), the cup of his happiness was literally full. It was a glorious ending to what had been, for him, a red-letter day.

When the banquet had passed through its final stages and Polton had retired triumphant to his own dominions, Thorndyke and I drew up our chairs to a rather premature but highly acceptable fire and filled our pipes. And, naturally, my thoughts reverted to the evening's researches and their rather surprising results. My colleague had seemed unwilling to discuss them at the time, though we had few secrets from Polton in these days, but now that we were alone, I thought he might be less reticent, and accordingly I ventured to reopen the topic.

"The presence in Gillum's chambers," I began, "of that mysterious stranger with the dyed hair seems to be a new discovery. At least, it is new to me. Have you any idea who he was?"

"Yes," Thorndyke replied. "I think that the facts in our possession enable us to form a fairly definite opinion as to his identity."

"You say 'the facts in our possession.' Shouldn't you rather say 'in your possession'?"

"Not at all," he replied. "Whatever is known to me is known also to you. As to the actual observed facts, we are on an equal footing. Any difference between us is in their interpretation."

This was so manifestly true that it left me nothing to say. It was the old story. I lacked that peculiar gift that Thorndyke had by virtue of which he was able to perceive, almost at a glance, the relations of facts which appeared to be totally unrelated. For some time I smoked my pipe in silence, reflecting on this unsatisfactory difference between us. Presently I remarked:

"You have put in a good deal of work on this case. Does it seem to you that you have made any real progress?"

"Yes," he replied. "I am quite satisfied."

"And have you marked out any further line of investigation?"

"No," he answered. "I am making no further investigations. I have finished. The details can be filled in by the police."

I looked at him in amazement. "Finished!" I exclaimed. "Why, I imagined that you had hardly begun. Do you mean to say that you have identified the blackmailer?"

"I believe so," he replied. "Indeed, I may say that I have no doubt. But there is one point at which I have an advantage over you which must be redressed at once."

He rose, and, opening the cabinet in which the "exhibits" connected with the case were kept, took out two sheets of paper, which he laid on the table.

"Now," said he, "here is the blackmailer's letter, which you have seen; and here is a sheet of paper which you have also seen. We found it in the tidy in Gillum's bedroom with a little bolt and nut wrapped in it. Do you remember?"

"I remember. But I thought it was the bolt and nut that were the objects of interest."

"So they were at the time," said he. "But I had a look at the paper, too, and then that became the object of interest. I have flattened it out in the press to get rid of the creases, so that it is now easy to compare it with the letter. See what you think of it."

I took up the two sheets and compared them. It was at once obvious that they were very similar. Both had been torn off a writing-pad; they appeared to be of the same size; the paper seemed to be the same in both – a thin, rather low-quality paper, ruled with very faint lines. When I held them up to the light, I could see in each a portion of what was evidently the same watermark; and the ruled lines were exactly the same distance apart in both.

"Your point," said I, "is that these two pieces of paper are identically similar. I agree to that. But is the similarity of any great significance? Writing-pads such as these sheets were torn from are made by the thousand. There must have been thousands of persons using pads indistinguishably similar to these at the time when this letter was written."

"That is perfectly true," Thorndyke agreed. "But now make another comparison. I put the two sheets of paper together, thus, both face upwards, as we can tell by the watermark. Now, see if all four of their edges coincide."

"So far as I can see, they all coincide perfectly."

"Very well. Now I turn one sheet over face downwards and again put the two together. Can you still make all four edges coincide?"

I tried, but found it impossible. "No," I replied. "They agree everywhere but at the bottom. One of them must be a little out of the square."

"Not one of them, Jervis," he corrected. "They must be both equally out of the square since all four edges coincided when they were both face upwards. And in fact they are. Test each of them with this set-square. You see that, in each, the bottom edge is out of the square with the sides, and in both to the same amount. I measured them with a protractor and found the deviation in both to be just under one degree. The reasonable inference is that they are both from the same pad."

"Reasonable," I agreed, "but not conclusive. The whole batch of pads must have presented the same peculiarity of shape."

"True," he admitted. "But consider the probabilities. Either these two sheets were from the same pad, or they were from two different pads in the possession of two different persons. Now, which is the more probable?"

"Oh, obviously, as a mere question of probability, they would appear to be from the same pad. But you seem to be suggesting that the blackmailer was Gillum himself; which is so improbable that it cancels the other probabilities. I shouldn't admit that the coincidence in the shape of these sheets is enough to support such an extraordinary conclusion."

"I agree with you, Jervis," he rejoined. "The coincidence alone would not justify that conclusion. But it is not alone. From facts known to us both I had already concluded that the blackmailing letters had been written by Gillum himself. The evidence of these two sheets is merely corroborative. But, as corroboration, it is enormously weighty."

"When you speak of facts known to us both," I said hopelessly, "you leave me stranded. I know of no such facts. But apparently you have worked out a complete case. What is your next move?"

"I am sending Miller the report of the inquest on Gillum's body and informing him that I propose handing the case over to him. That will probably bring him here by tomorrow evening at the latest to get the particulars. Then I shall, in effect, lay a sworn information."

"An information!" I exclaimed. "But against whom? You say that the blackmailer is a myth – that Gillum pretended to blackmail himself. But Gillum is dead; and if he were not, he would have committed, in effect, no legal offence. It was a pretence – according to your assertion; but it was not, in a legal sense, a fraud."

"Now, Jervis," said he, "tomorrow evening I shall show you the suggested indictment before Miller sees it. But I should like you, in the interval, to make a final effort to work this case out for yourself. You have all the facts. Turn them over in your mind without reference to any preconceived theory, and read Mortimer's narrative once again. If you do that, I think you will be forced to the conclusion that I shall propound to Miller."

I could do no less than agree to this. But I foresaw the inevitable result. Doubtless, I had all the facts. But alas! I had not Thorndyke's unique power of inference and synthetic reasoning.

CHAPTER SIXTEEN
The Disclosure

A telephone call shortly before midday making an appointment for eight o'clock in the evening, informed us that Mr Superintendent Miller had "caught on." Indeed, he was distinctly curious and would have liked a few particulars in advance, but as his call was answered by Polton, in Thorndyke's absence, these were not available. I sympathised with Miller and should have "liked a few particulars" myself; for I had re-read Mortimer's narrative before going to bed and cogitated on the case all the morning, and was as much in the dark as ever.

I saw little of Thorndyke during the day, for he went abroad alone, and even seemed to make a point of doing so. But we went out together in the evening for a rather early dinner at a tavern in Devereux Court; and it was on our way home that I had the unique experience of recognising Mr Snuper. We were just about to enter through the little iron gate that leads from Devereux Court into New Court when a man emerged from a doorway in the former and came along at a quick pace behind us. He followed us into New Court and there overtook us, and as he passed ahead, I observed him, though with no particular attention, noting, in fact, no more than that he was a nondescript sort of person and that he carried a large parcel.

It was this parcel that brought him to my notice; for, when he had got some little distance ahead, he seemed to get into difficulties with it and nearly dropped it; whereupon he halted to make some readjustments, allowing us to pass him. And it was at this moment, when he turned his face towards us and the light from a lamp fell on him, that I suddenly realised who he was.

Almost at the instant of the recognition Thorndyke seemed to change his direction. He had appeared to be heading for the passage that leads through into Essex Court; but now he turned sharply to the right and led the way down into Fountain Court, which he crossed to the left into Middle Temple Lane, following the Lane down as far as Crown Office Row and passing along the latter until we emerged into King's Bench Walk. And all the way I could hear the footsteps of Mr Snuper padding along behind us, and still, to judge by the occasional stoppages, wrestling with his parcel. When we came out into Kings Bench Walk he passed us once more, and, turning to the right, made for the pavement at the lower end, where presently he vanished into one of the entries.

It was a mysterious affair for the man appeared to be shadowing us; which was a manifest absurdity. I was about to seek enlightenment from Thorndyke when he forestalled my enquiries by producing from his pocket a small folded paper which he handed to me.

"That," said he, "is a copy of the statement that I am going to hand to Miller. You had better look through it before the interview so that you may be in a position to join in the discussion."

I took the little document very gladly; for it would have been rather humiliating if I had had to expose my ignorance to Miller. And it was none too soon; for even as we passed in at our entry, fully five minutes before our time, I caught a glimpse of the superintendent bearing down on us from the direction of Tanfield Court.

I hurried up the stairs to my bedroom and eagerly took out the paper, all agog to learn what Thorndyke's conclusions were. My expectations had been of the vaguest, but whatever they may have been, a glance at the little document blew them to the winds. I read it through again and again, hardly able to believe my eyes. For what it affirmed was not only astounding, it was bewildering and incredible. If the statement that it set forth was true, I had never even begun to understand the nature of the problem.

Slipping the paper back into my pocket, I ran down to the sitting-room where I found Miller already established in an easy chair with a big whisky and soda at his side and a cigar of corresponding size between his fingers. He greeted me with an affable smile as I entered and struck a match by way of getting the cigar going.

"Well, Doctors both," said he, "here we are again with another prime mystery in the offing. But I can't imagine what it may be."

"You have read the report of the inquest on John Gillum?" Thorndyke asked.

"Yes," replied Miller. "I haven't had time to read Mortimer's screed, but I have gone through the inquest carefully; and I have come to the same conclusion as the jury – a perfectly straightforward and obvious case of suicide. And I suppose I am wrong. Isn't that the position?"

"Yes," Thorndyke replied, "at least, that is my position."

"You are not suggesting that it was a case of murder?"

"I am not suggesting anything," replied Thorndyke, producing a small sheet of paper from his wallet.

"I am making a perfectly definite statement. This is what I say, and what I am prepared to prove; and you can have it in the form of a sworn information if you like."

With this he handed the paper to Miller, who took it, opened it, and read through the short statement. Then he read it through again, with deep attention and much wrinkling of the brow. Finally, he laid down his cigar and faced Thorndyke with an air of perplexity.

"I don't quite understand this," said he. "Of course the dates are all wrong. Clerical error, I suppose."

"The dates are perfectly correct," Thorndyke assured him.

"But they can't be," the superintendent protested.

"It's an absurdity. What you say is that you accuse Augustus Peck, a registered medical practitioner, that he did, on the night of the 17th of September, 1928, at 64, Clifford's Inn, London, maliciously and feloniously kill and murder one John Gillum. Do you say that you really mean that?"

"Certainly, I do," replied Thorndyke.

"But, my dear doctor," Miller protested, plaintively, "the thing that you are alleging is an impossibility. Gillum's body was discovered on the 18th of July, 1930. That is nearly two years after the date which you give as that of the murder. "You admit that?"

"Of course I do," Thorndyke replied. "It is the simple fact."

"But the thing is impossible," persisted Miller. "You are alleging, in effect, that the body which was discovered had been dead nearly two years."

"Not only in effect," said Thorndyke. "That is my definite statement."

The superintendent groaned. "But, doctor," he urged, "that statement is not reasonable, and what is more, it isn't true. It is contrary to all the known facts. That body was examined by a very competent medical witness who deposed at the inquest that it had been dead from six to eight days."

"*Appeared* to have been dead from six to eight days," Thorndyke corrected. "That is what he said, and I agree to the appearance."

"Very well," said Miller. "Appeared if you like. But the time he stated was about correct, for the man had been seen alive only ten days previously by Mr Weech; and Mortimer had seen him alive only a few days before that."

"My position is," said Thorndyke, "that neither Weech nor Mortimer had ever set eyes on John Gillum."

"Never set eyes on him!" exclaimed Miller. "Why, they both knew him intimately, and had known him for – "

He paused suddenly. Then, directing an intent look at Thorndyke, he added, slowly: "Unless you mean – "

"Exactly," said Thorndyke. "That is what I do mean. Weech and Mortimer and Penfield knew a certain man by the name of John

Gillum. But he was not John Gillum. He was Augustus Peck, made up so far as was necessary to play the part. And he played the part successfully as long as it was possible; and when it became impossible, he quietly disappeared leaving John Gillum's body to carry on the illusion."

Miller was profoundly impressed, but he was evidently not convinced, for he returned to the charge with further objections.

"You say he left the body on view when he disappeared. Then he must have had it in his possession. Where was it all that time?"

"It was lying hidden in a large coal-bin in the chambers at Clifford's Inn."

"But how was it that it didn't – well, you know, a dead body tends to undergo a good deal of change in two years. But the doctor said that it looked as if it had been dead not more than eight days. How do you account for that?"

"My dear Miller," said Thorndyke, "we live in a scientific age; an age in which natural processes are largely under our control. We can, if we please, prevent dead bodies from decomposing. And we do. In the Paris Morgue, bodies which have not been identified are now put into storage and kept, in a perfectly fresh state, ready for further inspections. I don't know how long they are kept, but, physically, there is no limit to the possible time."

"Yes," said Miller, "I see. Of course, you have got an answer to every objection. You would have. I might have known that you wouldn't propose an impossible case. But now, doctor, let us come down to the immediate business. As I mentioned when I phoned, I am not free tonight. In fact," he added, looking at his watch, "I must be off in a few minutes, but I should like to fix things up before I go. You have given me the substance of the case, a sort of sketch of an indictment. Now, I needn't tell you that that's no use even if you swore to it and signed it. Before I can make an arrest, I must have enough evidence to establish a *prima facie* case. When can I have that evidence? The sooner, the better, if we are not to risk a misfire."

"I agree with you as to the urgency of the matter," said Thorndyke, "for I suspect that our friend, Peck, has smelt a rat. I have him under close observation, but I fancy he has me under observation, too."

"The devil, he has!" exclaimed Miller. "I don't like that. What do you mean by having him under close observation?"

"I have got Snuper and a couple of assistants watching him night and day. You know Snuper?"

"Yes," replied Miller, "a capital fellow, a genius in his own line. But he doesn't meet the present case. He has no *locus standi*. He couldn't make an arrest unless he caught Peck committing some overt criminal act. And we don't want that. You had better give me his address and then I can detail one or two of our men to take over or act with him."

Thorndyke wrote the address on a slip of paper and handed it to the superintendent, who put it into his note-case and then resumed:

"We musn't let the grass grow, doctor. Watching is all very well, but we ought to get that gentleman under lock and key. If your statement is true he must be a pretty slippery customer. When can I have that evidence?"

" Can you come in tomorrow evening?" Thorndyke asked.

"Yes," was the reply. "I've got the whole evening free."

"Then," said Thorndyke, "what I propose is this: I ask you to arrange, if you can, for Anstey to lead for the prosecution, as he is used to working with me."

"The choice of counsel doesn't rest with us," replied Miller. "The Director of Public Prosecutions decides that, subject to the Attorney General. But I expect the Director will be willing to appoint Mr Anstey as you will be the principal witness. What then?"

"I shall assume that Anstey will be appointed and I shall get him to meet you here tomorrow night. I know that he will be able to. Then I shall lay before you a complete scheme of the evidence. How will that do?"

"It will do perfectly," replied Miller.

"I should like, also, if you agree," said Thorndyke, "to have Benson and Mortimer here. We can rely on their secrecy and discretion."

The superintendent was inclined to demur to this proposal. "It doesn't seem to be quite in order," he objected. "They will both be witnesses."

"They are not witnesses yet," retorted Thorndyke. "And you want to know what your witnesses are prepared to say and swear to. But apart from that, I think they may be able to give us some valuable help by answering questions on matters of fact."

"Very well," Miler agreed. "I don't much like it, but it's your funeral."

With this, he finished his whisky, and having been provided with a fresh cigar, rose to take his leave.

"And, look here, doctor," he said, as he shook hands; "don't you go taking too much outdoor exercise. If this fellow has rumbled you, it's a case for minding your eye and seeing that you don't make a target of the principal witness for the prosecution. We shall want you when the day comes, and for that matter I expect you'll want yourself. Keep an eye on him Dr Jervis, and by the same token, keep an eye on his invaluable coadjutor."

He shook hands again, and having lit the new cigar, bustled away. And as his footsteps receded down the stairs, we heard him apparently trying to whistle and smoke at the same time.

CHAPTER SEVENTEEN

A Symposium

The instinctive sense of simple hospitality which was the gift alike of Thorndyke and his devoted follower Polton, tended to impart a pleasant informality to what were essentially professional conferences. I noted it, not for the first time, when, on the evening following Miller's visit, we gathered round a cheerful fire to "hearken to the evidence" that my colleague had promised to expound to us. To an onlooker we should have seemed more like a party of cronies who had assembled for gossip and the exchange of "yarns" than a gathering of lawyers and police concerned with the detection and punishment of a capital crime.

Nevertheless, the attention of us all was concentrated on the business of the evening; and when Polton had provided for the comforts of all the guests, and, having placed on the table three wooden objects, one resembling an elongated brush-box and two shorter, upright boxes, had retired to the adjoining office (leaving the communicating door ajar) and the social preliminaries appeared to be getting unduly prolonged, Miller interposed with the blunt suggestion that Thorndyke "had better get on with it"; whereupon my colleague began his exposition without further preamble.

"I have considered," said he, "the most suitable way in which to present the scheme of evidence in this case and it has seemed to me that the best plan will be for me simply to follow the line of my own investigation; to produce to you the items of evidence in the order in which they became apparent to me. Do you agree to that, Anstey?"

"Undoubtedly I do," replied Anstey, "as that will be the order in which they will be best presented to the jury in the opening address."

"Very well," said Thorndyke, "then I will proceed on those lines. You have all read the report of the inquest on John Gillum's body and Mortimer's narrative of his relations with Gillum, and as those documents contain all the facts with which I started, I can refer to those facts as matters known to you all.

"The original inquiry was concerned with the identity of the persons who had blackmailed Gillum. That was the problem that Benson submitted to me. But though he did not contest the suicide – which seemed to have been conclusively proved – I could see that, at the back of his mind, there was a feeling that things were not as they appeared; that, behind the apparent facts of the case, there was something that had never come to light.

"Now, as soon as I began to look into the case, I had precisely the same feeling. The whole affair had a curiously abnormal appearance; so much so that it at once suggested to me the question whether the ostensible facts might not cover something of an entirely different nature. There were unexplained discrepancies. For instance, of the large sum of money that had been thrown away, no less than three thousand pounds had been money saved by Gillum in the course of his business in Australia. One naturally asked oneself how such a man ever came to have any savings at all. The result of these reflections was that I postponed the blackmailing problem and proceeded to a critical consideration of the case as a whole.

"Now, the outstanding fact of the case was that a sum of about thirteen thousand pounds had disappeared in less than two years. It had been drawn out of the bank in cash – in currency notes and, by special request, in notes which had been circulated and of which the serial numbers were unrecorded, and which it was,

217

therefore, impossible to trace. The explanation offered for this procedure was that this untraceable money was to be used for payments to blackmailers and for discharging gambling debts.

"So far as the blackmail was concerned, this explanation was reasonable enough; but not in connection with gambling. Why should a man take such elaborate precautions to make it impossible to trace the money with which he had paid his gambling debts? There was no reason at all. Gambling debts can be, and usually are, paid by cheque. Why not? Such payments are not unlawful and there is no valid reason for secrecy. Therefore I decided that the explanation offered was not adequate. It was really no explanation at all. But if one rejected the explanation, the original problem remained. Thirteen thousand pounds had disappeared, leaving no trace. Of that sum, about two thousand could be accounted for by blackmail. But what of the remaining ten or eleven thousand? Had it really been gambled away, or was it possible that the gambling was a mere pretext, covering the disposal of the money in some other way? Having regard to the inadequacy of the explanation, I was disposed to suspect that this might be the case; and this suspicion was strengthened by the fact that Mortimer – the only witness as to the gambling – had no first-hand knowledge of the matter at all. His belief on the subject was based on what Gillum had told him; and in reading his narrative I could not but be struck by the way in which Gillum had posed as a reckless and desperate gambler and the pains that he had taken to impress that view of himself on Mortimer.

"From this it appeared that there was really no evidence that any gambling – on a considerable scale – had ever occurred; and there was a reasonable suspicion that it was a myth invented and maintained to cover some other kind of activity. But what kind of activity? The entertainment of that suspicion raised a new problem. What reason – apart from blackmail – could a man have for drawing large sums of money out of his bank in such a form that it could never be traced? I turned this question over in my mind and I could think of only one case in which a man might behave in this way. It was that of a man who had got temporary control of another man's banking account. Such a man – obviously a dishonest man – would naturally seek to get permanent possession of the money under his temporary control. But how could he do this? He could not simply draw cheques in his own favour and pay them into another bank, for those cheques could be traced and the money recovered. And the same would be true of bank notes of which the serial numbers were known. The only plan possible to him would be that adopted by Gillum. He would have to draw the money out in untraceable cash. That cash he could pay into another bank or store for future disposal.

"That was the only alternative that I could think of to the gambling theory, and it appeared to be totally inapplicable to the present case. For the banking account was Gillum's own banking account and the money in the bank was his own money which he had himself paid in. What object could he have had in transferring that money to another bank, or hoarding it? I could imagine none.

"Nevertheless, I did not immediately abandon the idea, for the alternative – the gambling theory – was almost as difficult to accept; and there was a general queerness and abnormality about the case that disposed one to consider unlikely explanations. There was the suicide, for instance. Apparently it was a genuine suicide, but there had been no positive proof that it was. Actually, it was possible that it might have been a skilfully arranged murder. Accordingly, I decided to consider this imaginary case in detail and see whether it was as completely inapplicable as it seemed.

"First, I asked myself the question, how would it be possible for a man to get control of another person's banking account? Apparently, the only possible method would be that of personating the real owner. The case, then, which I had imagined involved, necessarily, the idea of personation. Accordingly, I set up the working hypothesis of personation and proceeded to apply it to the case of John Gillum to see how it fitted and whither it led.

"Now, when one sets up a hypothesis and proceeds to test it and deduce consequences from it, if the hypothesis is untrue it very soon comes into conflict with known facts and leads to manifestly false conclusions. But when I began to apply the personation hypothesis to the Gillum case, instead of conflicting with known facts it developed unexpected agreements with them; instead of evoking fresh difficulties, it tended to dispose of the difficulties that had at first appeared.

"The theory of personation involved the idea of two separate individuals; the personator and the personated. It was thus necessary, for the purposes of the argument, to decompose the person, John Gillum, into two hypothetical individuals: John Gillum of Australia and John Gillum, the tenant of Clifford's Inn. They had been assumed to be one and the same person. We had now to see what evidence there was to support that assumption.

"But the first glance showed that there was no evidence at all. The identification had been illusory. In effect, there had been no identification. Benson had identified the body as that of Gillum of Australia – whom we will call simply Gillum – but he had not identified it as that of the tenant of the Inn – hereinafter called the Tenant. And Weech and Mortimer and Bateman gave evidence referring to the Tenant, but their evidence furnished no proof that the body was the Tenant's body. There were really two sets of witnesses. There was Benson, who knew Gillum but had never seen the Tenant; and there were Weech, Mortimer, Bateman and Penfield, who knew the Tenant but had never seen Gillum.

"Thus the personation hypothesis did not conflict with the known facts. No evidence had been produced to prove that Gillum of Australia and Gillum the Tenant were one and the same person. Therefore, it was possible that they were different persons. But as soon as this possibility was established, two rather striking agreements with it came into view. Let us consider them.

"First there was the time of Benson's arrival in England. He arrived immediately after the suicide; or, to put it the other way round, the suicide occurred immediately before his arrival. But not only was it known that he was coming; the actual date on which he would arrive was known. Now, on the personation theory, the

Tenant of the Inn was some unknown stranger who was falsely personating John Gillum. He could not possibly have confronted Benson, for the fraud would then have been instantly detected. He would have had to clear out. But if he had simply disappeared, suspicion would have been aroused, whereas the presence of the body and the apparent suicide continued the illusion of the personation. Indeed, it did much more. For when Benson had identified the body as that of John Gillum, and that body had been accepted by Mortimer and Weech as that of the Tenant of the Inn, the personation seemed to be covered up for ever beyond any possibility of discovery.

"The second striking agreement is the state of the Tenant's finances. At the inquest it transpired that deceased was absolutely penniless and that he had no expectations whatever. The last payment of the purchase money for the sheep farm had been paid into the bank and drawn out. All the money was gone and there was no more to come.

"Now see how perfectly this agrees with the personation theory. What could have been the object of the personation? Obviously, to obtain possession of the ten thousand pounds paid for the sheep-farm and the three thousand forming Gillum's savings. Well, at the time of the suicide this had been done. The whole sum of thirteen thousand pounds had been drawn out. There was not a penny left in the bank and there were no more payments to come. Then the personator's object had been achieved and there was no occasion to continue the personation any longer. It was time for the personator to disappear; and disappear he did. Benson's arrival simply accelerated matters and fixed the date of the disappearance.

"So far, then, the results seemed to be positive. The more the personation theory was examined, the more did it appear to agree with the known facts. But there were other difficulties; and the most formidable of them was the body. If there had been personation, it must have begun immediately on Gillum's arrival in England and it had been maintained for nearly two years. But where was Gillum all this time? He could hardly have been alive; but if he was dead his body must have been preserved and kept somewhere ready to be produced at the psychological moment. For the pretended suicide must be assumed to have been an essential feature of the scheme.

"Of course, there was no physical difficulty. It is quite easy to preserve a dead body indefinitely, given the suitable means and appliances. The problem was how it could have been done in the circumstances of this particular case. But even while I was puzzling over this difficulty I received sudden enlightenment from Mortimer's narrative. You will remember that, on the occasion of his first visit to Clifford's Inn, he had a very remarkable seizure. From his admirable description it is evident that his symptoms were exactly those of rather acute carbonic add poisoning; and he notes that the room – the larder, or storeroom – in which the attack occurred was noticeably cold. Further, he mentions that, just before the attack, he had been shovelling up coal from a bin which he describes as occupying the whole of one side of the room.

"Now this combination of low temperature with a considerable concentration of carbonic acid gas was very impressive. It immediately suggested the presence, somewhere in the room, of a substantial quantity of solid carbonic acid; and as the gas appeared to issue from the coal-bin, it seemed probable that the solid acid was contained in the bin. But if that bin was of the size that Mortimer's description conveyed, it would be easily large enough to contain a dead body."

"But Mortimer says that it was full of coal," Anstey objected.

"It appeared to be," Thorndyke corrected. "But there might be room for a false bottom under the coal, and still room for the body under that. A false bottom would be a necessary feature of the arrangement."

"I think," said Anstey, "that we had better be clear about this solid carbonic acid. You know all about it, but we don't. Could you just give us a few particulars as to what it is like and what is its bearing on the case?"

"A very few particulars will be enough for our purposes," replied Thorndyke. "I need not go into the method of production. The substance, itself, is a white solid, rather like block table salt. It is simply frozen carbonic acid, just as ice is frozen water. And as ice has a maximum temperature of 0 degrees Centigrade – commonly known as freezing point – and becomes a liquid if it is raised above that temperature, so solid carbonic acid – sometimes called carbonic acid snow, from its resemblance to ordinary snow – has a temperature of minus 79 degrees Centigrade, that is, 79 degrees Centigrade below the freezing point of water. But, unlike ice, it doesn't melt into liquid when its temperature is raised. It changes directly into gas, intensely cold gas, which hangs round it and protects it from contact with warm air. If we were to place a block of it on the table, it would simply dwindle in size until it disappeared altogether, but it would not leave the slightest trace of moisture. And it would dwindle remarkably slowly; for the gas into which the solid snow changes is a very heavy gas and a specially bad conductor of heat."

"Thank you," said Anstey. "That is quite clear. There is only one other question. Is carbonic acid snow obtainable without any great difficulty?"

"It is quite easy to obtain," replied Thorndyke. "The snow is now manufactured on a considerable scale, as it is used for a variety of purposes. It is sold in two forms; the standard twenty-five-pound blocks, which are the most commonly used, and smaller, four-pound blocks, made principally for use in ice-cream tricycles to keep the cream frozen. You can buy the blocks, retail, without any difficulty, and they will probably be delivered in packages enclosed in insulating material such as silicate wool, or slag-wool. Is that clear?"

"Perfectly clear," replied Anstey. "Now we can return to the argument."

"Well," Thorndyke resumed, "you will now see the significance of the presence in this very cold room of free carbonic acid gas in conjunction with a very large coal-bin. It suggested a perfectly simple and efficient method of preserving a dead body for a practically unlimited time, and it thus disposed of what had been my principal difficulty. I was so much impressed by this new agreement that I abandoned the rather academic attitude in which I had considered the personation theory. For that theory was no longer a merely tenable hypothesis. It agreed with the facts much more closely than did the gambling theory. Indeed, it offered a perfectly reasonable explanation of those facts, which the gambling theory did not; and I began to feel that it was probably the true explanation of those facts.

"But there were still some difficulties; not very formidable ones, but still they had to be disposed of before the personation theory could be definitely accepted. There was, for instance, the question of resemblance and disguise. How far was it necessary for the personator to resemble John Gillum, and what amount and kind of disguise would be required to secure the resemblance? Now, it is important to realise that no very exact likeness was necessary. However much the personator had been like the personated and however skilfully he had been disguised, it would have been impossible for him to deceive any person who had really known John Gillum. On the other hand, in the case of persons like Penfield, Mortimer and Weech, who had never seen John Gillum, no resemblance at all was necessary.

"Yet, for other reasons, the personator would have had to bear a general likeness to the man whom he personated. The production of the body, for instance, must have been an essential part of the scheme; and its production involved the idea of its identification as the body of the Tenant. Therefore, the Tenant must have been so far like John Gillum that the body of the one could be mistaken for the body of the other. But for this purpose it would be sufficient for the two men to be alike in their salient characteristics.

"Now what were the salient characteristics of John Gillum? He was a tallish man – about five feet ten – with blue eyes, black hair and beard and upper front teeth which were very conspicuously filled with gold. He also, apparently, spoke with a slight Scotch accent. In all these respects, as we know from Mortimer's narrative, the Tenant resembled John Gillum; and as the body presented the salient physical features common to the two men, it was naturally recognised by Mortimer and Weech as the Tenant's body in the single hasty glance that they took.

"But how many of those characteristics must have been natural to the personator? Evidently, the stature and the eye-colour must have been real. The personator would have to be a rather tall man with blue eyes. But the other characteristics could have been produced artificially. Whatever might have been the natural colour of the hair and beard, they could easily have been dyed black. The only real difficulty would have been the teeth. But, even in their case, there would be no physical difficulty. It would be perfectly easy for the personator to have his front teeth filled with gold, or, preferably, covered with a removable gold plating; while, if he should happen to have false teeth, there would be no difficulty at all. He would simply have a duplicate plate made with gold-filled teeth in front. But either of these methods would require the services of a skilled dentist; and that was the fatal objection to them. They would involve an accomplice. But, since the personation would not only be a serious crime in itself, but would seem inevitably to involve a previous murder, the existence of an accomplice would constitute an appalling danger.

"However, as I have said, there was no physical impossibility or even any difficulty, and, accordingly, I accepted it provisionally as a practicable method, reserving further consideration of it until more facts were available.

"The next question was, assuming personation to have occurred, who could have been the personator? On this point, neither the report nor Mortimer's narrative gave any help beyond furnishing certain dates. But one saw at a glance that the personation would have had to begin almost on the very day of Gillum's arrival in England; for, immediately afterwards, the Tenant appeared in the Inn and at Penfield's office. From this it seemed to follow that, since Gillum knew nobody in England, the personator must be somebody who had travelled with him from Australia to England. Of such persons, only two were known to me. I learned from Benson that Gillum had had two cronies on board the ship; the purser, Abel Webb, and the ship's surgeon, Dr Peck; and as both these men had left the ship on its arrival in England, either of them might possibly have been the personator. There was no positive reason for suspecting either; but both fulfilled what appeared to be the necessary conditions. They had been Gillum's shipmates during the voyage, and both had left the ship for good at about the same time as Gillum.

"Of these two, poor Abel Webb was clearly out of the picture; and even if he had not died, he would still have been impossible as the personator. He was the wrong size, the wrong shape, and the wrong colour. There remained, then, Dr Peck, the only person known to us whom we could possibly suspect; and it was desirable to get into touch with him for two reasons; first, to ascertain whether his size, form, and colour were such as to render the personation possible, and second, to get some information from him respecting the passengers and personnel of the ship.

"This brings us to the end of what I may call the first stage of the inquiry. Up to this point I had been concerned with the original sources of information; with a critical examination of the report of the inquest, of Mortimer's narrative, and of the information supplied by Benson. The inquiry had started as a search for a hypothetical blackmailer. But examination of the material had brought into view a problem of an entirely different character; and the result of the first stage of the inquiry was the establishment of a *prima facie* suspicion of false personation against some person unknown. We now enter on the second stage, that of investigation proper; the search for new facts which might either confirm or rebut that suspicion."

CHAPTER EIGHTEEN

Circumstantial Evidence

"Hitherto," Thorndyke resumed after a brief interval, "I have followed the enquiry in the chronological order of events. But now, as we are dealing with an investigation *ad hoc*, it will be more convenient to consider it in terms of the particular items of evidence brought to light, maintaining the chronological sequence only so far as is practicable. The first stage of the inquiry had left us with certain matters of fact which required verification and certain others which had to be ascertained. Among the former was Mortimer's description of the coal-bin. From it I gathered that the bin was amply large enough to contain a human body, and I assumed that it probably had a false bottom to preserve an empty space under the coal. These were matters of vital importance; for if the bin should prove to be too small, or to have been kept completely filled with coal, my theory as to the disposal and preservation of the body would fall to the ground.

"Accordingly, my first proceeding was to get the keys of Gillum's chambers from Benson. Then Jervis and I went across to the Inn and made a preliminary tour of inspection. To come at once to the bin, we found it, as Mortimer had said, to occupy the whole length of the wall, and, on measurement, it proved to be of these dimensions: eight feet long, thirty inches from back to front and twenty-nine inches deep. It appeared to be brimful of coal; but when I took soundings through the coal with my stick, I came to a firm bottom nine inches from the top. Thereupon, we shovelled the coal away to one end, when there was brought into view a tray, or false bottom, of stout board, which we ascertained to be of the full length and width of the bin. A transverse crack showed it to be divided into two equal parts, and each half was furnished with a sunk iron ring. We brushed away the coal dust with a brush that hung close by – apparently for this purpose, as its hair was full of coal dust – and then lifted one half by means of the ring, when we found that the tray was of comparatively new wood, that it was supported by small wooden blocks which had been screwed on to the sides of the bin, and that its removal disclosed a cavity underneath nineteen inches deep and of the full length and width of the bin.

"Here, then, was a receptacle with a capacity amply sufficient to accommodate, not only a body, but also the mass of insulating material that would be necessary if that body was to be kept in a frozen state. The question of possibility was disposed of. It remained to ascertain whether there was any positive evidence that a body had actually been preserved in the manner which I have suggested.

"Having finished with the bin, we examined the little room in which it was situated. It had evidently been intended for a larder or storeroom and it had no fireplace or other outlet and only one window, which was about two feet six inches high by eighteen inches wide. But this window was fixed permanently as wide open as possible. The lower sash was pushed right up and secured in position by two wooden supports screwed to the jambs. Further, we found that a row of holes, each one inch in diameter, had been bored in the foot of the door; which, together with the permanently opened window, must have maintained a very free draught of air through this small room. And I may say that we learned from Mr Weech that the holes had been made and the window supports and the false bottom of the bin added by the Tenant – or rather by the Tenant's agent – at the beginning of the tenancy."

"The Tenant's agent!" exclaimed Miller. "Who was he?"

"Ah!" replied Thorndyke, "who *was* he? That is a very curious and interesting question. But the answer to it does not belong to this part of the story. We shall go into that at a later stage. At present we are considering the evidence bearing on the subject of refrigeration by means of solid carbonic acid.

"To resume: In the course of our survey of the chambers we found several mouse-holes which had been most carefully and efficiently stopped with Portland cement. There appeared nothing remarkable in this, as the Tenant had evidently taken pains to keep all food in metal or earthenware containers so as to avoid harbouring mice. But later, in conversation with Mr Weech, we got quite a new light on the matter. It seemed that he had learned from the lady who conducts the typewriting establishment on the ground floor that, up to the time when Mr Gillum came to the Inn, the house swarmed with mice to such an extent that she had seriously considered giving up her premises. But, as soon as Mr Gillum's tenancy began, the mice suddenly disappeared, and disappeared so completely that not a single mouse was ever to be seen. While we were talking, the lady herself came out of her office and fully corroborated Mr Weech's statement. Then it occurred to me to ask her whether her premises were still free from mice; to which she answered with natural surprise that they were not. Since Mr Gillum's death they had begun to reappear.

"This was a very remarkable fact. The disappearance of the mice might reasonably have been assumed to be due to the Tenant's care to keep all food covered, and especially to the very thorough stopping of all mouse-holes. But their reappearance after Gillum's death made it clear that there must be some other explanation; for the holes were still stopped and all the conditions were precisely the same. The disappearance had evidently been due to something connected with the Tenant himself."

"Yes," Anstey agreed, "that seems to be so. What do you wish us to infer from this fact?"

"I suggest that the behaviour of the mice is exactly what we should expect in the conditions which I have postulated. Let us see what those conditions would be. I assume that the bin contained a dead body kept frozen by means of solid carbonic acid. New supplies of the snow would be constantly fed into it, and this snow would be slowly but continually converted into the gas. Thus the bin would be filled with the icy gas which would be constantly increasing in quantity and finding its way out. Now, carbonic acid gas is an extremely heavy gas. It behaves almost like a liquid. You can fill a tumbler with it and you can pour it from one tumbler to another as if it were water. Like all gases, it diffuses upwards into the air, but while it is pure, it falls by its own weight.

"Thus, as the bin filled up with the gas, this would be constantly overflowing on to the floor and would tend to pour down through the cracks between the boards and especially to trickle down through the mouse-holes into the burrows, so that these and the spaces between the joists would be full of the gas. In such conditions, it would be impossible for mice to exist. They would all be either killed or driven away.

"My conclusion is, therefore, that these facts are completely consistent with the presence of solid carbonic acid in the bin and that there seems to be no other explanation."

"Yes," said Anstey, "I am prepared to admit that. What do you say, superintendent?"

"I agree," replied Miller, "that it seems to establish the point, subject to the condition that the theory is supported by other evidence."

"That is all I ask," rejoined Thorndyke. "This is only a single point. The charge against Peck rests on the whole body of evidence. But I have not completed the case for the carbonic acid snow. While we are on the subject, I may as well produce the rest of the evidence.

"Shortly after our visit to the Inn, Jervis and I made a call at the premises of the Cope Refrigerating Company. My object was twofold. First, I wanted to verify a description of Abel Webb, which, I may say, I did. But we will leave the case of Webb for consideration later. The other object was to ascertain whether the man known as John Gillum had ever had any dealings with Copes. I had reason to believe that he had obtained at least a part of his supplies from them and in this it turned out that I was right. For, when I interviewed a very intelligent gentleman named Small, I learned, among other interesting matters, that a man corresponding to the description of the Tenant had, on at least one occasion, purchased from him some four-pound blocks of solid carbonic acid; which, I also learned, were delivered in parcels roughly packed in insulating material. I ask you to note the insulated packing since the material used for that purpose is almost invariably silicate wool, or, as it is sometimes called, slag-wool.

"With regard to the identification, I may say that it does not seem to admit of any doubt. The man whom Mr Small served resembled the Tenant, as Mortimer has described him, not only in size and general appearance but even in respect of his teeth. Mr Small particularly noticed the extensive filling of the front teeth with gold and commented on the disfigurement that it caused.

"This completes the case for the carbonic acid snow, and you see that it is based on a remarkable body of evidence. There is the illness of Mortimer, exactly resembling carbonic-acid poisoning, occurring in a very cold room and close to the bin; the mysterious affair of the mice; and the direct evidence of the purchase by the Tenant of carbonic acid snow in blocks of a size exactly suitable for use in the manner that I have suggested. I submit that it constitutes conclusive proof that the Tenant had something in that bin which he was preserving by means of carbonic acid snow."

Both Anstey and Miller appeared to be profoundly impressed by this demonstration and the latter expressed the hope that the rest of the evidence would be equally convincing.

"Perhaps," said Anstey, "one might hesitate to use the word 'conclusive'; but even if one should not put it quite as high as that, still, it is difficult to imagine any alternative explanation. And I take it that the refrigeration theory is supported by other evidence."

"It is amply supported," Thorndyke replied; "and I shall now proceed to the consideration of some of the other evidence. To return to the chambers. My primary object in visiting them was to verify the dimensions of the bin. But there was another question to which I was anxious to find an answer, but had very little expectation of finding it. That question was whether or not the Tenant had artificial teeth. It was an important question, for there would obviously be great difficulty in fixing a false gold filling to natural teeth, though it would not be impossible. But with a dental plate there would be no physical difficulty at all. The only difficulty would be that the making of such a plate – obviously for the purpose of disguise – would involve the very dangerous complicity of a dentist. But that danger would exist equally in the case of 'faked' natural teeth.

"However, I had better luck than I had expected. In a rubbish basket I found an empty bottle labelled 'Cawley's Cleansing Fluid,' which is a sort of detergent lotion, principally used for filling the bowls in which wearers of false teeth put their dental plates at night so that they may be clean by the morning. Then, on the chest of drawers which served as a dressing-table, I found an earthenware bowl labelled 'Super-fatted Shaving Soap.' But, as the Tenant, whoever he was, wore a beard, he evidently had no use for shaving soap. And, in fact, the bowl was empty. But there were in it traces of the cleansing fluid, plainly recognisable by the smell. Apparently, the bowl had been used as a receptacle for a dental plate during the night; and, in confirmation of this, we found in the larder the handle of a dental plate brush, which had been used as a spatula for mixing Portland cement.

"Here, again, you will probably demur to the use of the word 'conclusive'; but the fluid, the bowl, and the brush, taken together, furnish very convincing evidence that the Tenant wore a dental plate. But if he did, he could not have been John Gillum, since it is known that Gillum had a full set of natural teeth and certainly did not wear a denture. I may add that we found a worn-out toothbrush of the ordinary kind and a small tin which had contained a toothpowder such as is used for cleaning natural teeth. So that, judging by these observations, it would appear that the occupant of these chambers was a man who had some natural teeth but also wore a dental plate. And I repeat, that man could not have been John Gillum.

"We made some other discoveries which I shall not deal with now. Among them was a piece of paper which was so exactly like the paper on which the blackmailer's letter was written that it was nearly certain that it was derived from the same writing-pad. But I leave that for your consideration later with the other letters and documents. You will probably decide to have these examined by an expert; and, at any rate, they form no part of my present case.

"The next stage of the investigation deals with the identity of the personator. I have already explained that Dr Peck was the only person known to me who could possibly have personated John Gillum. There was no positive reason for suspecting him; but he fulfilled the conditions that made the personation possible, and it was necessary that some enquiries should be made concerning him. Accordingly, I began by looking him up in the Medical Directory; and then the interesting fact emerged that he was not only a qualified medical practitioner, but also a fully qualified dentist. So that, in his case, the difficulty of getting the counterfeit gold teeth made did not exist. He could do whatever was necessary himself. This was, of course, no evidence against him; but it was another rather striking agreement.

"Dr Peck's permanent address was given as Staple Inn; and thither Jervis and I went to pursue our enquiries. We were fortunate enough to find the porter of the Inn a rather talkative person, so that a few discreet questions, just to help his conversational powers, soon put us in possession of all the facts that we wanted. And very striking facts some of them were. I need not reconstitute the conversation but will give you the substance of what we elicited.

"In the first place, we were glad to learn that Dr Peck was in England. He had just returned from a long voyage; a very long voyage, for it had taken him close upon two years. And what instantly struck me when I made a rough estimate of the dates was that he appeared to have started on his voyage just about the time when John Gillum's tenancy at Clifford's Inn began and that he had returned a short time after John Gillum's death. This must be admitted to be a very remarkable coincidence. And there were certain other circumstances that were at least rather singular. For instance, he went away with a full beard and moustache and came back clean-shaved; and he had not come back to Staple Inn although he had chambers there ready to receive him, and which he had always kept so that he should have some place to come to when he returned from a voyage. Instead of this, he had gone straight, as soon as he had landed, to some premises in Whitechapel where he had put up a brass plate and started in practice.

"All this was rather odd; but, of the facts disclosed by the porter's rambling discourse, I was most interested in certain preparations which Dr Peck had made before he had started on his voyage. These included a pair of portable bookcases in which he proposed to carry his travelling library, packed for transport and yet instantly available for use. Of these, the porter was able to give us fairly exact particulars; and, as he gave us the name and address of the man who had made them, I had – and took – the opportunity to fill in the precise details. And, as those details are highly material to the subject of our inquiry, I ask you to give very particular attention to them, both in regard to dimensions and construction.

"These bookcases were very ingeniously planned. The idea was that they could be filled with books in their proper order on the shelves and could then be closed by simply screwing on the fronts; when they would be ready for transport either by rail or sea. On arrival at their destination, they could be stowed in the doctor's cabin and the fronts removed, and they would be ready for immediate use. Furthermore, they could, if necessary, be quite easily taken apart for storage. There were no dovetails or other permanent joints. The parts were simply screwed together with well-greased screws, and when these had been withdrawn, the cases could be resolved into a collection of boards which would lie flat for stowage and take up a minimum of space.

"Now, as to the alleged disposal of these cases. They were delivered by the maker, Mr Crow, of Baldwin's Gardens, at Peck's chambers in Staple Inn, and, so far as I could learn, were never seen again. The statement is that Peck took them with him when he started on his voyage – he is said to have travelled overland to Marseilles and embarked there on a foreign ship – to have had them in use throughout that voyage, and finally to have sold them, with the books that they contained, to the captain of the ship from which he landed at Marseilles.

"That is the story. Now we return to the cases. They were made throughout of one-inch board, excepting the three equidistant shelves, which were of half-inch stuff and slid freely in grooves. Each case was three feet three inches high, twenty inches wide and fourteen inches deep. The depth, you notice, was inconveniently great, as the books which would stand in the nine-inch spaces between the shelves would not be more than six or seven inches deep. But the dimensions as a whole interested me profoundly. I wonder whether you notice anything significant in them."

"I certainly do not," said Anstey, glancing enquiringly at Miller, who shook his head with a hopeless expression; "in fact, I cannot imagine what possible bearing these cases can have on the matter that we are considering."

"Their significance," Thorndyke explained, "lies in the possibility of their conversion into something totally different. Each is three feet three inches high; the two placed end to end with the shelves and the adjoining ends removed, would form a long case with an interior capacity of six feet four inches by eighteen inches by thirteen inches. Such a case would hold quite conveniently the body of a tall man; and it would go into the coal-bin with eighteen inches to spare in the length, ten inches in the width and fifteen inches in the depth; of which ten inches must be subtracted for the false bottom, leaving a space of five inches. The two halves of the case could be secured together firmly enough for practical purposes by screwing to each side a short board such as one of the shelves."

Anstey looked at me with a somewhat wry smile. "This is ingenuity with a vengeance," said he. "It almost looks like perverted ingenuity; for even the Great Unraveller must admit that there are plenty of quite innocent containers which would accommodate a human body perfectly well. The mere suitability is of no evidential value excepting as corroboration of evidence showing that it was in fact so used."

"Exactly," Thorndyke agreed. "But at present I am merely proving that such a container existed. The other evidence comes later."

"But," Anstey objected, "the container appears to have been disposed of at Marseilles and to be, at present, somewhere on the high seas."

"My thesis," Thorndyke rejoined, "is that Peck's voyage was a myth; that the cases never went to sea at all, but were simply dismantled and conveyed piecemeal to Clifford's Inn. But may I suggest that my learned friend should allow me to produce my evidence in the appointed order and to defer argument until the facts have been presented?"

"I am sat upon," said Anstey. "Deservedly. I admit it. Let the demonstration proceed."

"I think," said Thorndyke, "that you hardly appreciate the extraordinary suitability of these cases for the use that I suggest. I thought it might be so, and I have accordingly asked Polton to make a set of scale models – two inches to the foot – to help your imaginations, and, if necessary, to produce in court. The models are on the table, but we shall have to find Polton to demonstrate the method of conversion."

The necessity of finding Polton, however, did not arise, for even as Thorndyke spoke, he emerged unblushingly from the office and enquired if anything was wanted. Miller greeted his arrival with a broad grin and bluntly accused him of eavesdropping; to which Polton made no reply beyond a bland and crinkly smile, but, producing from his pocket a pair of forceps and a watchmaker's screwdriver, bore down on the models.

"We will begin with the coal-bin," said Thorndyke, picking up the long, narrow box and handing it to Polton, "and I shall refer to the real dimensions, of which all these models are exactly one-sixth – two inches to the foot. This bin is eight feet long by thirty inches wide and twenty-nine inches deep. On opening the lid, you see the false bottom with a cavity above it nine inches deep – deep enough to accommodate a good supply of coal. But I need not continue the description. You can see the details for yourselves."

Our friends watched with profound interest while Polton picked up with his forceps the little sunk rings in the false bottom and lifted the latter out in its two halves, displaying in the cavity underneath a number of flat pads of cotton wool, which he picked out and laid on the table.

"What are those little pads?" Anstey asked.

"They represent the pads of insulating material," Thorndyke replied. "You will see their use presently. The actual pads were almost certainly made of silicate wool."

Having passed the bin round, Polton took up one of the model bookcases, and with his screwdriver extracted the little screws from the front, when the latter came off, displaying the interior with its three shelves. When he had repeated the operation on the other one, and passed both round for inspection, Thorndyke replaced them on the table.

"You have seen these cases," said he, "in their ostensible character as bookcases, and you will agree that their appearance is quite convincing. Now we shall see the transformation."

It was very interesting to observe how complete the transformation was. Polton began by drawing out the shelves, which slid freely in their grooves. Then, having extracted the lower screws, he let the bottom of each fall out. Next, laying the two cases on their backs, he brought the two open ends together, when they formed a long, narrow box, similar in shape to, but smaller than, the bin. Then he took two of the shelves, each of which was perforated by six holes, and laying them on either side of the long box across the junction of the two halves, fixed them in position with screws. Lifting the box, he demonstrated that the two cases had now become united to form a single structure with a continuous cavity.

When this had been passed round and examined, he took up one or two of the pads and laid them on the floor of the bin. Then he placed the box inside the bin, packed some more of the pads at the ends and sides, put the fronts on, laid the rest of the pads over them, and finally replaced the false bottom, which dropped comfortably into its place on top of the pads.

"You now see for yourselves," said Thorndyke, "how perfectly these cases are adapted to the purpose that I have suggested. The adaptability seems too perfect to be accidental. Not only is the long case exactly the right size and shape to accommodate the body of a tall man; it is also exactly the right size and shape to lie in the bin with enough space around it for the insulating pads and still room enough for the false bottom. There is not an inch to spare in any direction. Those cases have the appearance of having been carefully designed for this very purpose. And I submit that they were."

We were all deeply impressed by the demonstration, and Anstey expressed the sentiments of us all when he remarked:

"You were wise, Thorndyke, to have these models made. Seeing is not only believing; it is understanding. No amount of verbal description could have conveyed the extraordinary fitness of these cases for the purpose that you suggest. I take off my hat to you and Polton. I am even prepared to take off my wig; but I will defer that until you have produced the rest of the evidence."

The demonstration completed, Polton made as if to retire to the office, but before he could escape, Miller grabbed him and pulled him into a chair.

"What's the use of pretending, Mr Polton?" said he. "You know you have been listening all the time. Better sit here and listen in comfort"; which view, being endorsed by Thorndyke, was duly carried into effect.

"The fact that we have established," said Thorndyke, "is that these bookcases were capable of being converted into a receptacle which would hold the body of a tall man and which would fit the interior of the coal-bin. The objection to the suggestion that they were so used is that they are said to have been taken overseas and never brought back. I now proceed to deal with that objection.

"On the floor above Gillum's chambers at Clifford's Inn is a large lumber-room which has been used by the authorities of the Inn for storing old furniture and other bulky rubbish left by outgoing tenants in their chambers; but I learn that it has been out of use and undisturbed for some years. Now, it occurred to me, as a bare possibility, that the Tenant might, at the end of his tenancy when his proceedings would necessarily be somewhat hurried, find himself burdened with some objects which he would not wish to leave in the chambers but which he had no opportunity to take away or destroy; and, in fact, I had these very cases in mind. Accordingly, I decided to take a look round the lumber-room and see if anything appeared to have been deposited there; and did so, assisted by Jervis and Polton."

"Wasn't the room locked?" asked Miller.

"It was," Thorndyke replied. "A common builder's lock which could have been turned with a stiff wire. We actually used a provisional key."

Miller chuckled delightedly. "A provisional key," he repeated. "I must remember that expression. Sounds so much better than skeleton key. Yes, doctor; and, of course, you did find something."

"We did," Thorndyke replied. "Perhaps Polton will be so good as to produce our gleanings for your inspection."

Thereupon Polton retired to the office and immediately returned bearing a bundle of pieces of board which he laid out in order on the table.

"These," said Thorndyke, "we found hidden under a pile of much older lumber. The wood is obviously comparatively new and

239

the broken edges quite fresh. Let us fit those broken edges together and see what results. Here, for instance, are three pieces which fit together perfectly and form a rectangle with finished edges. It is three feet three inches long by twenty inches wide, the exact dimensions of the front or back of Peck's bookcases. Moreover, there are twelve countersunk screw-holes, each of which fits a number eight screw, and those screws are not only the same size as those in Peck's cases, but have the same distribution; namely, four equidistant holes on each side and two at either end.

"Then, here are two pieces which evidently formed part of a similar structure. They fit together exactly and their screw-holes are the same size and have the same distribution. Finally, here is a complete piece which corresponds completely with the sides of Peck's cases. It is three feet three inches long, thirteen inches wide, it has three equidistant half-inch grooves, and the screw-holes in the edges correspond exactly in size and position with those on the back and the front. But there is in addition an extremely interesting feature. At one end of this side are three holes which have been made by screws, showing that something, not part of the original structure, had been screwed on to the outside. Now, if you will look at Polton's model of the long case, you will see that the two halves are secured together by screwing on one of the shelves on either side, forming a sort of fish-plate; and I submit that these screw-holes afford evidence that a precisely similar procedure had been followed in the cases of which these fragments are part."

Miller and Anstey were both greatly impressed. Nevertheless, the latter objected:

"What you have proved, Thorndyke – and proved most conclusively – is that these fragments are parts of some structure which was exactly like one of Peck's bookcases. But you haven't proved that it actually was one of his cases."

"No," Thorndyke agreed, "I admit the objection, and I shall now proceed to dispose of it. I sent Polton with the complete back to show it to Mr Crow, who made Peck's cases. He shall tell you what Mr Crow said."

"I went to Mr Crow," said Polton, "and showed him the three pieces and we put them together on his bench. Then he looked up his book and compared the dimensions and the size and position of the screw-holes, and he said that the three pieces made up something that was exactly like the back or front of one of the cases that he had made for Dr Peck. I told him that we knew that, and I asked him if he couldn't be more definite. So he took another look at the pieces, and then he noticed this bit of American white wood," – here Polton pointed out the strip of foreign wood – "and that brought the job back to his memory. He remembered that he had then had a small piece of good American white wood left over from another job, and as the case was going to be stained, he thought he might as well use it up. So he did; and by that piece of white wood he was able to swear, and he was prepared to swear, that these pieces were actually the back of one of the cases that he had made for Dr Peck."

"I think that is good enough," said Miller; and, as Anstey agreed, the evidence as to the cases was accepted as complete, so far as it went.

"We are agreed, then," said Thorndyke, "as to the identity of the cases, and that somebody brought them from Staple Inn to Clifford's Inn. The next question that we have to settle is: Who brought them? Fortunately, we have some fairly conclusive evidence on that point. I have mentioned that the lumber-room had not been disturbed, or even entered, for at least several years. Apart from Weech's statement, this was evident from the appearance of the place. Everything in it, including the floor and the steps leading up to it, was covered with a thick, even coating of dust, almost like a thin covering of snow. Now, when we started to ascend the steps, we could see on them the very distinct footprints of some person who had gone up a short time previously; and when we reached the room, we could see a double line of footprints extending from the head of the steps to the farther end of the room – actually, as we found later, to the pile of lumber under which the fragments of the cases were hidden.

"As the dust must have been something like an eighth of an inch thick, these footprints were extraordinarily distinct. Like footprints in the snow, they were actual impressions, having a sensible depth and showing some detailed characters of the feet that made them; and their distinctness emphasised the fact that there was no trace whatever of any other footprints. As it happened that Polton had a camera with him in the chambers below, I asked him to photograph two of the footprints, a right and a left, selecting those which showed the most detail.

"This he did, laying a foot-rule beside each print to give a measuring standard and including the rule in the photograph. I produce here enlargements of the two photographs of the footprints, and I also produce photographs to the same scale, likewise including a foot-rule, of a pair of house-shoes which I found in the bedroom of the chambers and which seemed to correspond to the footprints. If you examine the two sets of photographs, you will see that the correspondence is quite unmistakable, even to the position of the brads in the soles and heels, which, as well as the various dimensions, you can verify with a pair of dividers and the foot-rule. I have done this, and I am prepared to swear, and to prove, that the footprints were made by these shoes. Whence it follows – since there were no other footprints, and the cases must have been deposited after the last previous visit to the room – that the fragments of the cases must have been put where we found them by the Tenant, whoever he may have been. Do you agree to that?"

"It is impossible not to agree," replied Anstey. "The proof is absolutely conclusive."

"Then," said Thorndyke, "we will consider the cases as disposed of, and I shall now pass on to another investigation which yielded evidence on two separate aspects of our inquiry. On Jervis' suggestion, I decided to make a systematic collection of dust from the floor of Gillum's chambers. The collection was carried out by Polton with a vacuum cleaner; and he not only kept the dust from the different areas separate, but, finding that the Tenant had used a carpet-sweeper, he extracted the dust from that and also carefully combed out its brushes. The same evening, we formed a sort of committee, with three microscopes, and went through the entire collection of dust. I need not trouble you with details of the procedure. Of the objects brought to light by our microscopes, there were only two kinds that are of interest to us; human hairs and particles of silicate wool."

"Silicate wool!" exclaimed Miller. "That sounds rather significant."

"It does," Thorndyke agreed, "but the hairs are, perhaps, even more illuminating, so we will deal with them first. We found, in all, nineteen hairs, of which seventeen were from the scalp, one a moustache hair and one a hair from a beard. Three of the hairs were taken by me from the pillow on which the head of Gillum's corpse had rested. Two of these were natural black hairs and one was white. We found, in the dust from the sitting-room floor, one other natural black hair. Of the other fifteen hairs, all were rather fair hairs dyed black."

"My eye!" exclaimed Miller. "Fifteen dyed hairs out of a total of nineteen! I suppose it isn't possible that they could have been Gillum's?"

"It is quite impossible," replied Thorndyke. "Not only were the black hairs from the pillow natural black, but one of them was white. And Benson will tell you that John Gillum's hair, both during life and after death, was black streaked with white. I need not point out to you that the presence of white hairs is incontestable evidence that the hair is not dyed."

"Let us, then, consider what we are compelled to infer from these dyed hairs. And first as to their number. Of the four natural hairs, three were from the pillow and had evidently come from the head of the corpse, while the fourth came from the floor of the same room. It had probably been detached when the corpse was moved either to or from the couch. At any rate, it was only a single hair. But there were fifteen dyed hairs collected from a fairly clean and habitually well-swept room. The unavoidable inference is that

243

the owner of those dyed hairs was the person who occupied those chambers. Of Gillum himself there is no trace excepting four hairs, three of which certainly, and the fourth most probably, came from the corpse. But there are abundant traces of a rather fair man with hair, moustache, and beard dyed black. In other words, of a man who was not Gillum, but who was disguised so as to resemble Gillum."

"Amazing!" said Anstey; "and all this impressive evidence from a few handfuls of dust!"

"Yes," said Thorndyke, "but we have not finished with the dust. Besides the hairs, we found, as I told you, particles of silicate wool. In the living-room they were few in number and mostly broken quite small by having been repeatedly trodden on. But Polton made a separate operation of the coal-bin; and when we came to examine the dust from that, we found it to consist entirely of coal and silicate wool. And the wool was not only present in large quantities; it consisted to a considerable extent of recognisable lengths of fibre."

"I need hardly ask," said Anstey, "whether you have preserved these tell-tale dust particles for production in evidence?"

"They have all been kept intact," replied Thorndyke, "so that they can be shown direct as well as by enlarged photographs; indeed, all possible exhibits have been carefully preserved. And now, you will be relieved to hear, I am getting near to the completion of my case. Only two more points of evidence remain to be considered, and I will take first that relating to the beginning of the tenancy at Clifford's Inn. I had the particulars from Mr Weech, and this is what he told me.

"One morning, towards the end of August, 1928, a man came to the lodge to enquire about some chambers that were to let. He thought that Number 64, which was empty, might suit him, so he was given the keys, and presently he returned and announced that the chambers would suit him and that he would like to take a lease of them. But he then explained that he was not taking them for himself but that he was acting as agent for a gentleman of means who was, at the moment, abroad, but wanted a set of chambers made ready for him to come home to. He was fully authorised to execute an agreement, to furnish references, and to pay whatever deposit might be thought necessary.

"As he produced a written authority from his principal, Mr John Gillum, and referred Weech to Mr Gillum's solicitor and banker, and was willing to pay a half-year's rent in advance, Weech accepted the tenancy. A provisional agreement was signed, the money paid, the keys handed to the agent to enable him to proceed with the furnishing and repairs, and the transaction was closed with one exception. The agent suggested that the references should not be taken up until Mr Gillum came into residence."

"Why did he stipulate that?" asked Anstey.

"His explanation – quite a reasonable one – was that Mr Gillum had lived abroad for some years and had done all his business with his solicitor and banker by correspondence and that neither of them knew him personally. This satisfied Weech, and the agent was allowed to take possession of the chambers and get on with the furnishing and the repairs. And it is interesting to note that those repairs included the false bottom to the coal-bin, the fixed window in the larder, and the holes in the larder door."

"What was the agent's name?" Miller asked.

"Weech is a little obscure on that point. He thinks it was either Baker or Barker or Barber."

"But," said Anstey, "there is the agreement with his signature."

"That agreement was destroyed when Gillum arrived and a new one executed."

"Then," said Anstey, "there was the agent's cheque. That ought to be traceable."

"There was no cheque," replied Thorndyke. "The money – twenty-five pounds – was paid in five five-pound notes."

"Then there must have been a receipt."

"There was; but it was made out to John Gillum. Mr Baker, as we will call him, left no trace whatever. But let us finish with Mr Weech's story.

"About three weeks after the signing of the agreement – on the seventeenth of September, to be exact – John Gillum came to the Inn, and the circumstances of his arrival were these, as related to Weech by the night porter: That night, between nine and ten, someone knocked at the gate, and when he had opened the wicket, he saw two gentlemen, one of whom was Mr Baker, whom he had seen once before. Accordingly he let them pass through and they went up the passage. Presently Mr Baker came back alone and said: 'By the way, that gentleman is Mr Gillum, the new tenant of Number 64. You might mention to Mr Weech that he has come.'

"The porter did so in the morning, and Mr Weech then called at the chambers. The door was opened by the man thereafter known as John Gillum; Mr Weech introduced himself and a new agreement was then executed and the old one torn up. So the tenancy began, and the mysterious Mr Baker was seen no more."

"How long did he stay that night?" asked Miller.

"There is no answer to that question. The night porter saw him go back into the Inn, and so far as I can learn he was never seen again."

"Did you get any description of him?" Miller asked.

"Yes," replied Thorndyke. "Weech described him as a tallish man, about his own height – that is, about five feet ten – fair complexioned, with light-brown hair, a tawny beard and moustache and blue eyes; apparently a gentleman with a pleasant, persuasive manner and a rather engaging personality. You notice that if his fair hair and beard had been dyed black, he would have seemed to correspond completely to Mortimer's description of the man whom he knew as John Gillum.

"I now come to the last stage of the investigation, and I must admit that I approached it with some anxiety. For if the result should not be what I expected, I should be left with the greater part of the inquiry to be begun afresh with no data to work from. I had assumed that Dr Augustus Peck was the personator of John Gillum, and that Mr Baker and Dr Peck were one and the same person. If these propositions were true, it followed that Dr Peck must be a man of about five feet ten inches in height, of blond complexion with blue eyes and light-brown hair. Furthermore, I should expect him to have some false upper front teeth. If he did not agree with this description, then he could not be the man; and I should have to look for another person to fill the role of personator.

"I need not describe our interview with him at length. When Jervis and I called on him, we were confronted by a rather spare man about five feet ten inches in height with light-brown hair and blue eyes. As he was clean-shaved, the colour of his beard was not ascertainable; but it could reasonably be assumed to agree with that of his hair. While we were conversing I was able to observe his teeth, as he had a short upper lip and showed them a good deal; and it was quite easy to see that there were several false teeth in the upper jaw and that these included the four upper incisors – the very teeth that had contained the gold fillings.

"Thus, you see, Dr Peck's physical characteristics agreed in every respect with those of the Tenant of the Inn, of the man whom Mortimer knew as John Gillum, and of the mysterious Mr Baker; and I affirm his actual identity with those persons. And I further affirm that, in view of that identity and of the body of evidence which I have presented, I have proved that Augustus Peck is the man who, on the night of the seventeenth of September, murdered John Gillum and thereafter falsely personated him at the Inn and elsewhere.

"And, as we say in court, that is my case."

CHAPTER NINETEEN
Re-Enter Mr Snuper

For sometime after Thorndyke had finished speaking, a profound silence prevailed in the room. We were all deeply impressed by the ingenuity with which the complicated train of evidence had been constructed and presented. And yet there was probably the same thought in the minds of us all. Despite the completeness and conclusiveness of the demonstration, the case seemed to be pervaded by a certain unreality. Something seemed to be lacking.

It was Anstey who broke the silence and put our thoughts into words.

"You have presented us, Thorndyke," said he, "with a most remarkable scheme of circumstantial evidence. I have never heard anything finer of its kind. The proof of your thesis appears to be absolutely conclusive, and it would seem almost ungracious for me to offer any criticisms. But, after all, the superintendent and I are practical men who have to deal with realities. It will fall to us to translate this scheme of evidence into action. And we are at once confronted with a serious practical difficulty. I dare say you realise what it is."

"Your difficulty, I presume," replied Thorndyke, "is that the whole case, from beginning to end, rests on circumstantial evidence."

"Exactly," said Anstey. "If we arrest this man and charge him with the murder, we have not a particle of direct evidence to produce against him. Now, the late Lord Darling once said that circumstantial evidence is more conclusive than direct evidence. But juries don't take that view, and I think the juries are right. If we bring this man to trial on the evidence that you have given us, we may easily fail to get a conviction; and there is even the possibility that some fact might be produced by the defence which would upset our case completely. You see the difficulty?"

"I do," replied Thorndyke. "I have seen it all along; and I have provided the means to meet it. Hitherto, I have dealt exclusively with the train of circumstantial evidence because that is really what the case rests upon. But I have borne in mind the need for some direct evidence to impart a quality of concrete reality to the other evidence; and I am able to produce two items which I think will satisfy you and Miller. The first is a set of photographs which Polton has prepared and which I will ask him to hand to me that I may show them to you."

Here Polton paid another visit to the office and came back carrying a small portfolio which he delivered to Thorndyke, who took from it two ten-by-eight mounted photographs and resumed:

"These two photographs are enlargements from small originals lent to me by Mr Benson. The first is a group taken by Mr Benson, himself, in Australia, and enlarged from the negative. I chose it because it had been taken in the shadow of a building and the faces were quite well lighted. What do you think of it, Benson? Is the likeness fairly good?"

Benson took the photograph from him, and having looked at it, replied:

"It is an excellent likeness. The enlargement has brought it out wonderfully."

"Then," said Thorndyke, "pass it to Mortimer."

"Has Mortimer seen it before?" asked Anstey.

"No," Thorndyke replied. "I thought it best that you should see the actual trial."

"You are pretty confident," said Anstey; and the same thought had occurred to me. But apparently his confidence was justified, for, after a prolonged and careful examination of the photograph, Mortimer announced:

"There is nobody that I know in this group."

"The man with the beard is John Gillum," said Benson.

"So I had supposed," replied Mortimer. "But I don't recognise him. He appears to be a complete stranger to me."

"Then," said Thorndyke, "we come to the second photograph. That is an enlargement from a small print and is not quite so clear as the other. It was taken by the first officer of the ship and shows a group of four men, one of whom is John Gillum. Look at the group carefully, Mortimer, and see if you can recognise Gillum this time."

Mortimer took the photograph and examined it attentively; and as he did so he appeared to become more and more surprised.

"This is really very curious," said he. "I recognised him at a glance. I suppose this must be a better likeness than the other."

"Show Benson which is John Gillum," said Thorndyke.

Mortimer turned to Benson, holding out the photograph and pointing to one of the figures.

"I say that this is Gillum," said he.

"Then," replied Benson, "you are wrong. That is the ship's surgeon, Dr Peck. The man standing next him is Jack Gillum."

Mortimer looked at him in astonishment – though I didn't quite see why, after what we had heard. Then, after another look at the photograph, he exclaimed:

"So that man is Dr Peck! Then the man I knew as John Gillum must have been Dr Peck, for the likeness is quite unmistakable. It is rather an appalling thought, though, considering the sort of terms we were on."

Miller rubbed his hands. "Now," said he, "we are getting down to brass tacks" (apparently he regarded the circumstantial tacks as being of an entirely different metal). "Mr Mortimer's evidence seems pretty convincing, but I think you said, doctor, that you had another item up your sleeve."

"I have," replied Thorndyke, "and I think it will be particularly acceptable to you."

He rose, and stepping across to a cabinet, opened it and took out an object which I recognised as the little roulette box that I had seen in Gillum's chambers. Having briefly explained its nature and origin, he continued: "I have fixed it to this board with a spot of glue so that it can be handled without being touched. You will see that it is marked all over with a multitude of fingerprints, many of them superimposed and most of them undecipherable. The grey powder with which I developed them doesn't show up at all well to the eye, but it photographs admirably; so I suggest that you give your attention to the excellent photographs which Polton has made of this box, which show the prints much more distinctly than they appear in the original."

He took from the portfolio a number of prints on glossy bromide paper and passed them to Miller, who examined them with eager interest.

"But these are not so bad, doctor," he said, when he had looked them over. "I can pick out at least half a dozen which our experts could identify quite easily. But what is the point about them? What do they prove?"

"The point is," Thorndyke replied, "that they are the prints of someone who had handled this box. But the box was the property of the Tenant of the Inn and the prints are presumably the prints of his fingers. At any rate, they were made by somebody who had been in those chambers; and Mortimer actually saw the Tenant handling this box. They furnish evidence, therefore, that the person who made them must, at some time, have been in John Gillum's chambers. And now cast your eye over this other collection."

As he spoke, he took out of the portfolio a sheet of paper on which there were two groups of fingerprints, apparently made with printing ink and accompanied by a signature of the same intense black. Miller took the paper and, after a careful scrutiny, compared the prints on it with those shown in the photographs.

"There is no doubt," said he, "that these fingerprints are the same as those that came from the box. But whose are they, and what are they? I should have taken them for lithographs. And what is this signature? That looks like a lithograph, too."

"It is a lithograph," replied Thorndyke, taking yet another paper from the portfolio. "I will explain how it was made. Here, you see, is a copy of the famous blackmailer's letter. I wrote it out myself on a carefully prepared sheet of lithographic transfer paper. When we called on Dr Peck, I gave it to him to read. When he had read it, I drew his attention to the attestation on the back, whereupon he turned it over, read the attestation, and turned it back. Thus his fingers and thumbs touched the paper at three different points, all of which I carefully avoided when I took the letter from him.

"Later, I called on a very skilful lithographer and got him to transfer both sides of the letter to the one and take off a few proofs. But first I asked him to write his signature on the letter with lithographic chalk so that it would ink up with the fingerprints and enable him to swear to the proofs."

"Then," said Miller, "these are Peck's fingerprints, excepting those at the upper corners, which I presume are your own, and it follows that the prints on the box are his, too. But that seems to put the coping-stone on your case, doctor, though, as this is a murder case, we could still do with a bit more evidence."

"You will find plenty of further evidence," said Thorndyke, "when you get to work with regular enquiries; evidence from the banks, from Copes and from various other sources. But you now have enough to enable you to arrest Peck. These fingerprints prove that he was in Gillum's chambers at the very time when, according to his own story, he was on the high seas at the other side of the world. Are you satisfied, Anstey?"

"Perfectly," he replied. "I should go into court confidently on what we have now, without depending on the further evidence that the police will be able to rake together. I see the shadow of the rope already."

It was at this point that Mortimer interposed a question.

"I have been expecting," said he, "to hear some reference to poor Abel Webb. Doesn't he come into the scheme of evidence?"

"He did," Thorndyke replied, "for the purposes of my investigation, but he does not for the purposes of the prosecution. I have not the slightest doubt that Peck murdered him. But I can't prove it; and without proof it would be useless to introduce any reference to the murder."

"Can you form any guess as to why Peck should have murdered him?"

"My dear fellow," exclaimed Thorndyke, "it is not a matter of guessing. It is obvious. Abel Webb was intimately acquainted with both John Gillum and Augustus Peck. Now, it happened that he saw Peck at his place of business, and he must have recognised him and have noticed that his hair was dyed black, that, in fact, he was disguised so as to resemble Gillum. He seems to have got Gillum's address − probably from the shipping office − and he certainly called at Gillum's chambers, apparently to make enquiries. There he met Peck, disguised and obviously impersonating Gillum. Then the murder was out. Peck had the choice of two alternatives; either to kill Webb or to abandon his scheme and disappear. Naturally, being Peck, he elected to murder Webb; and, accordingly, Webb was murdered immediately after his visit to the Inn − apparently on the very same day."

"While we are on the subject of explanations," said Benson, "could you give us just an outline of the actual events? A sort of condensed narrative of Peck's proceedings? I am not perfectly clear as to how the crime was carried out."

"To put it very briefly," Thorndyke replied, "I take it that the sequence of events was this: During the voyage, Peck learned a good deal about Gillum's affairs and, among other matters, two very important facts. First, that Gillum was coming into a large sum of money, accruing in instalments, and second, that he was a total stranger to England; that he knew nobody there and that nobody knew him. These two circumstances suggested to him the possibility of making away with Gillum, personating him while the instalments were being paid, and getting the money into his own possession.

"During the rest of the voyage, he must have devoted himself to finding out everything that he could about Gillum and his affairs and establishing himself as Gillum's intimate friend. Perhaps Gillum may have commissioned him to find a residence for him in London. At any rate, when Gillum went ashore at Marseilles, the friendship was already established and the two men must have been in communication while Gillum was travelling in France. That is clear from the fact that Peck knew when he would arrive in England and was able to meet him and bring him to the Inn, either as a guest or as the actual tenant of the chambers.

"As soon as Peck arrived in England, he set about the preparations to carry out his scheme; and he had the extraordinary good luck to find a set of chambers which contained an enormous coal-bin in an isolated room. When he had secured those chambers, his difficulties were practically over. He had merely to execute the necessary details; to have the bin made suitable for his purpose, to get a container to hold the body with the refrigerating material, to lay in a supply of slag-wool and solid carbon dioxide, to prepare the denture with the gold-filled teeth, and to obtain a suitable hair dye. All this he was able to do without committing himself in any way. If the scheme should prove impossible, he could simply call it off. He had done nothing unlawful or even irregular.

"Then, when Gillum arrived, everything was ready, even to the refrigerating chamber, lying on its bed of slag-wool, enclosed in the insulating material, and already charged with carbonic acid snow. The unsuspecting victim was led into the chambers, the oak was shut, and Peck proceeded quietly to convert the living man into a corpse. Probably he gave him food and as much liquor as he would take, with a moderate dose of morphia mixed in with it; and when this had taken effect and Gillum had fallen asleep, he administered the lethal dose with a hypodermic syringe."

"No marks of an injection were found at the post mortem," Anstey remarked.

"They were not looked for," replied Thorndyke. "But it would be easy for a doctor to give an injection to a sleeping man so that the marks would not be discoverable. However, the point is not material. The poison was administered, and when this had been done, Gillum was, in effect, a dead man. Peck was now irrevocably committed. He had burned his boats; and the instant, pressing necessity, was to get rid of the corpse. For if he should be found there with the dead man, he was lost. Probably, he proceeded with the disposal as soon as Gillum was quite unconscious; stripped the body, put it into the container with the carbonic acid snow, closed the lid, covered it with the slag-wool pads, fitted the false bottom over it, and emptied a scuttle or two of coal on to the false bottom."

"Do you mean to suggest," Anstey exclaimed, "that he put the living man into the refrigerator?"

"He wouldn't be a living man very long," replied Thorndyke, "in an atmosphere some fifty degrees below freezing-point. But that is what he must have done. As long as the dead body was visible in the chambers, he was in deadly peril; but as soon as it was put out of sight and covered up, he was safe. He could spend the rest of the night dyeing his hair and completing his arrangements for the morning. And when his hair was dry and his dental plate with the gold teeth substituted for the one that he had been wearing, he was ready to begin the personation and to carry it on as long as should be necessary in perfect safety, provided that he should never meet any person who knew Dr Peck or John Gillum, or, still worse, both of them.

"Moreover, you will note the completeness of his arrangements. Sooner or later, he would have to bring the personation to an end. What was he to do then? A simple disappearance would not answer at all. It would give rise to enquiries. But no disappearance would be necessary. At the appointed time, he could simply produce the body, properly staged for a suicide, and the exit of John Gillum would be perfectly natural. But he did not leave it even at that. He created in advance the expectation of suicide so as to forestall enquiries; and he prepared the blackmailing letters with such skill and foresight that they not only agreed with his drafts on the bank, but, if any suspicion should have arisen as to his connection with the murder of Abel Webb, they agreed with that, too. Actually, Jervis and I did, at first, connect the blackmail with that murder.

"Then, finally, observe the forethought displayed in the production of the body. As it was managed, it was practically certain that the corpse would lie undiscovered for several days at the least. But in that time it would undergo such changes as would effectually cover up any traces of either the murder or the refrigeration. Looking at the case as a whole, one has to admit that it was a most masterly crime; amazingly ingenious in design and conception and still more astonishing in the forethought, the care and caution, combined with daring and resolution displayed in its execution."

"That is true," said Anstey, "but what strikes me more is the callous villainy of the scheme and the way it was carried out. I am glad you told us the story, Thorndyke, because it has brought home to me what an inhuman monster we have to deal with. If he escapes the rope, it will not be from any lack of effort on my part."

We continued for some time rather discursively to debate the various features of this extraordinarily villainous crime. At length, Miller, having looked at our clock and then at his watch, remarked that "time was getting on" and stood up; and the others, taking this as an indication that the proceedings were adjourned, rose also.

"We will see you safely out of the precincts," said Thorndyke. "It has been a long sitting and we shall all be the better for a breath of fresh air."

Accordingly we set forth together, and having discharged Anstey at his chambers, sauntered by way of Tanfield Court to the

Inner Temple Gate, where we took leave of our guests. As we turned to retrace our steps, I noticed two men whom I had previously observed loitering opposite our chambers in the shade of Paper Buildings. Apparently they had followed us and seemed to be doing so still, for as we turned, they retired, and slipping round the corner of Goldsmith Building, moved away along the walk towards the cemetery. I drew Thorndyke's attention to them but, of course, he had already noticed them.

"I wonder," said I, "whether that will be Snuper and one of his myrmidons."

"It is quite possible," he replied. "I know that Snuper is keeping an eye on me. He divides his attention between me and Peck. But they may be a couple of Miller's men. The Superintendent is nearly as anxious about me as Snuper is."

He had hardly finished speaking when two shots rang out – sharp, high-pitched reports, suggesting an automatic pistol. At the moment we were crossing Tanfield Court and the sound seemed to come from the direction of the covered passage that leads through to the Terrace.

"That will be Peck," Thorndyke remarked quietly, and forthwith started off at a run towards the passage. It was extremely uncomfortable; for, though I would have much preferred to take cover and raise an alarm there was nothing for it but to keep close to Thorndyke. As we raced down the echoing passage, I caught, faintly, the sound of quick footsteps ahead, and almost at the same moment, similar but louder sounds from our rear, punctuated by the shrieks of a police whistle.

At the moment when we emerged from the passage on to the Terrace, I had a fleeting glimpse of a man running furiously, but even as I looked, he shot round the corner into Fig Tree Court and was lost to view. Here I would very willingly have called a halt to discuss tactics; for Fig Tree Court, with its two covered passages, both leading into Elm Court, afforded perfect opportunities for an ambush. It was about as dangerous a place as could be imagined for the pursuit of a man armed with an automatic and evidently bent on murder. But there was no choice. Thorndyke was leading; and when another shot sounded from ahead, accompanied by the shattering of glass, he merely noted the direction and bore down straight on the left-hand passage.

It was in Elm Court that the pursuit came to a sudden end. As we rushed out of the passage we saw two men sprawling on the pavement, engaged in a fierce and deadly struggle. One of them grasped a pistol and was trying to turn its muzzle towards his adversary, who, clinging tenaciously with both hands to the wrist that controlled the pistol, concentrated his attention on the weapon. But it was an unequal contest, for, even as we emerged, the man with the pistol was groping with his free hand under the skirt of his coat.

Thorndyke went straight for the pistol, and seizing it with both hands, wrenched it out of the holder's grasp; while I gripped the free arm at wrist and elbow and pinned it to the ground. And none too soon for, as I straightened out the arm, I saw that the hand held one of those deadly, double-edged surgical knives known as Catlins.

But the struggle was by no means over, for our prisoner seemed to have the strength of twenty men and the ferocity of a hundred. He writhed and twisted and kicked and even tried to bite. As I looked at his mouthing, distorted face in the dim lamplight – the face, it seemed, of a maniac or a wild beast – I found it difficult to connect it with the calm and dignified Dr Peck of our Whitechapel interview, but easy enough to recognise the murderer of Abel Webb and poor, confiding John Gillum.

The struggle ended as suddenly as the pursuit. It was only a matter of seconds, though it seemed an hour, before our two followers came flying out of the passage and instantly fell upon the prisoner. As one of them helped Thorndyke and me to drag the hands together – with an anxious eye upon the knife – the other produced a pair of handcuffs and expertly snapped them on to the wrists.

"There," said he in a soothing, persuasive tone, "that's fixed you up. It's no use wriggling, and you'd better let me have that knife"; which, in fact, he took possession of by a method which caused the prisoner suddenly to drop it.

Apparently, Peck realised the futility of further resistance, for he allowed his captors to raise him to his feet, when he stood glowering sullenly at Thorndyke, breathing hard but uttering not a word; while his original antagonist, who had risen unaided, regarded him with mild satisfaction and cast an occasional glance at a ragged hole in his own sleeve through which issued a little oozing of blood. Noticing this, I exclaimed anxiously:

"I hope you are not seriously hurt."

"Oh, no," he replied, turning to me with a smile, "it's just a matter of sticking-plaster and a tailor"; and as he spoke and looked at me, I suddenly realised who he was. It was Mr Snuper.

We accompanied the two officers and their prisoner up to the Inner Temple Gate and stood by until a police car arrived in response to a telephone call. Then as the door slammed and the car moved away, we turned back once more towards our chambers. Mr Snuper would have said good-night and faded away in his usual inscrutable fashion. But Thorndyke would have none of this.

"No, no, Snuper," said he. "You come back with us. We owe it to you that we are still alive and you were very near to giving your own life for ours. Neither of us is likely to forget your courage and devotion. But now you have got to come and undergo the necessary repairs."

The repairs were executed by me assisted by Polton (who positively grovelled at Snuper's feet when he heard the story) while Thorndyke attended to the hospitality; and, speaking as a surgeon, I am not sure that his methods were quite orthodox, even though it really was little more than a matter of sticking-plaster.

CHAPTER TWENTY

Epilogue

The trial of Augustus Peck lies outside the scope of this narrative. To follow it in detail would be merely to repeat what the reader has already been told. For there was practically no defence. Ingenious and convincing as the scheme of the crime had been, directly the alleged and presumed facts were challenged the whole edifice of deception collapsed. So overwhelming was the evidence for the prosecution that the jury agreed on their verdict of "Guilty" after less than ten minutes' deliberation.

The case for the Crown was based mainly, as Thorndyke had predicted, on the complete train of circumstantial evidence. But his prediction turned out to be correct in another respect. No sooner had systematic enquiries been set afoot by the police than an imposing mass of confirmatory evidence was brought into view. Inquiries, for instance, at Copes and other manufacturers of refrigerating material elicited the fact that Peck had kept himself regularly supplied with blocks of solid carbon dioxide. And an examination by experts of the various documents, including Gillum's holograph will, showed that the will and the letters received from Australia were clearly distinguishable from the skilfully forged documents executed by Peck; and this examination (together with Thorndyke's sheet blank paper) enabled the experts to testify that the blackmailer's letters had undoubtedly been written by Peck, himself.

But perhaps the most striking corroborative evidence came from the three banks at which Peck had kept accounts. When Miller, armed with an order of the Court, called on them to make enquiries, it was revealed that Peck had been in the habit of paying into each bank some thirty pounds a week in cash – mostly old one-pound notes – ostensibly the receipts from his Whitechapel practice, though, in fact, it was proved that the said practice was a pure fiction. As the money accumulated at the banks, it was promptly converted into gilt-edged securities, which Peck retained in his own possession and which were found locked up in his writing-table at Whitechapel.

But even more striking were the discoveries which were made in the strong-rooms of those banks; which included three large dispatch boxes, each crammed with old one-pound notes, evidently forced in under heavy pressure and forming a solid, compact mass. On counting them, the total amount contained in them was found to be just over ten thousand pounds; which, together with the securities and the combined credit balance, came near to accounting for the whole sum of thirteen thousand pounds which had been withdrawn from Gillum's bank.

"If one were disposed to moralise," said Thorndyke, as he laid down the newspaper in which an account of Peck's execution was printed, "one would lament the misuse of the remarkable gifts with which Augustus Peck was undeniably endowed. He was a very unusual type of criminal. I do not recall any other quite like him. He was clearly a man of some culture; he was gifted with a constructive imagination of a high order and with inexhaustible ingenuity and resourcefulness. He avoided risks whenever they could be avoided, and when they could not be, he took them with a courage and resolution that would be admirable in any other circumstances. Consider his murder of Abel Webb. The risk of committing a murder in a public thoroughfare was enormous. But yet, as a matter of mere policy, the risk was justified. For when he had taken the immediate risk and escaped, the very publicity of the crime was a safeguard so complete that though we were certain that he had committed the crime, we could never have brought it home to him. And Abel Webb was silenced for ever.

"Nevertheless, he suffered from the inherent folly that is characteristic of all criminals. The paltry thirteen thousand pounds was not worth the risk that he took; and his ridiculous attempt to murder you and me when, I suppose, he had to some extent lost his nerve, was sheer imbecility. For he still had a sporting chance of escape.

"But, at any rate, the world is better without him, and I am not dissatisfied to have been the means of his elimination."

"No," I agreed. "You have done a brilliant piece of work, and as to the result of your labours, as Mr Weech would express it: *Finis coronat opus.*"

R Austin Freeman

The D'Arblay Mystery
A Dr Thorndyke Mystery

When a man is found floating beneath the skin of a green-skimmed pond one morning, Dr Thorndyke becomes embroiled in an astonishing case. This wickedly entertaining detective fiction reveals that the victim was murdered through a lethal injection and someone out there is trying a cover-up.

Dr Thorndyke Intervenes
A Dr Thorndyke Mystery

What would you do if you opened a package to find a man's head? What would you do if the headless corpse had been swapped for a case of bullion? What would you do if you knew a brutal murderer was out there, somewhere, and waiting for you? Some people would run. Dr Thorndyke intervenes.

R Austin Freeman

Flighty Phyllis

Chronicling the adventures and misadventures of Phyllis Dudley, Richard Austin Freeman brings to life a charming character always getting into scrapes. From impersonating a man to discovering mysterious trapdoors, *Flighty Phyllis* is an entertaining glimpse at the times and trials of a wayward woman.

Helen Vardon's Confession
A Dr Thorndyke Mystery

Through the open door of a library, Helen Vardon hears an argument that changes her life forever. Helen's father and a man called Otway argue over missing funds in a trust one night. Otway proposes a marriage between him and Helen in exchange for his co-operation and silence. What transpires is a captivating tale of blackmail, fraud and death. Dr Thorndyke is left to piece together the clues in this enticing mystery.

R Austin Freeman

Mr Pottermack's Oversight

Mr Pottermack is a law-abiding, settled homebody who has nothing to hide until the appearance of the shadowy Lewison, a gambler and blackmailer with an incredible story. It appears that Pottermack is in fact a runaway prisoner, convicted of fraud, and Lewison is about to spill the beans unless he receives a large bribe in return for his silence. But Pottermack protests his innocence, and resolves to shut Lewison up once and for all. Will he do it? And if he does, will he get away with it?

The Mystery of Angelina Frood
A Dr Thorndyke Mystery

A beautiful young woman is in shock. She calls John Strangeways, a medical lawyer who must piece together the strange disparate facts of her case and, in turn, becomes fearful for his life. Only Dr Thorndyke, a master of detection, may be able to solve the baffling mystery of Angelina Frood.

'Bright, ingenious and amusing' - *The Times Literary Supplement*

OTHER TITLES BY R AUSTIN FREEMAN AVAILABLE DIRECT FROM HOUSE OF STRATUS

Quantity		£	$(US)	€
☐	THE ADVENTURES OF ROMNEY PRINGLE	6.99	9.95	13.50
☐	AS A THIEF IN THE NIGHT	6.99	9.95	13.50
☐	THE CAT'S EYE	6.99	9.95	13.50
☐	A CERTAIN DR THORNDYKE	6.99	9.95	13.50
☐	THE D'ARBLAY MYSTERY	6.99	9.95	13.50
☐	DR THORNDYKE INTERVENES	6.99	9.95	13.50
☐	DR THORNDYKE'S CASEBOOK	6.99	9.95	13.50
☐	DR THORNDYKE'S CRIME FILE	6.99	9.95	13.50
☐	THE EXPLOITS OF DANBY CROKER	6.99	9.95	13.50
☐	THE EYE OF OSIRIS	6.99	9.95	13.50
☐	FLIGHTY PHYLLIS	6.99	9.95	13.50
☐	FOR THE DEFENCE: DR THORNDYKE	6.99	9.95	13.50
☐	FROM A SURGEON'S DIARY	6.99	9.95	13.50
☐	THE FURTHER ADVENTURES OF ROMNEY PRINGLE	6.99	9.95	13.50
☐	THE GOLDEN POOL: A STORY OF A FORGOTTEN MINE	6.99	9.95	13.50
☐	THE GREAT PORTRAIT MYSTERY	6.99	9.95	13.50
☐	HELEN VARDON'S CONFESSION	6.99	9.95	13.50

ALL HOUSE OF STRATUS BOOKS ARE AVAILABLE FROM GOOD BOOKSHOPS OR DIRECT FROM THE PUBLISHER:

Internet: www.houseofstratus.com including synopses and features.

Email: sales@houseofstratus.com
info@houseofstratus.com
(please quote author, title and credit card details.)

OTHER TITLES BY R AUSTIN FREEMAN AVAILABLE DIRECT
FROM HOUSE OF STRATUS

Quantity		£	$(US)	€
	The Jacob Street Mystery	6.99	9.95	13.50
	John Thorndyke's Cases	6.99	9.95	13.50
	The Magic Casket	6.99	9.95	13.50
	Mr Polton Explains	6.99	9.95	13.50
	Mr Pottermack's Oversight	6.99	9.95	13.50
	The Mystery of 31 New Inn	6.99	9.95	13.50
	The Mystery of Angelina Frood	6.99	9.95	13.50
	The Penrose Mystery	6.99	9.95	13.50
	Pontifex, Son and Thorndyke	6.99	9.95	13.50
	The Puzzle Lock	6.99	9.95	13.50
	The Red Thumb Mark	6.99	9.95	13.50
	A Savant's Vendetta	6.99	9.95	13.50
	The Shadow of the Wolf	6.99	9.95	13.50
	A Silent Witness	6.99	9.95	13.50
	The Singing Bone	6.99	9.95	13.50
	The Stoneware Monkey	6.99	9.95	13.50
	The Surprising Experiences			
	of Mr Shuttlebury Cobb	6.99	9.95	13.50
	The Unwilling Adventurer	6.99	9.95	13.50
	When Rogues Fall Out	6.99	9.95	13.50

ALL HOUSE OF STRATUS BOOKS ARE AVAILABLE FROM GOOD BOOKSHOPS
OR DIRECT FROM THE PUBLISHER:

Tel: **Order Line**
0800 169 1780 (UK)
International
+44 (0) 1845 527700 (UK)

Fax: **+44 (0) 1845 527711 (UK)**
(please quote author, title and credit card details.)

Send to: **House of Stratus Sales Department**
Thirsk Industrial Park
York Road, Thirsk
North Yorkshire, YO7 3BX
UK

PAYMENT

Please tick currency you wish to use:

☐ £ (Sterling)   ☐ $ (US)   ☐ € (Euros)

Allow for shipping costs charged per order plus an amount per book as set out in the tables below:

CURRENCY/DESTINATION

	£(Sterling)	$(US)	€ (Euros)
Cost per order			
UK	1.50	2.25	2.50
Europe	3.00	4.50	5.00
North America	3.00	3.50	5.00
Rest of World	3.00	4.50	5.00
Additional cost per book			
UK	0.50	0.75	0.85
Europe	1.00	1.50	1.70
North America	1.00	1.00	1.70
Rest of World	1.50	2.25	3.00

PLEASE SEND CHEQUE OR INTERNATIONAL MONEY ORDER
payable to: HOUSE OF STRATUS LTD or card payment as indicated

STERLING EXAMPLE

Cost of book(s):..................... Example: 3 x books at £6.99 each: £20.97
Cost of order:...................... Example: £1.50 (Delivery to UK address)
Additional cost per book:.............. Example: 3 x £0.50: £1.50
Order total including shipping:.......... Example: £23.97

VISA, MASTERCARD, SWITCH, AMEX:

☐☐☐☐☐☐☐☐☐☐☐☐☐☐☐☐☐☐☐☐

Issue number (Switch only):

☐☐☐

Start Date: Expiry Date:

☐☐/☐☐   ☐☐/☐☐

Signature: _____

NAME: _____

ADDRESS: _____

COUNTRY: _____

ZIP/POSTCODE: _____

Please allow 28 days for delivery. Despatch normally within 48 hours.

Prices subject to change without notice.
Please tick box if you do not wish to receive any additional information. ☐

House of Stratus publishes many other titles in this genre; please check our website (**www.houseofstratus.com**) for more details.